Black
Papyrus

Black Papyrus

A Year in the Life of an African Village

by Bret Galloway

Unlimited Publishing
Bloomington, Indiana

Distributing Publisher:
Unlimited Publishing LLC
Bloomington, Indiana

http://www.unlimitedpublishing.com

Contributing Publisher:
Bret Galloway

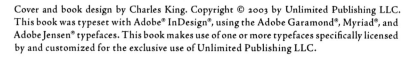

Cover and book design by Charles King. Copyright © 2003 by Unlimited Publishing LLC. This book was typeset with Adobe® InDesign®, using the Adobe Garamond®, Myriad®, and Adobe Jensen® typefaces. This book makes use of one or more typefaces specifically licensed by and customized for the exclusive use of Unlimited Publishing LLC.

Unlimited Publishing LLC provides worldwide book design, printing, marketing and distribution services for professional writers and small to mid-size presses, serving as distributing publisher. Sole responsibility for the content of each work rests with the author(s) and/or contributing publisher(s). The opinions expressed herein may not be interpreted in any way as representing those of Unlimited Publishing, nor any of its affiliates.

This is a work of fiction. All characters, products, corporations, institutions, and/or entities of any kind in this book are either the product of the author's imagination or, if real, used fictitiously without any intent to describe their actual characteristics.

Special thanks to editor Anna Cousins.

First edition.

Copies of this book and others
are available to order online at:

http://www.unlimitedpublishing.com/authors

ISBN 1-58832-088-x

Unlimited Publishing
Bloomington, Indiana

Preface

THE READER will find a glossary at the end of this book to help in understanding the many foreign terms used throughout. Most of the words by far are in Setswana, the national language of Botswana. English shares the honored place of being one of the two official languages and it is spoken, if somewhat imperfectly, by much of the population. Nonetheless, Setswana is unquestionably the language of daily intercourse in Botswana regardless of tribe. Thus, it is no surprise that this language infuses the pages of this book. The glossary is intended as a reminder for words that are often used and these will, over the course of reading the book, become familiar to the reader. Words that are used only once are immediately explained in the text.

In any case, the words or phrases that are used again and again are generally interjections or short phrases such as greetings that do not measurably alter the meaning of a story if not understood. Learning the words will lead to a fuller experience and a closer link to the characters in the stories, but at no time is an understanding of them necessary to understanding the stories themselves.

It is worth mentioning two of the most important reasons for using so many foreign words. First, the way of life and the manner of thinking of the characters in this book are profoundly different from those found in the technologically advanced countries, and while the individual words used in these stories provide only paltry windows through which the outsider can glimpse the world of these people, taken together they help to drive home the point and keep the reader aware of these differences. What, to the Western mind, will seem a belabored emphasis on greetings is an integral part of the cultures in sub-Saharan Africa; this is just one example that cannot be ignored if one is to have some understanding of the people in this book. Secondly, the area in which the stories of this book take place is highly multilingual and reflects the constant interchange of cultures that occurs. Setswana, Simbukushu, English and, to some extent, Afrikaans are used every day and may even on occasion be mixed together in one sentence. Eliminating all non-English words would fail to convey the diversity and richness of these people and misrepresent the daily life in a village like Shakawe.

Contents

Preface .... *vii*

Map of Botswana.. *x*

Prologue... *xi*

Part I: Pula (Rain) **1**

Under the Baobab (January) 3

Queen of Kgadi (February) 13

Footprints (March) 23

Cool Dark Waters (April)........................35

Part II: Legodimo (Sky) **55**

Ke Moloi Ene (May) 57

Badge of Honor (June) 71

Go Hithla Motho (July)........................... 89

Eggshells Are for Drinking (August) 111

Part III: Phefo (Wind) **133**

Fa Ele Jalo (September) 135

A Burning White Sky (October) 149

Part IV: Mbu (Earth) **163**

Black Papyrus (November) 165

Pula (December) 179

Glossary *197*

Botswana

Prologue

FAR AWAY in the central highlands of Angola near the town of
Huambo, the second longest river in southern Africa, the Okavango,
begins its transient life. It slides down green hills, over sloping rocks
and sturdy boulders into the bush-savanna of the southeastern low-
lands where, being fed by tributaries such as the Cuatir and the Cuito,
it grows markedly in size. The young and vigorous river then turns
eastward for almost four hundred kilometers, symbolically divid-
ing the relatively lush Angola from the very arid Namibia. There
was a time in the past when this was the richest stretch of the river
where the slower currents bred fish, birds, and hippopotamus; where
herders could cross their cattle in shallows or gentle bends; where
access was easy for even the smallest goat. But a war of politics and
petty egomania has ravaged Angola for almost fifteen years and left
the entire northern bank a ghostly wasteland where nothing moves,
not even animals, only an occasional acacia branch nudged by a
plaintive gust of wind.

After running straight east for some distance, the river plunges
several meters down a fault line in the earth's crust and turns its path
to the south where it plows through the deep sands of the Kalahari
until, growing weary, it slows, dies and then is reborn as the verdant
swamps of the Okavango Delta.

Between its turbulent eddies and rocky whitecaps in Namibia
and the turgid marshes of the delta, the river meanders firmly but
slowly through a narrow flood plain of reed and papyrus, bounded
on either side by steep, tree-lined banks. Many hippopotami live
here, wading and yawning in their favorite backwaters; and this is
also prime breeding ground for crocodiles, which love to gather in
the heat of the sun on long white sandbanks. Many kinds of birds
flourish in the rich wetlands, and snakes thrive in the dense twist-
ing underbrush along the upraised banks. And wherever the main
channel sweeps against the shore, there are people in abundance:
washing, bathing, fishing, gathering water for the house or bringing
their livestock down to drink.

This part of the Okavango was never inhabited by any one people long enough for them to call it their homeland. The Khoi-san, or Bushmen, had been here first hunting and fishing, but then they had never been very numerous nor is it their custom to live in any one place for long. If any can call it home, it is the Hambukushu and the Bayei. Centuries before, there had been more water in the region and travel was possible by canoe from the Okavango eastward to the Kwando and Chobe rivers, and from there onward to the mighty Zambesi. Originally from what is today eastern Angola and western Zambia, the Hambukushu and the Bayei migrated first to the Kwando river region in what is now the eastern Caprivi Strip of Namibia. Later, they gradually moved southwestward along a quiet and unpretentious waterway, the Makwegana, which was still open in those days and ran between the tip of the Caprivi and the Okavango. They settled in the delta and along the panhandle of the Okavango River to the north. The river was expertly fished by both peoples and the fertile land of the flood plains was diligently farmed. They were adept at working iron, the Hambukushu the better of the two, and so they bonded in marriage with the land and shared in its beneficence. To this day, it is most closely associated with these two tribes, although it now falls under the dominion of newcomers from the south, the Batswana.

As the eighteenth century gave way to the nineteenth, there came from the south a splinter group of the Bamangwato tribe of the Batswana whose leader, or *kgosi* as he is called in Setswana, was named Tawana. He and his descendants brought the restrictive and aggressive social forces of a pastoral people, who despite having little in the way of arts or technical skills, nevertheless rose above and engulfed the tribes already in the area through their greater administrative organization and more highly developed social hierarchies. Of the Bayei, they made slaves and servants, then later vassals; the Hambukushu further to the remote north were sometimes enslaved, but more often ignored so long as they acknowledged Batawana sovereignty, for the Hambukushu were feared and respected as powerful rainmakers. Gradually, the matriarchal ways of the Hambukushu and the Bayei were replaced by those of the patriarchal Batswana. They soon called their headmen *kgosi*, too, and they began to feel the taint of shame for the color of their skin which was jet black and not chocolate brown like the Batswana, who had mixed in their veins the blood of the Khoi-Khoi, the Bushmen and the Europeans from the south. The peoples of Ngamiland even adopted the language of their lords, Setswana, and relegated their own tongues to the darkness of their huts or the open bush far from disapproving ears.

Today, the modern world has reached these people, but its influence is still new and undigested. Having been dominated by a foreign tribe for over a century, and standing now before the onslaught of another less tangible one, these people of the Okavango are placed precariously on the threshold of their destiny. The door is closing quickly behind them, and soon they could find themselves shut out just as much in front as well.

Shakawe, a village near the Namibian border on the western bank of the Okavango, is just such a place. Its two thousand inhabitants awake peacefully each morning in their reed huts to the sounds of crowing roosters and whining goats. The women still work for the most part from sunup to past sundown: chopping wood, cooking, cleaning, washing, nursing babies, tending gardens, weaving baskets, sewing clothes. The men plow fields, fish, herd cattle or work as laborers, but often they simply drink beer and talk about community affairs. Children run around with dirt-encrusted bodies, phlegm trailing from their noses and pus oozing from open sores on their legs. Few people of Shakawe have modern cinder-block houses nor do many have jobs. Still, all wear Western clothes no matter how ragged, none wear loincloths any longer. The old ways are falling away gradually like autumn leaves, while the new ways from down south and from across the oceans burst open with tentative exuberance like spring buds. The old Mumbukushu shakes his or her head as the young ravenously grab at the new styles and constantly berate their elders for their backwardness.

There is no tarred road to the village, only a long set of parallel lines in the shifting sands. Neither are there many modern jobs that generate cash income nor are there telephones, televisions or even a bank. A feeling of timelessness still hovers in the air. Summer days move slowly through a thick haze of buzzing locusts below the swollen white bodies of thunderclouds.

Mornings find the women, like colorful elegant oil derricks, rhythmically pounding maize meal with large wooden mortars and pestles. Goats wander unmolested, and people shuffle lazily when they move at all. Day is still governed by the sun-beaten habit of countless generations, while night still crawls silently under the fearsome rule of poisonous snakes, lurking predators and malevolent spirits.

But, one wonders, for how long.

Part I

Pula   (Rain)

Under the Baobab

(January)

Under the Baobab

WARM MUSTY RAIN, like whispers; sky, purple-gray. Rolling, swirling clouds: so dark. Spread my arms and catch the rain. Rain feels good running down my nose and chin. Let it fall: on the chest and run between my breasts, spread out happily in my dress against my belly. A delta. Not a teacher. The Okavango delta! I am the Okavango river and the delta. I am the delta and the rain that soaks me. I am wet. I am mad!

I am.

Rain, love rain. Every drop is a mother's caress. Please, keep falling. See how the small trickles flow down the packed sand, past my feet and down to the river. Leaf caught in a tiny pool. Turning and turning wants to escape to become one with the river. Push it; go on; there, it's moving now. All things go home, all things return to their mother. Rain. Feels warm soft. Beautiful rain without wind, like this rain, so peaceful so soothing so embracing so forgetful. Rain is forgetting: forget Motsholathebe. Not so easy. Think only of the rain. Rain rain rain rain rain rain. Forgotten. Only the tickling between my breasts and the itchy drops on the ends of my chin my nose my ear lobes. Wash away all memories, return to happiness. Clean, pure, fresh. Getting cold. Should go in. Will the cold help me forget? No, not like the rain; don't seek it out, don't want to bury myself in it. Funny, cold is not feeling and yet one remembers; rain is all feeling and one forgets. Must go in but don't want to. Forget. *Jo, jo, jo, mosadi,* mustn't forget the water jug. Can't come all this way and leave the water; too far to come back. No longer remember the small things. Sethunya, have the *badimo* bewitched you? Got to be careful.

Exams. I must mark the exams this afternoon, but first make some *bogobe* and a salad . . . Is there enough cabbage? No, must go to Dumfries' maybe they have some don't want to walk all the way out to Alexander Karapo's farm. But I might see him at Dumfries'. Don't want to go. Have to, though. This path is so overgrown. Hope

I don't tear my dress: too expensive. Maybe send for another through the mail-order catalogue, the deep blue sun dress with white flowers or the beige two-piece. Not polyester, smooth but too hot, must get a cotton blend. Anyway, have to wait till month end; not enough money now. There, finally at the top of the hill. Easier going. Will pass the baobab tree soon. Had forgotten. But can't forget. Try! Should've gone another way. Exams. Must do . . . the rain is so soft. Almost like the time when he and I . . . must forget. Forgetting is happiness; happiness forgetting.

> Here we go round the forgetting bush,
> The forgetting bush, the forgetting bush,
> Here we go round the forgetting bush,
> So early in the morning.

Too much teaching. Singing nursery rhymes, foreign nursery rhymes. Nursery rhymes *are* foreign. Reminds me: still have to mark exams. Will take five times thirty-six times two . . . six hours. All day. Should've become a . . . what? Nothing to do in this country, let alone this faraway corner. Maybe a bookkeeper or . . . or what? Isn't much. Coming up to the baobab. Forget. Why did I go to teachers' training college? To learn, to read and think, to make some money. To discover there wasn't anything to read in this country, no one to talk with and nothing to think about, nothing but hot sun and deep sand. Better off without it. No opportunity for an educated woman. No, not completely true. At least there's more money being a teacher. Might build a house in a few years. Yes, better than the past. Just frustrated and hurt. Being silly and selfish, and . . . oh no, Motsholathebe! Where to go? What to do? Too late; must act calm, unconcerned.

"*Dumela*, Sethunya."

"*Dumela*." Walk on, keep going. You've said hello. Now go.

"*Waii*, pretty lady, you are going to make yourself sick, walking about in the rain like that. Come and let me share my tree with you. It'll keep you dry."

The same Motsholathebe. Talking smoothly . . . like some kind of conniver. Isn't, though; not a conniving hair on his body. Just his way. Must avoid, must go.

"*Ija*, I am not a lion, you know. *Tla kwano, mosadi*. Come out of the rain. It hurts to see you suffering so." Knows I want to walk on.

6

Sees it in my eyes, my body. Tense. His smile. "You can leave when the rain stops, pretty lady. It's my promise."

Everything spinning confusion what to must go just like a dust devil *tshus lu tshus lu* goes the dust devil round and round and I must go. Wait. He looks ill; pale and thin. Eyes floating and blank; no lust no anger.

"You're not well. What is it?"

The smile again. "Nothing pretty lady. I'm the same strong Motsholathebe as ever." Wants me to believe him; knows I don't. "Don't look at me like that, Sethunya. You frighten me. I'm not a dead cow drifting down the river. *Gao, wena*, you are always worrying." He knows. "Nothing is wrong. Couldn't be better." Smile is empty.

Leave now. *"Go siame."*

"Mosadi, you will get wet. Really you will."

A flash in his eyes. Something still there. Is it . . . no, must forget. Thought about it too much already. Can't do it again. There, feet are moving. Going away, leaving, forgetting. Happy. No, don't be so foolish: not happy and nothing forgotten. Must I remember again? I am getting wet; he is right. Usually is. Didn't look well at all. Should've stayed . . . no, better to leave. All is quiet again; only the rain whispering. Beautiful rain. Why did he have to betray me, why did he have to lie? *Ijo*, feel so tired now. Go home and rest. Do the exams tonight. Just rest. And forget.

Sethunya remembers nevertheless. Thoughts crowd in and toss all others about. She must calm them and so she sits upon the grass along the top of an embankment and looks out over the flood plain. Let the memories come on, she thinks.

"Waii, the moon is beautiful tonight."

His first words. Not hello and not hey baby you are beautiful. He said: The moon is beautiful tonight. He saw that in my eyes, in the reflection. Switched places and I saw too. He was right, always is. But what a romantic way to be right. *Ijo*, the most romantic man around and he doesn't even know it. Truly innocent. Maybe the reason why. Was he lying that night? No, you know he wasn't. But. And the other times? The Fridays when you met in front of Dumfries' General Dealer? The times he walked with you and laughed? Making love beneath the baobab tree? What is lie and what is truth—how can I know? Did he lie the first time? No. The others? Too many questions. Think, remember, feel. *Nyaa*. No, he didn't. I always said he did, though, or said he did that one time. But did you ever really ask him? No. Much easier to say he lied. He was with Seonyana, though, I'm sure of it because . . . because even she said so. Isn't that enough? He must've been bewitched. Maybe Seonyana or her father paid an *ngaka*, maybe cast a spell on Motsholathebe. Doubt, so much doubt. Fills my mind all the time; instead of listening, trying to find answers, close my ears and try to forget. Should know better. *Ijo* but it makes me so angry to think about . . . Why should it happen to me? Because you feel Seonyana is better, more popular. Only natural. Natural? That crane huddled in the upper branches of that tree is natural. She suffers like me. When it stops raining I will go about my business, she hers. But I'll still remember and punish myself with it; she'll move on. If only I could pull out my mind like a rotten tooth. Be like the crane. No, can't be, you know that. All gifts come with a price; high for us. All my fault. Stupid stupid stupid stupid. You are a fool, Sethunya. I hate myself, I hate Seonyana, I hate Motsholathebe's treachery. But don't hate Motsholathebe. Can't. Won't. More than that, though, *it isn't right, doesn't feel right.* He couldn't have and I know that. Wasn't lying when he kissed me in the rocking *mokoro* in the middle of the river. Or when he said I was the only one he thought of, that he could tell . . . Isn't that what bothers you, stupid Sethunya, that you know he couldn't but you think he did? I'm so tired.

Rain has stopped. Sun breaking through the clouds. Orange-green, husky purple, dusty black, pearl white, pristine blue. Air smells heavy but clean. No, Sethunya, mustn't forget. Must remember and solve. Ask. Learn. That is the way to your salvation. *Waii*, but you sound like a Christian missionary! All right, remember and think. It's the only way.

And in consideration of her comforting revelation, the sky bursts out in color as a tall thin rainbow arches its way across the land; as if Sethunya has passed through a terrible passageway of fetid darkness and finding her way into the light, has looked back to see that the dank tunnel had all along been bright and brilliant when seen from the other side.

"Sethunya. Come quickly." Twamanine is breathing hard. Why? What's happened? Panic in his eyes. "Motsholathebe, he's really sick. You've got to come help. I don't know what to do and I can't find Lebogang."

"What about Seonyana? Can't you find her?" Petty vengeance. Have to prod my anger.

He won't answer. Embarrassed, of course. No . . . confused, doesn't understand. "Why? I didn't think . . . she wouldn't come, anyway. She doesn't care." Frustrated. Doesn't even understand hatefulness in my question. "*Retsa!* Motsholathebe is sick. He needs someone to help him. If you won't do it . . ."

"No! I'll come . . . I'll . . . just a moment. Wait." What's going on? Must change clothes; bring some blankets, towels, bandages . . . bandages? Don't even know what's wrong no no no Sethunya don't panic try to think what to do hurry what to bring hurry what next. Can't be seen hurry in these slacks. H-u-r-r-y. Put on green sun dress. Got to hurry. Should bring food; no, he won't eat, too much to carry; tea, yes bring some tea. I'll need . . . maybe he'll have some. Come on, hurry Sethunya. How about some . . . no, never mind. Where's Twamanine?

"*Go siame. Are tsamaya.*" Let's go let's go let's go.

"*Ee.*"

Hot today. Getting thirsty. *Ke dirang, nna? Ruri o a tsenwa, mosadi.* What are you saying? You're truly mad. So nervous about this meeting with Lebogang. Have to begin with her, though. Have to listen to her at last. Been trying to tell me, but I refused to hear. *Ke a ganne.* I refuse. I refused. Will refuse . . . to be so emotional in the future. Promise? Promise. *Ijo, mosadi,* what nonsense you talk. There I go again: promises curses praises decisions. Too much thinking. Too much feeling. Which? Neither; usually just doing. That's the way, isn't it? No, like this: feeling doing *then* thinking. Some think first—some of the old ones—but most never think at all. Better that way. Why always such a problem since meeting Motsholathebe? Never bothered me before, never tossed me around like this. Calm down. There. *Waii,* the heat! Probably won't rain today.

Look at that fool Porridge Pot driving around in his '*bakkie.*' Try convincing him that it isn't there! Nobody sees a thing. But he does. That's what counts, I suppose. Wonder what people think when they look at me. Probably see nothing; nothing of the dust devil of memories that haunt me like an angry *modimo* spirit. *O a tsenwa tota—jaaka Porridge Pot yole*: just as crazy as that Porridge Pot.

Ehe, there is Lebogang. Got to look natural; as if nothing out of the ordinary.

"*Heela*, Lebogang, *le kae?*"

"*Re teng. Wena?*"

"*Ee.*"

"So, you are not teaching, *mosadi yo montle.* I am always surprised to see you outside the school compound." Smiling. Wide and white. Eyes prettier, though.

"*Ee.* I also sometimes think I should have special prison clothing." She looks relaxed. "Found any good trouble for yourself lately?"

"*Waii, mosadi*, you know I don't tell about such things." Laughing. "But I've been pretty busy with a BDF friend, now that you mention it." BDF. Botswana Defense Force. Green, well-starched uniforms. Ready cash. Young men, very young, bored to the end of their sanity. Looking for a good time. Lebogang looking for a good time, too. Until . . . what? All of us, looking for a good time, an escape, a forgetting. Until something we don't know yet. No, not all, not always. Old people much better at never remembering in the first place. If it's painful, it's forgotten fast, because it's *someone else's* fault. Convenient. Sssoooo easy. And me too. Used to. Was happy then.

"What's his name? Or does he only have a number?"

"*Naa*, he's got a name, but I think the number suits him better. Let's just call him BDF number one. If another comes along, he'll be BDF number two." Have to laugh. She's right. "Not much choice, you know, *mosadi.*"

"'There are plenty of wild animals, but only a few dappled bulls!' That's what you used to say." *Diphologolo di dintsi, dipoo tse difatshwa di dinnye. Dintsi. Dinnye.* Many. Few.

"*O bua nnete, mosadi.*" I speak the truth. Yes, I speak truly but I don't speak the truth. Falling into confusion. Stop. *Di dintsi di dinnye, nnete maaka*: many few, true false. Must ask; now's the time.

"*Retsa*, Lebogang, about Motsholathebe . . ." She's interested, prepared, understands. Keep going. "Please tell me . . . I want to know. I know I didn't want to hear before."

"*Ao, tsala, a bothata.*" Come on Lebogang, help me. Don't look so pained. "Really? Before you kept on . . . I don't know. It's hard to change so quickly."

"I've seen him. He's been very sick with malaria and I've been taking care of him. But he's still too weak to say anything and . . . *waii*, Lebogang, I can't ask him. You know, I just can't."

Wait. She waited while I wallowed, now I must wait, too. No need
for words. *A bothata*, she said. Yes, such troubles. Angry but can't
help feeling I'm the fool. Makes it more difficult to face. Come on,
Lebogang, come on. Wait; can't wait. Speak.

"*Naa*, this is the story, Sethunya, so listen well. Alright?" Alright.
This is the story. Yes. This is . . . alright . . . the story. She is speaking
and words come out like mating butterflies. But which words are
the truth? *Nnete, maaka*. True, false. Maybe all of them. So many
of them, so many butterflies, so many colors, so fast. Listen. Soon
they will be gone: you must remember.

So, that's it. Now, she has told me all. The meetings between
Motsholathebe and Seonyana in the village, the ones I stumbled upon
causing me so much doubt and pain, all innocent. Motsholathebe
innocent, that is. Not Seonyana. Patiently planned and arranged
like a leopard. Knew she probably couldn't turn Motsholathebe,
couldn't wrap him around her fat crusty finger, couldn't even make
him interested; easier to set a trap, let appearances do what she could
not. Rumors and light remarks dropped here and there, this person
and that, bit by bit. Soon a reasonable story: believable makes sense
rings true seems to prove becomes. Most important of all . . . even
though important, the words flicker confusingly past like winged
termites at mating time . . . his disappearance that weekend was
only an emergency job in Gumare. You fool, Sethunya! Set up by
Seonyana and her father. Set up, arranged, fixed. Motsholathebe
to take the bait like a wide-eyed dog. Doesn't suspect a thing. No,
he wouldn't. Never suspects anything. Only is. Exists, taking all
things as they come. Clever and so foolish at the same time. Like
me, he is, I can think and yet I can't; let the most obvious lies crawl
into my ears and stick to me like leeches. Leechy lies. Lies like
leeches. Fool. Fell fool to foul feeling. Words words words words.
But they have meaning; not in their sounds, somewhere in between.
And thoughts, are they words or something else? *Waii*, Sethunya,
can't you ever stop thinking? No, can't. Known the truth all along
someplace inside. Another part wouldn't let me see clearly, though;
covered in the darkness of anger and hurt and pride and silliness
and . . . so many others. Doesn't matter. Feel good suddenly, lighter
and more hopeful. Not even embarrassed, no meaning to being
embarrassed. Feelings free once more to fly like swallows. Or maybe
termites. *Jo, jo, jo*. Won't you ever stop such foolishness? If anyone

knew your thoughts!. Send you straight to an *ngaka*. Too late. I'm already bewitched.

And hot. Good thing it looks like rain.

Life is balanced again. How odd. Sitting here beside him I cannot imagine my anger or the separation between us. It was not real. Maybe a spell cast by some *ngaka*. Who knows. I should know better, taught to think differently in school, but who knows. Hard to change old ways, old customs, old feelings. Maybe just too tired from it all. Emotions made numb, like cattle in a long drought; but now new life, like rain. Rain. Thirst gone and everything green; was that 'dry season' only a dream? No. Rays of sunlight coming through the slits in the wall. Reed wall. Needs to be repaired. But how wonderful it is, this moment, the light coming through all golden-white, specks of dust floating through. A fly. Odd. I can almost *hear* the light.

He's opening his eyes. Needs something to drink. Water. "Here, drink slowly. Only a little!" Eyes look better. Still weak but getting better.

"*Kana, o mont'e jang, wena!*"

Calling me beautiful when he can barely speak. Typical. Knows it bothers me more than flatters. Means it, though.

"It's hot."

"Tsst. Don't speak. You need to rest." It is hot, though.

"*Naa, mosadi*, will you do one thing for me?"

"What?"

"Soon I'll be well." Throat's still dry. Give more water. That's better. "Next Friday. Friday night, meet me under the baobab. *Go siame?*"

Warmth. Even in my fingers and ears and . . . the knees. How stupid. The knees! Sethunya, what a strange creature you are. How strange. And how happy. We'll be whole again when we meet under the baobab. *Ee, rra, ee.* Knows already from my eyes. Tell him then. Say it out loud.

"*Go siame.* Under the baobab."

Queen of Kgadi

(February)

Queen of Kgadi

So, you want to know who I am and what I do? *Waii*, what makes you think I will tell you? Don't you know it's rude to ask someone such prying questions? Only someone who wants to harm another would be so interested in such things. *Xx, monna*, do not look so sad. I am only teasing you. Of course, you are a *Lekgoa* and do not know these things. But I can see you have a kind face, so do not worry, I'll tell you. You don't think I can tell all about you from your face? I can see you do not believe me. But you are mistaken, *monna*, that is what I do. I read men's faces and tell them what they need to know and what they want to hear—*waii*, sometimes they are even the same thing! Ha, ha. That's right, sit down over here and let me get you a cup of *kgadi*.

What is *kgadi*? Mother's milk to men, that's what it is. It comforts them and smoothes away the harshness of life. It's a magic potion that lets them fly over the land like a bird and see things that others can't. It's a spirit that brings men together when used wisely and breaks them apart when used foolishly. I brew it in a way nobody else can in that steel drum over there, the rusty dark green one. You'd call it beer, sorghum beer, I think, but it is nothing like that woman's drink they sell in the bottle shops in brightly colored tins. No, *kgadi* is life itself, and I, Kotlo Kutupura, I am its queen. Heehee!

Bona, do you see all of the men sitting around here? They are my worshippers. *Naa, tsala*, I speak more truly than you think. They come to me to rid themselves of their worldly troubles and the devils that eat away at them inside. *Ehe*, I know, many people in the village say bad things about me—*ke itse sent'e*—but then those are mostly the women, and they are jealous of me. You know why? Because I can give their men the one thing that they cannot: peace of mind. Ha, ha. You are laughing with me, *tsala*. That is good. *Retsa*, it is still early in the day and there are some hours of sunlight left. Stay a while and then you'll understand what I am talking about.

Bona, do you see that old man leaning against the fence, the one wearing the gray jacket? No, no, the one laughing. That is

Nyambe Tuvumbudara. His mother's mothers were some of the first Hambukushu to settle in Shakawe long ago, long before the *Makgoa*, the Whites, came and long even before the Batawana tribe had arrived down south in Toteng. He is a proud man, but he has also seen many changes in his lifetime and it makes him sad to watch the old ways pass by. And can you blame him? It is one thing to be saddened by the death of someone you have known, of a relative. This is truly painful. But is it not true that new life is always coming to take the place of the old? A child is born and takes the place of a parent or a grandparent who has passed on. But the young people now do not feel this. They do not respect the old ways and they do not have concern for the other people in their village. *Jo, jo, jo,* they think only of themselves and always they are looking far away over the bush and the great ocean to where the *Makgoa* live. They even fill their walls with color magazine pictures of their heroes. They are no longer thankful to *Modimo* for what they have been given, they only complain about what they don't have or what they cannot buy. So, no longer do cows give birth to other cows, now they bear hyenas. Who wants that? That's why Nyambe is sad and that is why he comes here, because we understand him and because with *kgadi* he can protect himself from the dry thorns of this new world of the young.

And the one next to him, see him? The man with the narrow face and the walking stick. That is Kuvumbira Nyangana. His mother's sister's son is the headman, the *kgosi*, of Shakawe and the surrounding villages. Since he was a baby, Kuvumbira has grown up under the protection, and the shadow, of the *kgosi*'s battle-axe and his spear. He has been able to say that he is a royal person, a kind of *mogol-wane*. But, really, he is only a man. He has no title, he has no power, and the *kgosi* does not seek his advice. His boys look after the few cattle he has so that he does not starve or lose all respect. He comes here because we are his friends. We do not see the royal cloak on his shoulders, but we also do not point out its absence. For him, it is there. He sees it in his mind. It is a heavy cloak, you see, and he is always worried about it. When he is with us here, the cloak does not exist and neither does his concern about it.

Waii, as for me, *monna*, I can only tell you that I am a simple woman. I have lived many years and seen many oppressive events. I have seen the cattle killed many times by drought, by hoof-and-mouth disease, by sleeping sickness . . . I have seen too many dead. But I have seen the good years also and I have seen this village grow.

It was only a small group of reed huts when my family moved here from Andara. Have you been there? It is just there, just across the border in what is now called 'Namibia.' Andara was the capital of the Hambukushu once when the Hambukushu were a nation and ruled everything in this area and to the north. *Ruri, ke bua nnete,* we controlled the trade between the many tribes around us and we were respected for our ability to bring the rain. We were not a warrior nation like the Matabele, no, but we were feared all the same. Then the time came when the Batswana pushed on us from the south and the Gcereku from the north and . . . *naa,* but that was long ago in the time of my grandfathers. They are just memories now.

And do not think I am a wicked woman because I sell *kgadi*! We must all live the way we can, whatever it is. *Ruri.* My husband—he is the man sitting in the *kgotla* chair under the tree—he has a sickness and has not been able to work for some years. He cannot plow the fields as he used to and he cannot visit our cattle post often. So you see, I must take care of him. *Fa ke bua nnete,* to tell the truth, I have always done that. Don't worry, he can't hear us. Anyway, at least now he cannot run after the women as he used to do—in actual fact, I became accustomed to the other women, but he made me too angry the way he spent all our money on them. That was what bothered me the most and caused the worst fighting between us. All the money running away like frightened *duiker.*

So, anyway, here I live with my husband and one of my daughters, who helps me with the chores. She has not found a husband and stays with us. *A o itse,* she might have left us for a big village like Gumare, or even Maun, like so many others do. My other daughter is married and lives in Sepopa. So strange, in the old days a husband would come to live with his wife's family. Sometimes they still do, but mostly they behave like the Batswana now. Or the *Makgoa.* It is too sad and . . . sorry, I must fetch those men some more *kgadi.*

What was I saying? *Naa,* it doesn't matter. Now things are good. The *kgadi* brings in enough money to buy food and clothes and even a cow sometimes! The missionaries and the civil servants will say I am a bad person. *Jo, jo, jo.* But what is the harm I do? To make people happy and keep myself and my family alive at the same time? *Waii,* this is just silly talk. It is easy for them to talk, they live in nice beautiful houses and always wear new expensive clothing and they have so much food it rots away and what-what. Easy for them to talk. *Xx!* So easy.

Bona, let me explain. See that man approaching? Over there. The fat one who thinks he is a *kgosi*? That is Kitchener Semumu. He is the Village Development Committee chairman and a representative of the Land Board for Northern Ngamiland . . . *waii, monna*, I don't think I could say all of that twice in one month. Every day in the hour before sunset, he comes to my place and drinks *kgadi*. He enjoys the drink, and he enjoys conversation with his friends. And yet, there are times when some government official puts pressure on him to announce a new policy and he will stand up in the middle of the *kgotla* and say terrible things about how disgusting and corrupting *kgadi* is. He will say some bad words about my business and demand I stop brewing at once. At the end of the day, he will come to drink as usual and nothing will be said and in the end nothing will be done.

And the missionaries! They will say, Kotlo, why do you make that wicked *kgadi*? Why can't you live 'righteously' like us? That's the word they always use: righteous. I don't even know what it means. Anyway, I have visited their houses and seen the kitchens overflowing with food and the big dry rooms and the beautiful soft furniture and their gardens full of delicious vegetables. Yes, I have seen them and I tell them, "Let me live in your house and I will stop brewing *kgadi*." But they just smile and say, "Poor Kotlo, you do not understand. You must be a good person and cut wickedness from your life. Do not seek such things of this world." And then they walk back into their beautiful houses saying, "Poor Kotlo, poor Kotlo." *Naa*, so you see, *monna*, I cannot waste my time worrying about these people who say I am wicked. As I see it, I am simply a part of people's lives. I give them something to do. And they are too lucky because I don't charge them for my services. Only for the *kgadi*. *Ijo*, speaking of *kgadi*, I must get some more for that fat hippopotamus, Semumu.

Bona, the sun is falling behind the trees. That is good. Soon it will be cool. Today was hot, truly. It has not rained for two weeks, and yet I could feel that it was trying very hard today. Do you not feel the wetness in the air? The longing? An *ngaka* from the other side of the river has been over here for three days trying to make rain. Have you not heard the drums at night? Really, the rainy season this year has not been helpful to us. There has almost been enough for the crops to grow, but the sorghum is small and thin. That is why they have hired an *ngaka* to make rain. If the rain can come one or two times more, the harvest will be large enough to keep us fed until next year.

There have been better years; but then there have also been worse years. In the evening, our village *ngaka* Letlonkana Mokumbwanjira will come here for some *kgadi*. Maybe he will tell you more about making rain—after he has had a few cups, of course.

Naa, do you feel it? The cool air? It is crawling up from the river. You can only feel it curling around your ankles now, but soon after the sun is asleep it will rise up quickly. The cool air will bring different customers, you'll see. Some of the men just drink here during the day and others only at night. The night customers will take the place of the day ones, just like the cool air takes the place of the hot air at nightfall. *Bona*, here comes Abel Sirumbu. Let me get him a cup of *kgadi* before I continue.

Sorry. Back again. *Ao*, my back is aching. I think maybe I am beginning to grow old. *Ijo!* Where was I? *Ehe*, Abel there works as a gardener for the junior secondary school. It is a good job for him as he is clever with plants. It is also good because he works alone and no one can bother him. You see, his mother's mother was a Mosarwa, a Bushman. You can see it in his eyes and his wrinkled skin. If you know him well you can also see it in the way he loves the bush. He is never quite happy in the village. The people, they are sometimes cruel to him and he will never have a good position in the village. But then again he is only partly Mosarwa. If he were pure Bushman, he would probably be in the bush with them right now. His brother Isaac lives with the Basarwa at Tsodilo Hills. He is a guide for the tourists there. Sometimes, I think it would be better if Abel was to live at Tsodilo with his brother, but I also know he would miss the village too much. The Mumbukushu in him is too strong. Even though he is oppressed here, he can't think of living anywhere else. Really, he is a good man. He often brings me tomatoes and cabbages from his garden, and in return I give him free *kgadi* when he has no money at month end.

The night has come, *tsala*. It is for the young ones. The old men go home to their wives and daughters. The only ones left are the young or the unmarried ones like Abel. You see that tall young man way over by the *motsaudi* tree? The good-looking one talking to that young girl? That is Motsholathebe Modibu and next to him is his girlfriend Sethunya Dishero. I think they will be married soon. *Waii*, that Motsholathebe, he works too hard. Always trying to do business and make money. He is a plumber, you see, and they are too rare in our country. Some day he will have many cattle, and people will treat him with respect. You wait. *O tla bona.* But now the people are so often jealous of him and so some of them say bad things about him. *Xx,* no one can believe what is said of him if it is bad. Such foolishness. *Naa,* the *badimo,* they care for him as they would a strong bull. Really, he is blessed.

And what about that man on the other side of the *motsaudi* tree with the cane in his hand. That is Jackson Sedumedi. He thinks he is so beautiful that he falls in love with himself whenever he looks in a mirror. That is why he is standing next to the tree—he doesn't want the wind to blow any dust on his beautiful clothes. Every *thebe* he makes goes for clothing. There is one funny story about Jackson and his new clothes. Dunkirk Dumfries, the owner of the general dealer store, had finally managed to marry off his ugly daughter—a little over a year ago in November, I think it was. Rra Dumfries has lots of money, but she was so bad-looking no man could stomach the idea of marriage to her, even for a fortune. Anyway, he found a willing suitor, a nephew of the *kgosi.* The poor young man needed a lot of money quickly to pay some debts to an angry government minister. There was to be a large wedding in the village. Everyone was invited and Jackson thought it would be a good chance to show himself off. So, he took all his savings, borrowed about three times that amount, and with the whole lot he sent off to one of the mail-order houses in South Africa for one of their most expensive and fashionable suits. I think it was white with thin black stripes. So, the day of the wedding came and Jackson put on his new suit. Everyone he met said how beautiful his suit was and Jackson was happier than I had ever seen him before. He nearly fainted from all the praise. Then a sudden thunderstorm came rushing across the flood plain. There had been so much noise at the wedding party and most of the men were so drunk that no one noticed the storm until the wind began blowing terribly. People ran in all directions looking for some shelter. Poor Jackson became so confused. His admirers had all disappeared! He stood in the same place for several minutes looking around like a lost heifer. Before he knew what was happening, he had been surrounded by a dark gray cloud. The storm had run across a brush fire and pushed all the smoke and ashes in front of it as it moved forward. Jackson began to run away from the storm at last, but it was too late. In all the smoke he could not see his way well and he tripped on a small bush. He ripped his sleeve in the fall and the front of his suit became dirty from the gray sand on the ground. He got up and looked at his suit with much anger. It was then that the rain started falling. The drops of rain were black from the brush fire and as fast as a bolt of lightning Jackson's suit was all black as if he had dressed for a funeral. He began crying, he was so saddened. I felt badly for him at the time, but when I see him strutting proudly like a male ostrich now, I can't help remembering the story and laughing. Really, I shouldn't be so hard on Jackson. He is a kind man and never hurts anyone. Maybe if he found a woman, he could forget his clothes for a while.

Waii, monna, I have talked too much. I have been telling you only of these gentlemen and you wanted to know about me. But you see, that is what I do. I talk to them, they talk to me. I serve them *kgadi* and they drink it. This is why I can tell so much from the face of a man. I have seen many and talked to many. Every day you will find me at this place serving my *kgadi* or brewing it inside the compound. I have watched the river rise and fall many times, sometimes it has flooded and sometimes it has seemed to disappear. I have seen all this while making my *kgadi*. I will continue to do so. You want me to read your face? Don't look so frightened, *monna*. There are no storm clouds in it.

Here, take another cup. No, you must. Take a drink. Do you feel the cool smooth grains of the sorghum? Do you feel it passing down to your stomach and do you feel the swelling of the air in your nostrils? Do you feel the soft rush through your head like a river current swirling round your legs? Listen, do you hear the tree frogs beginning to tinkle and the bullfrogs as they bellow and the stars waking up in the sky? And do you not feel the men around you—are you not a part of them? Yes? Good! Then there is no need to explain any longer. You want to know who I am and what I do? Now you understand. I am Kotlo, the Queen of Kgadi.

Footprints

(March)

Footprints

I WISH JOSEPH hadn't been so interested in microscopes. Ever since the day Mr. MacEwan showed us what cells looked like in our science course, Joseph had treated microscopes with all the devotion of Christian missionaries for their cross. He was always impatient for Mr. MacEwan's class and he thought up new excuses each day for staying late in the afternoon so that he could put his eye against the metal lens-guard. Perhaps I am putting it too strongly; he really wasn't obsessed. There were other things that interested him, but, I must say, there was nothing else in school that held his attention so much as microscopes.

Really, Joseph had been different from the beginning. But that was to be expected. After all, he was a Monoka, one of the remaining Basarwa people, the Bushmen, who lived along the river and in the delta of the Okavango. In actual fact, that is what Monoka means in Setswana: a river person. Being a Mosarwa you can imagine his appearance—the small size, the light coppery complexion, the puffy squinting eyes and the buttocks even larger than our own. So, of course, everyone made fun of him, even me sometimes. But I can't say that he was as ugly as those awful *Makgoa* like Mr. MacEwan or Miss Compton with their clever little eyes, pointy chins, sickly pale skin, huge sharp noses and flat buttocks. As children we called them *dipodi*, "goats," because that is what they looked like to us, especially the men with their scraggy beards. And yet we all respected the *Makgoa* in a hateful sort of way, for they were undeniably powerful. But the Basarwa were just dirty uncivilized animals as far as we were concerned. Good for tracking, yes, but not much else.

Joseph Nxwere. I suppose I am telling you about him because our lives walked closely together for a while. Really, mine was held strongly in his. Never before had anyone or anything touched me so deeply and in so unusual a way. Strangely, it was as if I could see myself from a distance, like I was sitting high up in a tree. What I saw was not good. Some of the ugliness came from knowing that I could be so cruel to another person, but I was more shocked to see how common this hateful trait was in all of us in the village. Where I come from we are brought up thinking that all the bad things in life, as well as many of the good, come from the actions of the spirits of our ancestors, the *badimo*. Sometimes they act directly and sometimes they act through humans using magic. The people in my village, they think everything happens because of things outside of themselves. We are always the victims of these forces and never the cause. Sometimes I think we fear taking responsibility for our actions more than even death. Because of Joseph, I saw that this was not true. Although I still respect the powers of the *badimo*, I know they are not responsible for all unfortunate things in life. After I learned this, I was pained to find myself alone among the people I had grown up with—like Joseph in a way. That was what really frightened me.

Joseph had been abused by all of us ever since he first came to our junior secondary school in Shakawe. He had been sent to stay with his mother's cousin because it was closest to where they lived on the other side of the river. In this way I was similar to Joseph because I am a Moyei and not a Mumbukushu like most of my classmates. My mother and I are originally from Sepopa, and we only came to Shakawe because she got a job as a teacher at the primary school. So, in a way you could say that I was also an outsider from the beginning, although the Bayei and Hambukushu are not so far apart. As I was saying, we teased him constantly. We girls would laugh at him and tell him how ugly he was. The boys would call him names and even physically bully him. I don't know what made us angrier, his appearance, his cleverness or his refusal to show the pain he must have felt at our assaults. Most probably, it was all three that made us hate him so much.

Hate.

I hated him, too, and I didn't know why. As I look back, I cannot understand where this feeling came from. There was no reason for it. Joseph never hurt anyone, never spoke badly of anyone, never insulted or betrayed anyone. And for this he was hated. No, that's not it. I know better now. It wasn't hate, it was fear; but fear of what I am still not sure.

On one occasion, I remember how some of the boys had trapped him in the bushes while he was defecating. We all used the bush for the toilet sometimes—this was how we grew up—but we mostly used the pit latrines on the school grounds as we were told to do by the teachers and the government. Joseph never did. He said it was much too strange to him and seemed dirty. And so this one time, some boys followed him as he left the school grounds, and then while he was squatting in the middle of some bushes, they attacked him from all sides. They threw sticks and pieces of concrete left over from construction at the school. He was hit several times, but the worst injury seemed to have come from the shame he felt as he came out of the bushes with his pants around his ankles. I am told he tripped several times trying to get away while pulling up his shorts.

The boys also did things such as take the schoolwork he had just finished in study hour and tear it up so that he would have to start over again. They would trip him up and kick him when playing football or sometimes the girls would pretend to knock his bowl over at lunch and make his porridge run down his shirt and into his lap. Although we played these kinds of pranks on others, we never did it so spitefully as with Joseph.

Then last year on the final day of school before the Christmas holidays, something happened that jarred my thinking like a sudden stormburst. The following day I would leave for my family's farming lands where I would have to work by cooking, cleaning, chopping wood and planting. Since I would be gone for six weeks and was in no hurry to begin this drudgery, I decided to go home the slow way back along the flood plain. As I walked along the crest of the banks, I noticed Joseph squatting in some reeds down below and ahead of me. Something odd in his behavior stopped me from calling out to him.

It took me some time, but finally I understood what it was: even with his back to me, I could tell by his movements that he was crying.

I was confused and walked away taking the inland path so he wouldn't see me. The picture of him huddled like that in the reeds stayed with me during the holidays. Of course, I didn't expect him to enjoy the taunting, but I never allowed myself to see him as really human. That distance was no longer possible and I remained troubled by it.

One night while at our *masimo*, our farm lands, I had a dream. In it several large lions had surrounded a springbok, which stood on a termite hill high above them. It remained motionless while the lions growled and roared below, seemingly afraid in spite of their strength and sharp claws to climb up the mound. I too was one of the lions, and I could even taste the desire for blood on my lips. The springbok refused to move. I and the lions became angrier and angrier. It was then I noticed the termite mound becoming wet. Soon small streams of water were running down its side and washing up against the paws of the lions. We all grew suddenly silent. I noticed that I was once again a person and marveled at that fact for some seconds. When I looked up, I saw that the streams of water were all coming from the springbok's anguished eyes. Soon, its tears began to wash away the mound, which seemed to make the lions even angrier. At last, the mound disappeared into the ground, and the springbok with it, as if it had been made of sand all along.

I could no longer hate.

I wanted somehow to tell Joseph this, but it was difficult to do. When I returned from the holidays, I watched him more closely, looking for some excuse to talk to him and come to understand him better. My chance came several weeks later in the middle of February when some of the boys began taunting him again by taking his porridge bowl away from him. They eventually ran away with it and threw it into the bushes. I happened to see one of the boys throw it over the fence and knew where it landed. After they had left, I went and got the bowl. I waited until after school when no one was watching and then returned it to Joseph. He said nothing, but I could see that he was thankful. That, I think, was the beginning of our short friendship.

It was hard to get to know him. One reason was that he rarely talked about himself. In actual fact, he rarely ever talked—at least in the beginning. The more important reason was that a hobble was put on me by the villagers because they would never accept someone having an open friendship with him. At the same time, as much as I could relate to Joseph on an equal level, it wasn't easy for me to throw off the opinions of my schoolmates and my people. I was embarrassed to be seen with him. The situation was worse because I was a girl and he was a boy. Too much time spent together would quickly cause gossip.

However, once I came to know him, we had some long talks; and even though they were few, each one was very meaningful. In that way they were like the years of good rain: rare but bountiful. I learned that many of the things I had formerly thought about him were not true. For example, we had thought him to be arrogant and overly serious because he never laughed or took part in our activities. *Ijo!* Of course, now I see that we were foolish to expect him to join us when we treated him so badly. I understood when one day, as I walked along the road to school, I was startled to see him laughing and joking with an old Monoka who was passing through the village. I could sense that they were strangers, and yet he seemed so completely at ease and so much different from the way we knew him. We had cut him off and abused him, and we had done everything we could to make him feel unwanted and uncomfortable. Was it strange that he seemed proud and serious? Once I knew him better I found I was right. With me, he was much more relaxed and we spent almost as much of our time together laughing as doing anything else.

One day, a few weeks after I had returned the bowl to him, he and I went to bathe after school in one of the shallow pools on the edge of the flood plain. The day had been too hot and all of the students were covered with sweat from sitting in the stifling classrooms. The river had been rising for a couple of months, and places where we had once been able to walk up to the river's edge were now covered with a meter of water. It was hardly noticeable because the reeds, papyrus and tall grasses disguised the difference in water level. If you knew the area well, though, you could see the change by the small inlets of water that had formed in various places where the land dipped down to the level of the flood plain. When we arrived, many of the others from school were already there. They were having too much fun in the water to think of bothering Joseph, so for once spiteful thoughts were forgotten and everyone became lost in enjoying the feeling of cool water on our hot skin.

All at once the wind began to blow strongly and the clouds darkened. Some of the boys and girls left for home fearing the storm, but the rest of us were too caught up in the fun to think about leaving. It wasn't until we saw bright flashes of lightning and heard the groaning thunder that we came out of the water to find shelter. The others ran back to the school, but Joseph motioned for me to follow him. As we trotted along he said he knew a place where we would be safe. We zigzagged through thick acacia and sour-plum bushes and then came to a very large water fig, its large teardrop-shaped leaves hanging down to the ground in heavy sadness. There was a small, barely noticeable opening which Joseph began to go through. He saw me hesitate, so I told him that I was worried about snakes. He said it was okay, because he came there almost every day and he had long ago killed all the snakes around there.

I followed him into a large open space inside. I think it could've held four or five adults. Hundreds of branches thick with leaves fell down on all sides and formed a kind of living cave. There was no other way in and there was no way anyone could tell the place existed by looking from the outside. The growth was just too dense. I asked him if anybody else knew about this place and he said no, all those who had come close to finding it were turned away by the narrow opening and the thought of snakes that might be waiting inside, just as I had been.

The storm broke and the rain began. Between the noisy bursts of thunder we could hear the heavy drops of rain as they fell against the outer leaves. I was surprised to find that none of them came through. We began talking after a few minutes, mostly about things at school. I was still amazed at how dry it was inside the water fig and I asked Joseph if he spent a lot of time there. He said he did, but he didn't like it. I thought it very comforting and very safe in a way, so I asked him why. He said he felt much better in the open spaces, just wandering through the bush where there weren't many humans. This was difficult to do in the village, though, and he had used this place as an escape from the people there. Although the hideaway was confining, he thought it was much better than facing the villagers.

What I remember most, however, was that near the end of our conversation the rain eased up and a deep quiet followed on the back of the storm. In the background, we could hear the random sound of drops of water as they fell from the leaves higher up and down to the ground and bushes below. Joseph was clasping his knees and had his chin buried in his legs. All at once he said that someday soon all I would know of him was the shadow of his footprints. I did not understand what he meant by this, and for some reason the calm of the moment was so strong that I didn't feel comfortable asking him to explain. The rain had stopped and we left to go home, our secrets remaining behind in the water fig.

You shouldn't think from all of this that Joseph felt unhappy all of the time or that I thought he was somehow perfect. He shared many traits with other boys, and could be mischievous in his own way. On the other hand, I always felt that he was in some way much deeper and more experienced. He was—how should I say—somehow more developed. I am thinking maybe developed isn't the right word; more complete might be a better way of saying it. Of course, that was one reason others around him thought him so suspicious. He didn't ignore his weaknesses as easily as they did.

For all that, though, he had his playful side. One afternoon a few days after waiting out the storm in the water fig, he told me about some of his pranks. My favorite was the one he pulled on the nasty police chief Big Boy. Big Boy, who came from the Bakwena down south, hated all of us in the village and we in turn all hated him. We could never do anything right to please him, and he never missed a chance to curse us and tell us how backward we were. Well, Joseph did have some acquaintances in the village he talked to regularly, and he rarely forgot anything they told him. He learned from a friend that whenever Big Boy went to the toilet after drinking at *Ema Re Nwe* he would regularly come up behind the clerk Naledi on his way past the bar and grab her by the buttocks. It really irritated Naledi, of course. She always pushed his hand away with a sneer, but he always did it again on his next visit. Joseph went up to her one day and told her about an idea he had, and she quickly agreed to it. The next evening, Joseph waited outside the shop until he saw Big Boy approaching the store. Joseph ran inside and pretended to help Naledi behind the bar. According to plan, when Big Boy got up from his table after his third beer, Joseph sprayed Naledi's backside with ironing starch and then emptied a small bottle of finely ground chili peppers on top. Big Boy soon came up and seeing her attention elsewhere, crept up behind Naledi, grabbed her backside as usual. She brushed his hand away as she commonly did, and Big Boy giggled while passing on to the toilet. Within minutes, Joseph and Naledi found their revenge. He began sneezing terribly and couldn't seem to shake the mysterious source of his irritation. Next he started rubbing his right ear forcefully, there apparently being a strange tingling irritation in that area as well. Big Boy was putting up a good front; he had to because he didn't want his guests, Kitchener Semumu and Mokgwasho Nkape, to think him odd. Naledi and Joseph nearly died from holding in their laughter as they watched him try to ignore the growing irritation. The best, though, came when Big Boy began to cross and uncross his legs every few seconds. His drinking partners began to notice this strange behavior. Suffering too much to hide it any longer, Big Boy started to scratch his crotch roughly. They finally had to ask if he was feeling ill. Big Boy muttered something about gas pains and ran out of the bar into the darkness. Knowing Big Boy as I do, even I had to laugh at this story.

Other than casual greetings at school, I only spoke with Joseph a few more times. I had much work to do at home and it was difficult for me to get away, but I did get to go for a walk with him on Saturday a couple of weeks later. Having grown up in Ngamiland, I knew the berries of many plants, which were edible and which were not, and about which trees made good firewood and which ones contained magic. And yet, Joseph made me feel as if I knew none of them, so great was his knowledge. He had a name for every single plant and he would talk and talk at length about the uses of each. He could even tell a story for most of them. I knew he was clever in school, but there it was not so obvious because he didn't say much. He was at home in the bush and his cleverness stood out for anyone to see. We walked for three hours, and I was so interested in what he had to say that I thought only a half hour had passed when we ended up back at the edge of the village not far from where I lived. He joked about something, said good-bye, and walked back into the bush.

It was the following Tuesday that it happened. Mr. MacEwan found one of the microscopes missing from the science classroom. He questioned each class, one after the other, but without success. No one knew anything about it. His efforts to remember the last time he had seen it and who had been using it were of no use since his recollections changed each time he thought about it. At lunch hour, my friend Masego told me that she had seen Teapot Saudu with something like a microscope in his hands the day before walking along the banks of the flood plain on his way to the village. He was so stupid to have done that, I told myself, but I thought nothing more of it. What did it have to do with me? The foreigners, the *Makgoa*, would buy us another one. They had plenty of money; and if they didn't, then the government would.

But there were problems the next day at school. In the morning, I saw Teapot and his friend Leshulo go in with a parcel and talk with Mr. MacEwan. After lunch, Mr. MacEwan waited for our class to arrive and then told Joseph to report to the headmaster. Mr. MacEwan then began the lesson as if nothing had happened. Something had happened, though, and I couldn't help looking out of the window across to the central building where the headmaster's office was. As always, Joseph walked calmly.

It took until the next day for me to learn from rumors that Teapot and Leshulo had blamed Joseph for lifting the microscope. They claimed that they had seen him running away from school with it and had followed him. They said they eventually stopped him and questioned him. Satisfied that he had stolen the microscope, they took it from him and brought it back the next day. That was their story. Joseph denied it, of course, but no one believed him.

I begged Masego to go tell the headmaster, Mr. Ndlovu, what she had seen. She refused. There were no other bystanders, and if she did bring the issue up, she herself risked being accused of slander at the *kgotla*, the tribal court. Even if there were no official punishment, she could expect secret vengeance by those she had betrayed. I explained what the terrible results would be for Joseph, but she would not give in. I then told her that if she would not do it then I would. I demanded that she tell me again everything that she saw. What she had seen would become what I had seen. Once away from Masego, though, my courage failed me. As much as I wished to clear Joseph of these lies, I still felt the heavy weight of my schoolmates' judgment. If I supported Joseph, I chanced being cast out by the villagers. I looked for him all that day so that I could talk the matter over with him, but I couldn't find him anywhere. I went home confused and very tired.

That night I had another upsetting dream in which I floated down the river at night in a *mokoro*, a dugout canoe, watching as a brush fire crept insidiously along the riverbanks. Soon it threatened our family hut. All I had to do was shout for help, to warn others what was happening, and the family would be saved. Try as I might, though, I could not make even the smallest sound. I feared the crocodiles in the water, feared that if I even made one sound they would know I was on the river and then eat me. No matter how much I tried I could not bring myself to cry out. I woke up as the flames surrounded our hut.

As soon as I arrived at school the next morning, I went in to see Mr. Ndlovu. I explained Masego's story as if it were my own and told him of the terrible things the others had done to Joseph in the past. Fortunately, Mr. Ndlovu was from Zimbabwe and was not so likely to take sides. For him, one tribe of people in Botswana was like any other. He thanked me for coming forward and said he would question Joseph and the other boys again in order to learn the truth.

It didn't matter. They waited for several days to speak with Joseph and then it became clear that he had run away. He was clever enough to realize that he would not be believed. Anyway, as I saw it, he needed very much to be in the open bush and our ways were too painful to him. I suppose the trouble with the microscope just gave him the excuse he needed to leave. I know he must have been suffering if the only place he could find peace in Shakawe was in the dark interior of a water fig (which, by the way, I did check—he was not there). Just as a villager finds the towns dangerous and frightening, so Joseph did even our small village society.

In the days that followed, I wandered around the edges of the village hoping to see some sign of him in the bush. Of course, I didn't, but in all of that searching I began to see invisible traces of him in all the places we had been together and in all the plants he had told me about. Now, I understood what he meant by the shadow of his footprints. Although I was sad for Joseph, I was perhaps even sadder for my people. Or was it just people in general? I don't know. So many things have changed.

Being a girl I could never hope to make others think differently, and yet I felt that I must do something. I could study very hard and obtain a first-class pass for my Junior Certificate. Then I could go on to a senior secondary school, and afterwards maybe even to university—maybe even in the UK. If I could do that I could make people listen and make them open their hearts. I'm sure of it.

You will possibly be laughing at me, thinking, *waii*, this little girl, this Pono Kenyaditswe, her high ideas will fade soon enough and she will become sensible like any other woman in Botswana. But something died in me when I saw the shadow of Joseph's footprints. Something was born, too. The dead must be buried and the young cared for, that is the way of life. My classmates have somehow turned that around; now I see that they loiter like children over the crumbling graves of their own hearts. No, there is no turning back for me, Joseph saw to that. Someday I will make others see his footprints, too.

Cool Dark Waters

(April)

Cool Dark Waters

SEOBO'S FACE brightened into a hollow grin. Her five remaining teeth obstinately refused to accept the notion that a full set were somehow an integral part of a successful smile. She beamed. You could see it in the crinkled corners of her mouth and the waggle of her tongue and the wetness of her eyes. How could she help smiling? Little Tebogo was trying to pet his grandmother's dog as only a two-year-old can, namely, with an open-handed slap that was less like a caress and more like an attempt to hammer the object into the ground.

"*Ijo*, Tebogo," cried Seobo, "maybe we should put you to work pounding sorghum with the women!"

This good-humored jab at Tebogo's manhood had no effect and he continued to pound away at the oblivious dog while Seobo laughed and chided. A younger woman would have covered her mouth and turned her head to temper such a display of emotion, but at her age Seobo could ignore such social niceties. Certainly, the many sufferings she had already endured and her advanced age gave her a great deal of license. Even she wasn't exactly sure of her age. When asked, she would only shrug her shoulders. All she knew was that she had been born during the final reigning years of the last great Tawana king Sekgoma Letsholathebe. Many doubted the claim since that would put her at well over eighty.

Thin as a reed and having all the resilience of one, she had weathered one husband, two children, many lovers and more droughts than she had wrinkles. Her withered body did not so much bear the mark of decrepitude or mortality as it expressed tenacious endurance. Her scars and wrinkles were testimonials worn like a soldier's medals proclaiming her bravery in the face of life: the dry burning heat of the sun, innumerable illnesses, childbirth, the daily washing of clothes and the scrubbing of floors, the witnessing of death, beatings suffered and the loneliness of old age. Her head was covered with a knitted purple balaclava and she wore a torn dress that had once been brilliantly yellow and green. Both were now faded from the sun's uncompromising rays and covered with ash and dirt. Around her right shoulder and left hip hung a cream-colored shawl, draped like a foot soldier's bedroll. Crusty bare feet stretched out in front of her, always ready to carry her along the stony path of life.

She called Tebogo to her and told him what a fine looking boy he was. Wasn't his mother lucky, she asked, and wasn't she so proud? Completely naked to remain comfortable in the heat, Tebogo peered back with eyes open wide as if in disbelief—not that he knew what to believe or disbelieve at the age of two and a half years. Seobo asked him if he was a gentleman and said that a gentleman should always be clean. She tickled him under his penis and scrotum and then brought her finger near her nose and sniffed. She made a teasing grimace to indicate that this boy was not yet a gentleman and then repeated the process over and over. Tebogo continued to look at her, entranced by her movements and speech. Finally, he burst into laughter, beat the air with his arms and stamped his pudgy legs. While it might be tempting to say that he was responding to Seobo's gestures, it would be more truthful to say that he was simply happy. He liked being with her and he liked the sun warming his face and the warm sand under his feet and her funny face. He was happy.

He and Seobo sat on a sandy incline above a backwater of the Okavango. Behind them, a tall sausage tree rose from the crest of the gentle bank giving them shade, its large elongated seeds suspended like dark rueful corpses; before them, an open expanse of flood plain, the river itself being out of sight beyond a wide stretch of reeds and floating papyrus; directly below them, a narrow pool of water that lay separating the sandy bank and the green papyrus. Tebogo's mother Leahaditswe was busy washing clothes in the pool, her skirt hitched up above her knees, pulled between her legs and tied in a knot up front. On her head was a bright red bandanna, which bobbed hypnotically up and down as she scrubbed the clothing almost as if she were a slender crane feeding in the shallows.

Seobo couldn't help noticing the beauty of Leahaditswe's dark glistening legs where the water had splashed them. Tsk, tsk, tsk, she thought, that's about all she has, those shapely legs and a pretty face. That was all right, young as she was, but one needed more character to survive the long bitterness of life, and of that Leahaditswe had none.

A flock of egrets, brilliantly white against the darkening cumulus clouds in the distance, caught Seobo's eye as they flew above the flood plain following the river upstream. Hardly had they disappeared from sight when a large but graceful heron came slowly in their wake.

"*Heela!* Leahaditswe, don't take too much longer. *Ao utlwa?* The rain, it is coming."

Leahaditswe nodded and then turned back to her work. She understood. It was a good twenty minutes back to her mother's compound where she lived. The compound was situated on the southern edge of Shakawe and only a hundred meters from the flood plain, but there was no open water accessible in that area. It was wildly overgrown with reed and papyrus, and the banks were thick with thorny acacia bushes, and so they had to walk downriver to where they were now. There was a better spot further on. When the water was low, as it was now, one could walk out to where a broad shallow sandbar lay at the inside of a sweeping bend in the river. It was easy to keep watch for crocodiles there while one bathed in the cool clean water, but they rarely went to the river bend because Leahaditswe's mother, Nyetsana, strongly disapproved of it. It was too dangerous, she had said—too many crocodiles and hippos; and besides, Leahaditswe didn't know how to swim. She was right and so they mostly came to this tiny lagoon where the water was murkier but safer.

Leahaditswe finished, gathered up the wet clothes in a basket and hoisted it onto her head. Seobo gathered the giggling Tebogo on her back and bent over to keep him there while she tied him to her back with her shawl. She picked up her walking stick and joined Leahaditswe. They walked up and over the bank, following a worn sandy path through the underbrush. As they approached the compound, they were met by three friends of Leahaditswe's mother who had just come from visiting her. Maiphetlho Tsheko was the most domineering of them. Her lean, haggard looks framed powerful eyes that constantly flitted back and forth like an eagle's, always searching and recording. Nyaleditse Thabo was taller than the others, and with her stiffly erect posture, she gave off a profoundly aristocratic aura. Fat Mabela Mange was the most physically imposing of the three, but was so vacuous of mind that she served more as a backdrop to the group than as a member.

Maiphetlho was the first to speak. "*Moroke, maopinduka?*" Good day, how is it with you?

"*Maopinduka thuana, hakamadi.*" Leahaditswe answered politely that she was doing well.

"So, you are returning from the river?"

"*Ii*," affirmed Seobo. "Leahaditswe was doing the washing."

"*Ijo!* Such hard work," said Maiphetlho pouting, "and now you carry the heavy clothes on your head." She gave a knowing glance to her friends.

"*Waii*, I don't mind," said Leahaditswe smiling.

"*Ii, muanangeana*, I wish I had half of your youth," Maiphetlho chuckled. "But tell me, don't you think the child should be with you? You are the mother."

Leahaditswe laughed. "There are many times during the day when I carry Tebogo, maybe too many. Seobo is being kind to carry him."

"If you say so, you know what is best." Mabela spoke distastefully, the words seeming to slide grudgingly down the bridge of her nose.

Maiphetlho sought to soften Mabela's rudeness. "You are quite right, little one," she said, a forced smile exposing her brown and yellow teeth, "it's only that we want to help you more. Perhaps, we could take care of Tebogo for you next time. After all, we are your mother's closest friends."

"That's kind of you, but I don't want to bother you. I am sure you have more important things to do. Besides, Tebogo adores Seobo, don't you Tebogo?" She pinched his cheek. "Of course, if you are around, you are welcome to come along with us."

Maiphetlho glanced briefly at Seobo. "Yes, perhaps we could do that," she said.

"*Naa*, I must hang this washing on the line before it rains so they will get their second rinse." She waved and rushed off for the compound.

Seobo bowed her head and said good-bye, then followed. As she waddled along, she could feel the weight of the other women's eyes on her back, and in spite of the heat of the sun and the warmth from Tebogo's body, she felt a cold wave run up her spine, like a shadow creeping upwards at sunset.

She was grateful for the smile that greeted her as Nyetsana let her in the door. Her joy crumbled, though, when she glanced over her shoulder and saw the three women still waiting where she had left them like dyspeptic vultures.

The following week was a hot one. No more rain had come and the torpid sun seemed to hang heavily in the dense air like a bubble in honey. It seemed to be the final gasp of summer before the cool dryness of winter set in. Seobo had not felt well for the last few days and had at first attributed it to the weather. She went to Leahaditswe's as usual to play with Tebogo, but the strain grew more burdensome with each day and she finally realized that she was in fact sick. She lived in a small reed hut on the edge of her sister-in-law's compound. Her only two children had died in infancy and their father had never married her. Thus, she was now alone. Her elder sister had inherited the family compound in the center of the village, and Seobo would have lived there were it not for the overcrowding. There were fifteen people living at her sister's compound including her husband, four of the sister's children, one of the husband's cousins and eight grandchildren. Being in the middle of the village, there was no place to expand and the compound seemed to be growing in on itself.

At last, Seobo sent for her brother's grandson.

"Opadile, you must help your *naueana*. Go fetch Letlonkana Mokumbwanjira, the *ngaka*. Tell him I'm not well." Opadile hesitated, apprehensive about the thought of going before a traditional doctor by himself. Perhaps she would change her mind.

"Don't worry, little one," Seobo said with a faint smile, "he will not harm you. He is someone who helps in difficult times. Go."

It was late morning by the time Opadile and Letlonkana arrived. There were beads of sweat on Letlonkana's face as he entered Seobo's hut. All of Seobo's brother's family was waiting inside, for immediate family members were an important part of traditional therapy. Letlonkana greeted them all and then sat down on a stool beside Seobo's bed.

"*Maopinduka*, Mma Ramphisi."

"*Maopinduka, tate.*"

"Opadile," said Letlonkana turning his head, "get me some water. It is very hot today." He turned back to Seobo and pulled out a handkerchief to wipe his forehead. "So, you are sick."

"*Ii, tate.*" Yes sir.

He smiled. "*Re tla bona.*" We shall see.

Opadile returned with the water and Letlonkana drank slowly from the enameled tin cup, his Adam's apple rising and falling rhythmically.

"That tastes good," he said wiping his lips. "Let's begin."

Letlonkana bent down and grabbed his *kgokong*, a kind of brush or whip made from the tail of a wildebeest. First, he lightly whipped

Seobo across the chest and legs, and then he had her roll over and did the same to her back. Next, he reached for an old mealie meal bag, which served as his *moraba*, the bag holding his divination bones. He had Seobo blow into it, then he shook it briefly and emptied the bones onto the floor. He had asked no questions yet about her condition. There was no need, for the bones would tell him most of what he needed to know. He studied them now with deep concentration, sometimes mumbling to himself. For a moment he seemed mildly startled, but gradually this expression gave way to one of curious puzzlement.

Mokumbwanjira finally spoke up. "You have been having stomach pains and infrequent bowel movements."

"*Ii, tate.*"

"You are not often hungry."

"*Ii.*" No, she wasn't.

Mokumbwanjira picked up the divination bones and put them back into the bag. He had Seobo blow into it and then he tossed the bones onto the floor again. He pointed to a polished black stone that lay on the edge of the scattered group to Seobo's left.

"This tells me you have spent much time away from the family. Have you been traveling?"

Seobo was embarrassed. "*Nyaa*, I have just been to a nearby compound . . . to help take care of the child of a friend."

Mokumbwanjira gathered the bones together and cast them once more. He studied the pattern for some time and then sat back.

"You have *diphilo*, that is clear. It is not serious, although it will take most of a day to cure. I can see that the cause of your illness is the *badimo*. They are unhappy that you have neglected your family at the compound in favor of this friend and they have brought on this illness to warn you. However, your transgression is not great. The treatment will be easy."

Seobo's brother, Moikokobetsi, awkwardly asked how much it would cost.

"I will require a goat. This is necessary for the treatment. I will only ask for the two hindquarters as payment. *Go siame?*"

"*Ee, rra, go siame.*" Seobo knew that Moikokobetsi was not haggling; he simply knew how much the services of an *ngaka* could run. His wife had been sick lately, too, and he had already paid out one hundred pula to treat her. He could afford a goat, but not much more than that.

"*Naa, go siame.*" Letlonkana put his bones back in the *moraba* and stood up. "I am going now. I'll return tomorrow. Until then, you must rest." Seobo nodded.

Seobo felt better now that Rra Mokumbwanjira was attending to her, and she was grateful for the support of her family. Nonetheless, she spent a restless night tormented by dreams in which lions stalked her in the bush, pounced on her, and tore her apart with their long sharp claws. Then hyenas came to devour her flesh and she cried in horror as they fought vociferously amongst themselves for the privilege. And yet none of that was as terrible as the quiet chilling darkness that slowly surrounded her afterwards and left her so utterly alone. She woke up and found herself shivering in spite of the relative warmth of the night.

Rra Mokumbwanjira came early the next day and ate some porridge while the family fetched one of their seven remaining goats and tethered it to a tree. Some of the family members gathered around the compound, some in the doorway of the hut and some inside. Mokumbwanjira finished eating and then instructed several of them what they should do. When the goat was prepared, he came out and brushed it several times with his *kgokong.* Then he had them slaughter it while he softly muttered some phrases over it. He had them remove the kidneys from the dead and skinned animal, from which they made a stew. After it had simmered for an hour, he added herbs from the *totamadi* and *sekaname* plants, and then the medicinal stew was allowed to simmer for much of the day. In the meantime, parts of the goat were stewed and others roasted for eating. Mokumbwanjira gossiped with Moikokobetsi and the other men and from time to time he would look in on Seobo. It was unbearably hot, so Mokumbwanjira waited until the late afternoon to serve Seobo the kidney broth. The entire family was in attendance while she drank this.

"You must drink some of this broth," said Mokumbwanjira, "four times a day until it is finished. You may not leave the compound for seven days following that—your friends may visit you, but you cannot go out. When you are well, I would advise you not to go as often as before or you will make the *badimo* upset again."

Seobo drank up the last of the broth, gave the bowl to Mokumbwanjira and then they left her to rest. Mokumbwanjira feasted with the family on the remains of the goat until sunset when he left with Opadile, who carried the two hindquarters home for him.

Seobo did as she was told and by the third day she was feeling much better. Mokumbwanjira came back to check on her, staying only long enough to be satisfied that she had recovered properly. Nyetsana, Leahaditswe and Tebogo also came several times to visit her. This eased her mind considerably and made her confinement tolerable. Seobo did feel guilty about having spent more time with Leahaditswe and Tebogo, but it certainly hadn't been out of dislike for her family. The fact was that she enjoyed little children immensely and yet her youngest grandchild was already eleven years old. Although all of her brother's grandchildren who lived on the compound loved Seobo, they were growing or had already grown independent and when they weren't busy doing chores or going to school, they preferred to be with their friends. She felt needed when she was with Leahaditswe and Tebogo.

Her spirits improved with every day, and on the fourth day of her confinement Opadile came home with Porridge Pot, the village "idiot." The unfortunate Porridge Pot was forever stuck in the fantasy that he was driving a four-wheel-drive vehicle wherever he went. Indeed, he sported a pair of empty driving goggles, a large steering wheel rummaged from a wreck and a dented sky-blue porridge pot for a helmet—hence his name. He traveled far and wide in these trappings, spluttering all the while with his tongue and lips and engaged in what was for him the very serious business of driving. Seobo knew Porridge Pot well and the mere sight of him was not enough to cause any unusual reaction. However, on this day Opadile came up to ask her if they had a spanner in the compound that Porridge Pot might use to repair his vehicle. Seobo looked over at Porridge Pot and saw that he appeared quite distressed. She had to laugh and wanted desperately to do so; but she instead told Opadile to ask his grandfather because she thought he had an old pair of pliers that might do. She had to go inside her hut to let loose her swelling mirth. She later learned that the grandfather did have pliers and that they were successful in repairing Porridge Pot's *bakkie.* Laughing to herself, she thought, "It seems I've been repaired, too."

Seobo went to visit Tebogo and Leahaditswe as soon as her full seven days of confinement were over. She understood that she must not go as often as before and she planned not to do so, but then so many days in the same hut and the same compound had worked on her nerves. She just had to get out for a while and the only place she really had to go to was Nyetsana's. The day was hot and the sky was full of large shimmering white clouds that seemed to claw their way upwards in search of cool relief. There still had been no rain for over two weeks, but Seobo could sense that a storm would soon be coming.

Nyetsana's three friends Maiphetlho, Nyaleditse and Mabela were at the compound when Seobo arrived. Tebogo was sitting in Maiphetlho's lap, but as soon as he saw Seobo he climbed off and ran toward her with his hands flapping and yelling "Zobo! Zobo!" She picked him up and kissed him.

"So," said Maiphetlho, "you are feeling better, Seobo?"

"*Ii.*"

"That is good. We are so happy."

"But shouldn't you be staying in your compound?" asked Mabela with her usual crudeness.

"Why do you say that?" replied Seobo.

Mabela winced and then smiled, "*Ijo,* it is nothing, only what is being said."

"*Ehe,* no doubt by that good-for-nothing Mothsithsi," laughed Seobo. Mothsithsi was the village gossip. She added sternly, "Don't worry, I am allowed to leave the compound when I wish."

At that moment Leahaditswe came out of the hut and greeted Seobo. Nyetsana, too, stepped out and said how happy she was to see her visiting again. Grimaces fell across the faces of Nyetsana's three friends.

Seobo lifted Tebogo into the air. "He is looking strong and happy."

"Of course," said Maiphetlho, "he has been well taken care of. Even the three of us, we have been here every day to look after him."

"*Ii,* you know how much we like him. He is like our own grandson," echoed Nyaleditse.

Seobo knew differently and thought their exaggerated concern strange. But, she did love Tebogo dearly and welcomed anything that might improve his welfare. She quickly put the three of them out of her mind and turned her attention to Tebogo. She put him down several times as she conversed with Nyetsana and Leahaditswe, and each time the three friends would try to coax him over to them, but he would not go near them and instead went to Seobo or to his mother. Maiphetlho, Mabela and Nyaleditse were clearly upset and yet they did not leave or make any further show of annoyance. After a while, Seobo said that she had to go. Although she felt better, her energy had not fully returned yet. She promised to stop by again soon.

Dark rain hovered reticently in the puffy cumuli that gathered each day. By mid-afternoon they would grow gracious and tall, tinged with purple below, but still there was no rain. While the build-up of clouds helped block the sun and kept the temperature from running wild, the increased humidity made it uncomfortable all the same and smothered any hope of relief. Seobo kept her promise and only visited Tebogo and Leahaditswe every few days, but the indecisive weather only caused her to suffer more during the absences and she wished greatly for the end of summer.

Then, near the end of April, Nyetsana came to visit Seobo. She said that her brother-in-law had died in Ncamasere and she had to go to the funeral the next morning. She asked if Seobo could stay with Leahaditswe and Tebogo while she was gone. She was worried about leaving them alone, especially as she didn't fully trust Leahaditswe's judgment.

"I know you are not supposed to visit so often," she added with concern, "but I'm sure the *badimo* would see this as a special situation. It is to help another family in need." She paused and rubbed her hands gently. "I would rest easier if you could do this. Somehow I have this terrible feeling . . ." she said in a faraway voice. "*Ga ke thlaloganye tota.*" I just don't understand.

A mystified Seobo tried to comfort her. "I would be happy to, but . . . what about your friends Maiphetlho, Mabela and Nyaleditse? They have offered so many times to help."

"*Waii*, I have known them since I was a little girl and they will always be around me, but that does not mean I trust them. They can't take care of a lightheaded girl like Leahaditswe. Besides, Tebogo doesn't like them."

Seobo smiled. "I will be there tomorrow."

She passed up her porridge the next morning and rushed straight over to Nyetsana's. Nyetsana was already dressed for the funeral and carried a small cardboard valise, which held a change of clothing and gifts of food for the bereaved family. Leahaditswe, who carried Tebogo on her back, was trying to help Nyetsana gather everything together for the trip when Seobo arrived.

"*Ehe, moroke* Seobo." Nyetsana beckoned her into the hut. "Come in, come in. So, you have come. *Ke itumetse thata.*"

"*Moroke.*" Seobo greeted them.

"Moroke, Seobo. *Maopinduka?"* Leahaditswe was smiling charmingly as usual.

"Ii. So, you are ready, Nyetsana?"

"Ii. I was just thinking over what things Leahaditswe must do while I am in Ncamasere. I don't have to tell you what they are, Seobo. I know you have a good head. But you must promise me one thing—it has been hot lately and there has been no rain. Even though Tebogo has been irritable, I don't want Leahaditswe to take him swimming in the river. Not even if the sun itself should sit on top of the roof of this house. It's too dangerous. Will you see that they don't go?"

"Ii. There are other ways of staying cool. Don't you worry."

Nyetsana sighed in relief. *"Naa,* I am leaving then. If I am to have any chance of getting a lift before noon, I must be at the *morula* tree while it is early." The large *morula* tree beside the main road was a central gathering point for those seeking lifts out of Shakawe. She hugged Leahaditswe and Tebogo, then gathered her bags together and marched off past several grazing horses, dressed in her hot funeral black, her valise on her head and her wobbly high heels sinking perilously into the sand.

The next two days were spent quietly trying to ignore the heat. Seobo played with Tebogo as usual while Leahaditswe went about her chores. Maiphetlho, Nyaleditse and Mabela stopped by on their way to the river on the second day. They said it was simply too hot and they were going to cool their feet in the shallow river bend nearby. When they suggested that the three of them come along, Seobo repeated Nyetsana's prohibition and politely refused. Maiphetlho appeared mildly surprised at this and asked several questions. Before too long, however, the heat compelled them to go the river and they said good-bye.

"Couldn't we go for just a short time?" asked Leahaditswe. "The water there is so clean and cool."

"Ijo, Leahaditswe, you know what your mother said. But we can go to the wading pool if you like."

Leahaditswe sulked while she gathered Tebogo on her back. Seobo saw that the heat was working on everyone's nerves and she hoped that the wading pool would provide enough relief to ease tempers and restore some clear thinking.

The wading pool, a kind of backwater, was the same area that they washed clothes in, standing between the papyrus and the riverbank.

Although the water was shallower, more static and thus warmer than the water in the river, it was refreshing all the same, especially for Tebogo, whose body was small enough for them to submerge easily. They spent the entire afternoon there, alternating between the coolness of the water and the dry comfort of the shade under the sausage tree. This excessive heat so late in the year worried Seobo. Such unusual events were often accompanied by misfortune. The same swollen clouds she had seen for almost two weeks looked down on her. When will this end, she wondered.

The heat began to subside in the afternoon and they returned in better spirits. Leahaditswe is lucky, thought Seobo; she only lives with Tebogo and Nyetsana. How could she make Leahaditswe understand that any loneliness she must sometimes feel was nothing next to the drudgery and back pains she would endure if she were married or had a father and brothers to take care of. How many young women had Seobo seen drawn into the relentless maw of domestic toil in the service of idle men? She could not begin to count the fresh girls she had seen turned into withered hags long before gray began to streak their hair. With men to care for, she would have to work from dawn to dark. Count your blessings, child, she thought, count your blessings.

Seobo slept unevenly that night. There were drums playing nearby, possibly for a church service, and they seemed to toss her thoughts around like a *mokoro* caught on stormy waters. When she woke early the next morning before daybreak, she immediately heard the low soughing of a moderate wind and sensed the world's delicate balance finally beginning to change. She stuck her head out of the door and felt the warm wind mingle with the cool air of morning. Yes, she thought, it will rain today.

She went out to chop some kindling and when she came back Leahaditswe and Tebogo were awake. Seobo made some porridge while Leahaditswe dressed Tebogo and straightened up inside the hut.

Leahaditswe came out of the hut yawning, "*Ao,* it's so warm already."

"*Ehe.* It will rain today. Then it will be cooler, you'll see." Seobo stirred the mealie meal that was cooking in a three-legged pot.

"Perhaps."

Seobo smiled to herself. She wasn't insolent, but this Leahaditswe had all the traits of young people these days. They thought they knew everything and looked upon the elders as one might a keepsake—valued for the memories they evoked but otherwise useless. She tried to think back to her youth. Had she and her friends been any different? Yes, they had been, she decided. They certainly had not been perfect or angelic as many older people liked to remember, but they had never been so self-absorbed, so removed from their roots. Then again maybe she was looking back through a wishful mist as well. She knew she was not immune to such tendencies.

They used the cool morning hours to stamp the millet so it could be cooked, and then they cleaned the compound in preparation for Nyetsana's return the next day. It was already uncomfortably hot when they finished at midday, the higher humidity making it more unbearable than the day before. Seobo looked to the northeast and saw a low-lying bank of clouds stretching above the horizon. *Pula etlatloga ena*, she thought: the rain is coming.

Leahaditswe prepared lunch while Seobo played with Tebogo. After they had eaten, Leahaditswe rocked Tebogo to sleep in the shade of the *utara*, the reed overhang, and the two women sat down to rest as best they could in the heat. The afternoon swooned in a sea of hot rising air as the lazy swells of buzzing locusts came to them like far-off waves. Seobo nodded off.

She awoke after a while and looked curiously around at the dusty compound; at the dozing figures of Leahaditswe and Tebogo; at the sun-baked walls of the *rondavel*; at an empty galvanized pail; at the tall grass and the dark, green trees of summer in the background; at the towering bodies of storm clouds building above. The tops were flattening out into anvils and the bottoms were growing menacingly dark. *Pula etlatloga ena.*

Leahaditswe awoke as Nyaleditse, Maiphetlho and Mabela entered the compound. "*Waii*, it is too hot," grunted Mabela as she wiped her forehead with a handkerchief.

"*Maopinduka*," said Maiphetlho in greeting.

"*Maopinduka*," answered Seobo. "Would you like some water?"

"*Ii.*"

Leahaditswe got up and brought a full cup to each of them one at a time.

"*Ijo*, truly it is hot," said Maiphetlho after drinking the water. "So, you are resting. But we are going to the river to fetch water. Why don't you come with us?"

"But . . ."

"*Waii*, come Seobo, just for a little while. It is too hot."

Seobo could see a grain of desperation in her eyes. "But it will rain soon, there is no need to go. We will just have to run back."

"*Naa*, you always say that and it never rains." Leahaditswe's knowledge that this was not true was clouded by her pouting.

"*Ija*, you are too hard on the child," said Nyaleditse snorting. "One would think you were her mother." Seobo winced.

"Anyway," said Maiphetlho, "my granddaughters are down there bathing now. They will look after Leahaditswe and Tebogo."

"*Bona*, there is nothing to worry about, Seobo!" Leahaditswe was standing in the doorway of the hut, Tebogo strapped to her back. "I am going."

Seobo sighed, "*Naa*, I'm coming."

They set off down the path to the flood plain. A small herd of cattle was grazing on their left, their sated stomachs dulling the curiosity in their eyes as they leisurely chewed and watched the women pass by. A thick stand of tall trees and an increase in undergrowth rose up before them, marking the area neighboring the flood plain. Seobo could sense the baleful presence of *badimo* hidden among the branches of the dark trees and walked on with her head sunk in her shoulders.

"Leahaditswe, let's turn here and go down to the wading pool," she implored. "There's no need to go so far. When it rains, it will be a long way back to the compound."

Leahaditswe pretended not to hear and Nyaleditse merely looked back with the same haughty expression that had been chiseled in her face since birth. The others ignored her and walked on. Seobo followed again, sometimes haltingly, as if ineluctably drawn onward like a wounded kid. Her anxiety increased as they began their descent down the bank and into the open. From the edge of the bank she could see the approaching storm. Although it was still mid-afternoon, a sheet of dark purple already stretched across the northern sky surmounted by lofty clouds that rose up sparkling white in the middle and then golden at the top. They looked like eerie phantoms swirling on a sea of woe.

Seobo began to say something, but the others steadfastly walked on heedless of her, and so she lowered the arm that she had started to beckon with. Once more she trailed doggedly after them. She wandered through the tall reeds that flanked her on either side and occasionally felt the soft earth below, which had been left spongy by freshly receded floodwaters. She tried to block out the foreboding she felt by concentrating on the soft light green of the new grass shoots beside the path, thinking of the times she had played in such grass by the river as a child.

There was no one at the sandbar when they arrived. Seobo asked about Maiphetlho's granddaughters and received the terse reply that they must have gone home. The heavy Okavango pushed past them, bits of reed and grass floating persistently downstream. Leahaditswe stood with apprehension at the river's edge. Seobo could see that she was watching the swift spiraling eddies created by the bend in the river that rolled out boldly toward the opposite bank like spinning tops let loose.

Seobo tried once more with quiet firmness, "Leahaditswe, let's go back to the wading pool. You know what your mother said." She realized too late that those last few words were a mistake. Leahaditswe simply turned her head and looked back at her with a blank expression. Several beads of sweat fell down her face.

"*Ao*, Seobo, you are always worrying," chided Maiphetlho. "Can't you see that the sand bank is shallow here? No crocodile can surprise you, and the current is not a problem so long as you stay in the shallow part. *Ijo*, you see bad things everywhere." She hitched up her skirt above her knees. "*Naa, mpona.*" Just watch me, she said. Then she waded out several meters to where the water came up to her knees. Indeed, the current flowing past her legs did not look dangerously strong. "*Waii*, the water is so nice. Come in."

Nyaleditse and Mabela complied, walking in up to mid-calf but no further. At first Leahaditswe stood at the edge without any hint of inclination to enter, seemingly devoid of emotion. Suddenly, however, Tebogo, who had been lulled to sleep by the heat of the day and the rhythmic bouncing of their walk to the river, woke up. Finding himself uncomfortably hot and sweaty on his mother's back, he began to cry. This brought Leahaditswe out of her stupor. She bent over, untied the cotton-print wrap and swung him off her back. The sand was too hot for her to set him on it, so she sat down and put him in her lap. Seobo, too, sat down on a grass-covered hump at the edge of the shoreline. The three old women came back out of the river and also sat down on grassy clumps, though at a distance from Seobo.

"*Heela*, Leahaditswe," cried out Nyaleditse, "go into the water. Don't sit there like a lizard in the sun. Go on or you will shrivel up like a Mosarwa."

Seobo could see the storm clouds moving closer. The air was brutally hot. The edge of the front had not yet reached the western sky and the sun still shone with all its usual ferocity. Leahaditswe was sweating profusely and Tebogo was showing increasing signs of discomfort.

"The rain will soon be here," Seobo beseeched Leahaditswe. "Come, let's go back."

Leahaditswe seemed not to hear and only gazed out at the water while Tebogo cried on. All at once she stripped all of her clothes off, picked up Tebogo and stepped into the water.

Seobo jumped up pleading, "Leahaditswe! Don't . . ." But she was suppressed by the jeers of the three old women, who told her to stop complaining.

Leahaditswe went out to where the water came up above her knees. She dunked Tebogo in and out several times, and it was obvious that the cool water was pleasing to both of them. She then lowered herself up to the chest, all the while holding Tebogo so that his head was well above water. She splashed water over her face and hair using her free hand, while Tebogo beat the water with his open hand, just as he had pet the dog, and laughed at the splashes he made. She laughed, too, and amused him further by raising him up above her at arm's length and bringing him down into the water. He loved this.

Leahaditswe turned to look at Seobo and said, "You see, Seobo, it's beautiful, the water." Her smile and the brightness on Tebogo's face bore their way through Seobo's concern and compelled her to drop her nagging for a moment and smile back. She thought she had never seen anything so beautiful in her life: the sun reflecting off Leahaditswe's teeth, a white flame in the rich rounded darkness of her face; her head turned delicately and casually towards them as if she were a slender graceful crane.

Leahaditswe tossed Tebogo into the air again. His body was slippery, though, and on the third toss she lost her grip. He came loose from her right hand, but she still had a grip on him with her left as he hit the water. She panicked and quickly tried to grasp him again with her right, which only pushed her farther out in the process. Seobo rose to her feet and ran to the edge of the water. Leahaditswe was now only waist deep and there was no reason she should have had any great trouble recovering, but she was frantically occupied with holding on to Tebogo. Suddenly she lost her footing.

She and Tebogo were swept downstream and into deeper water before she realized what had happened. Seobo ran to the water's edge and saw the two of them floating down the river—Leahaditswe desperately pawing the water. Maiphetlho and the others joined Seobo and they all watched in stunned silence as mother and son drifted like bobbing clumps of papyrus in the river. A hundred meters down, an exhausted and panic-stricken Leahaditswe went under, reappeared several seconds later, and then went out of sight, never to come up again.

There was a moment of silence, and then Seobo collapsed onto her knees and began crying. The others looked at one another in shock. The look of confusion in their faces was followed by anger. All of a sudden, Maiphetlho thrust her arm out and while pointing at Seobo yelled, "She is responsible! She has wanted this all along. Because she could not have Tebogo to herself she chose instead to kill them both."

Seobo looked up in amazement. Although tears still fell from her eyes, she had stopped her moaning. To her feeling of shock at the sudden loss of Leahaditswe and Tebogo was added a sense of the fantastic by these comments of Maiphetlho.

"*Ii,*" said Nyaleditse, "*O bua nnete.* Was she not conspiring with an *ngaka* recently? How do we really know she was sick? I think she is a *moloi.*" A *moloi* was a witch.

"Truly, that is my view," hissed Maiphetlho. "How else could she have enticed Leahaditswe down here to swim? We all know that Leahaditswe's mother forbade her to come to this place, and she was always an obedient daughter."

With abrupt vehemence Mabela shouted at Seobo, "You! You killed her. You must die."

Incredulous, Seobo got to her feet and backed away.

"*Moloi!* You have killed her, and now you must pay," cried Maiphetlho.

"Kill her!" echoed a wild-eyed Nyaleditse.

Seobo tried to run, but the three women quickly caught her. Her appeals for mercy were covered by the passionate screams of the three hags. In their primal rage they clawed at her and beat her with their open hands. Seobo tried to get up again. This angered them even more and, when she slipped, they fell on her with renewed fury. They no longer hit her—they bit into her and pulled out chunks of flesh with their teeth. When Seobo tried to push Mabela's face away,

Mabela bit down on her finger and cut cleanly through. Like hyenas, they ravaged her body, the blood only sharpening their appetite.

They only stopped from sheer fatigue. Seobo had already been dead for several minutes. Their chests heaved with panting. After some minutes had passed, Maiphetlho got it into her head to wash herself off in the river. The other two did likewise and when they had finished they stood on the shore and looked at the bloody mess on the edge of the reed bed. The storm clouds were now close and a chill went over them.

Maiphetlho spoke at last, "We must throw her in the river. People will think she has been attacked by a *moloi* or killed by an *ngaka* for body parts."

"But what about the blood?" asked Mabela.

Maiphetlho looked over her shoulder. "The rain will wash it from the earth. Come."

And so, they dragged Seobo's body out to the river, having to make several trips for chunks of flesh that remained behind. The blood briefly formed a bright ring around the remains of her body and then evaporated from sight, leaving only the gaping wounds and the faded yellows, reds and blues of her dress to be seen.

Thunder groaned loudly and a brisk wind arose, pushing waves across the surface of the river. Maiphetlho, Nyaleditse and Mabela watched as Seobo's body began bobbing up and down, a colorful speck in the Okavango's cool, dark waters.

"There," said Mabela full of venom. "She's where she belongs."

The others grunted in agreement. A flash of light and a sharp peal of thunder startled them. Without saying another word, all three moved as one and walked back along the path towards the village, huddling against the increasing drops of a chill and angry rain.

Part II

Legodimo (Sky)

Ke Moloi Ene

(May)

Ke Moloi Ene

LETLONKANA MOKUMBWANJIRA watched a man approach from the river. The man walked heavily through the sand; he wore no shoes, his gray slacks were full of holes and his T-shirt was stretched, ripped and faded. Letlonkana knew him to be Mukambe Umstwe from one of the islands in the flood plain. That he possessed a T-shirt, even a torn one, betrayed his relative affluence for an islander. Letlonkana waited patiently under the protective shade of an *utara* overhang as the other came up timidly.

"*Dumela, rra. O tsogile?*" Mukambe greeted him while glancing down to the side.

"*Dumela*, Mukambe. *Ke tsogile. Wena, o tsogile?*"

"*Ee.*"

Letlonkana pretended to rummage around his pouch. "So, you have come from the river?"

"*Ee, rra.* I have come from our island, from Xanekwa."

"*Ehe.*"

"*Ee.* I have come to ask for your help. The people of Xanekwa, they think my aunt is a *moloi*. *Waii*, the people, they are too angry. I am worried."

"*Ke a bona.*" I see, said Letlonkana. "*Naa*, I'm almost done here. Wait for me at the river. I am coming."

Letlonkana finished smearing the *morao*, an herbal mixture used to protect a house from evil powers, around the doorway of the reed hut. The inhabitants stood nearby anxiously watching every move he made. They had been bothered by an unusually high amount of snakes in the past few months and wished to put an end to it. Letlonkana had agreed to treat their house for twenty pula—half the price of a lean goat. In addition, he had told them he would throw in protection against *baloi*, or witches. A large tree beside a compound not far from theirs had been hit by lightning last month, a possible sign of magic. He knew this and sensed their concern about being next in line for harassment by a *moloi* when the rainy season returned the following year.

He then dipped a small branch from a *mopane* tree into the *morao* and fastened it above the door. He had already placed eight other *mopane* branches around the house, four at the corners and four facing the sides, and had sprinkled herbal water on the floor of the house. As an added measure, he had made them cut up a recently killed snake into five pieces. He had then given the family an herbal powder and told them to make four small fires around the inside edges of the compound and a fifth at the doorway into which they were to throw the sections of the snake and a portion of the powder. They should start the fires and apply the herbs, he said, so that the protective forces would be more closely linked to them personally.

Lastly, he grabbed his *kgokong* and repeatedly whipped the outside walls of the hut while walking around it. After five circuits, he informed the family that he had finished.

"*Re itumetse, rra, re itumetse thata*," they said thanking him profusely.

He waved off their gratitude gently. "I will send my grandson tomorrow to be sure everything is all right." This was an indirect way of claiming payment that avoided embarrassing the client and diminished the commercial nature of his services. The price had already been discussed and agreed to, and therefore there was no need to mention the issue openly again.

Mukambe was waiting patiently at the river. He waved for Letlonkana to step into his *mokoro*, his dugout canoe, and soon they were on their way upstream. Mukambe followed the farther shore where the water was often shallower and where he could firmly plant his pole. Being next to land also provided quicker egress to safety in case of a hippopotamus attack.

Summer had given way to early winter and the nights were already quite cool. Letlonkana welcomed the chance to warm his body in the sun. Like a table knife sinking through warm butter from its own weight, so too the tremulous but sharp heat of the sun cut through the cool air surrounding his skin and felt lightly refreshing. The soft rocking of the *mokoro* soothed his spirit and lulled him into a state of peace.

However, this business about the *moloi*, the witch—that unsettled him and brought his thoughts always back to what was for him the world of shadows. People's feelings usually ran high over such matters and invariably they were wrong. Letlonkana had seen *baloi*, had cured many in his lifetime and knew that they existed, but he also knew that there were fewer of them than people supposed. So many of them were created in people's own minds. Although he had often tried to explain it to them, the people refused to understand that supernatural powers were not completely and unconditionally under the grasp of any individual who wanted them—even for an *ngaka* like him. For an *ngaka* to make contact with the Great Spirit, *Modimo*, or lesser ancestral spirits like the *badimo*, his intentions had to be beneficial, not selfish and insidious. An *ngaka* who called up spirits out of spite or a desire to injure quickly lost control of them and ended a slave of their anger rather than their master. To abuse these powers was to abuse nature. No deity, not even the Christian devil, would ever allow itself to be so casually manipulated. There were those who had the knowledge and the intent to misuse these powers, but they were few and usually not long-lived.

He closed his eyes and sighed. So very tired. Such foolishness in the world. He had been deeply saddened by the recent death of old Seobo. Saddened because she had been wrongfully labeled a *moloi*, and saddened because her body had been mutilated and then burned without any respect. It was true that some unscrupulous *dingaka*, traditional doctors, used parts of the human body in an effort to link the two universes of spirits and humans, but they did not mutilate a body so viciously as in her case. What's more, the discovery of the two other bodies of Leahaditswe and Tebogo down river made it even more unlikely that an *ngaka* was involved. And while it was possible that the three of them were the victims of a *moloi*, Seobo certainly was not the instigator. No, someone weak had mutilated her, someone who feared and hated—feared whatever they did not understand or could not control or could not have.

He knew this for certain because he had cast the bones for Seobo a few weeks before her death to diagnose an illness of hers. There had been no indication of witchcraft, nor even any evidence of malicious manipulation by unfriendly spirits. Still, he *had* sensed the presence of death in the bones at that time and it had bothered him greatly, especially since there had been no clear connection to the illness at hand, which was clearly minor and inoffensive. The feelings of death in the bones had been subtle and imprecise, like a fleeting scent in the wind. Things to come were often like that in divining. The bones told much about the forces at work in and around an individual, which helped the *ngaka* to determine what the sickness was or what malevolent powers might be present. They displayed the past insofar as the past had gone into shaping the individual as he or she existed at the time of the casting of the bones; but the future was usually something indistinct and ambiguous.

Letlonkana opened his eyes again and watched the bright green papyrus as it passed by on the right. He looked at the blue cloudless sky above and the dark water beneath him. That is what others see, no doubt, he thought—blue and green and black. Simple shapes and simple colors: what lay behind them none knew and all feared to know. He saw differently. He saw them growing and heard them breathing. He saw forces moving and spirits swirling within them. That he could see things which others could not was a gift; that others often resented and even hated him for it was a curse. This special vision held him apart from humanity while doing nothing to protect him from the loneliness engendered by its powers. He looked aft at Mukambe, who smiled at him and poled in tranquility not sensing any of this. Sometimes Letlonkana was not sure which one of them was the better off.

They passed a herd of hippo that was playing in the deeper waters on the far side of the river. Mukambe stayed close to the shore and remained alert while pushing on smoothly and nonchalantly. A couple of hippos yawned lazily, revealing their pink mouths and huge incisors. The others snorted or spun their ears around to shake out the water, one ear circling comically in the opposite direction from the other in a rapid twirling motion.

Soon after, Mukambe guided the *mokoro* into a narrow side channel and beached it about thirty meters from the river. They stepped out into in the middle of a wide marshy field covered with thick grass and began walking. The footing was soggy at first, but the ground rose as they reached a line of trees and then became noticeably firmer. Some areas of these islands would remain above water all year round, while the exposure of others varied greatly with the seasonal water level throughout the year. The islands were little used from December to May when the river was high, except as fishing outposts; by June they would be dry enough to bring in cattle, which would feed on the abundant grass until the rains came again the following summer and raised the water level up again. Mukambe and Letlonkana skirted the edge of the woods for a while and then emerged once more onto a broad open plain of low light green grass. There were some marshy patches here, too, but they took a footpath that followed dry terrain and made for easy going.

The serene beauty and the comforting calm of the landscape gradually dissolved as they came near a cluster of huts. Voices that had first been heard as a low hum soon grew into a hideous clamor as they moved closer. Letlonkana saw a group of men and women shouting curses and denunciations, their arms flailing in staccato jabs in the air. In a corner between the main hut and a protruding reed wall sat an older woman cowering with fear, her hands held across her face. An older man, perhaps her husband, argued with the others and kept them from getting to her. He was the first to see Mukambe and Letlonkana walk up, and as his expression changed the others fell quiet and turned to see what had caused it.

"*Moroke. Maopinduka.*" Letlonkana greeted them first as a visitor should.

"*Moroke, tate . . . maopinduka . . . ii, moroke,*" came the varied responses of the startled members of the group.

Mukambe smiled and gestured with his clasped hands. "*Arume,* this is Letlonkana Mokumbwanjira, the *ngaka* from Shakawe. He has come to help us settle this problem."

The rabble looked at each other doubtfully, clearly puzzled about how to react. Finally, the older man who had been defending the woman thanked Letlonkana for coming and motioned for him to sit down. Letlonkana did so. From the chair, he slowly moved his eyes from one person to the next. He said nothing for several minutes, preferring to let the silence be his introduction. Just when the group was beginning to grow restless, he stated plainly, "*Naa,* I hear you are having problems."

A tall, lanky man with a torn and tattered shirt, its sleeves ripped off, jumped forward and thrust a finger at the woman. "*Ke moloi, ene. Ke moloi!*" She is a witch, that one. She is a witch!

Several men and women stepped forward and started shouting in a jumble, "*Ke moloi . . . ruri, ke moloi mosadi yoo . . . tate, re a tshabe thata kagore ke moloi . . . re thusa.*" Once more the gathering became a chaotic clashing of brute fury. So loud were they that no more than a few shouting words could be heard from any one person.

Letlonkana raised his hand for silence. "*Naa,* you say she is a witch?"

"*Ii, tate,*" said a plump woman. "She has many more crops than any of us. We all have fields, but, really, no one else's mealie grows like hers. You must beat the magic out of her or else . . ."

He silenced her with his hand. *"Naa, mpolelela. Ke ngaka, wena?"* So tell me, are you an *ngaka*? The woman shook her head meekly to say no. With chilling calm he said, "Then, *naueana*, do not tell me how to do my work." He paused and looked over the group. "You people know nothing."

He changed his tone to be more reassuring and to lower the tension, "I will look into this matter directly and let you know what I find. Before I make my diagnosis, I would like to walk around her field and some of yours, if I may. That will help me to sense any evil forces that may be present." He stood up and began to walk away, then turned to the group, who had not stirred, and added, "There is no need to bother that woman while I am away. If she is a *moloi*, I will handle her properly when I return. If she is not, I think you will be greatly ashamed afterwards if you should do anything to harm her."

He called to Mukambe and asked to lead him to the fields. Normally, Letlonkana would not have walked around like this nor even asked questions at all. Rather, he would have immediately cast the bones for an explanation of an illness or for an indication of the presence of a *moloi*. That presupposed, however, that he knew the people well who were involved and that he knew the organic pulse of the village. That was not the case here. He knew some of the residents of this island and he had been here before, but his familiarity was not as sound as it was in Shakawe. For this reason he had come up with the excuse for the walk. It would give him a better perspective from which to interpret the divination bones later, and, perhaps more importantly, it might make the angry group cool down some.

They first came to the accused woman's field. Indeed, the mealie plants were healthy and plentiful. A brief survey of her crops told Letlonkana that she had been meticulous in planting solid rows of seed around the edges of the floodwater. As it receded, which it had been doing for the last month, she had planted successive rows behind the water. Thus, the plants increased in size the further they were from the water. This was not a new method—it had been around for a long time—but it was not traditional or pervasive. The reason was that it required diligence on the part of the planter to take good advantage of the process. Most people would only haphazardly plant two or three times as their only concern was to produce just enough to eat and they preferred to spend as little time outdoors in the heat as possible. As seeds would obviously germinate best in the very moist soil just at the edge of the water line, the woman had taken full advantage of this by planting every few days.

The two of them walked on to another field and Letlonkana's suspicions were confirmed. The others had done three bulk plantings, filling one large area at a time. The moisture in the soil was variable across the surface of each planting, the side farthest from the water being drier than the area beside the edge of the floodwaters, and as a result the seeds had germinated unevenly yielding plants of variable size and robustness. The next two fields were similar. Letlonkana did not yet know whether this woman was a *moloi*; he certainly could declare her a superior farmer.

"Come," he said to Mukambe, "it's time to go back."

The rabble was shouting again when they returned. Letlonkana had expected no less. They grew quiet, however, on noticing his presence. He sat in the same chair as before, which was near the besieged woman, Seitseng Nthupi. From the satchel slung over his shoulder he pulled out his snakeskin bag, his *moraba*, which held his divination bones. The group of onlookers closed in for a better view, forming an oppressive wall.

"*Ditsala*, if you must come so close, some of you will have to sit down, otherwise it is too difficult to breathe." The men sat down in front where they had the best view.

Letlonkana held the *moraba* bag out for Seitseng to blow into, and as he did so he noticed the abject fear in her eyes. At that moment, he knew that the bones would only tell him what he now saw from her expression: she was no *moloi*. A *moloi* might show hate or ecstasy or power in the eyes, but not fear. He blew into the *moraba* after she had done so, shook it, and then cast the bones onto the ground. They were called "bones" because they had originally been made primarily from animal bone and horn. Nowadays the sacred bones could actually be stones, animal hooves, seashells or even bits of glass and plastic. In fact, the central piece for this session, the *Kgadietona*, was an old binocular lens that Letlonkana had found one day in the sand beside the northern road out of Shakawe. It represented the subject woman for the reading.

Kgadietona had fallen near the center with its convex side facing upwards. This was a good sign for the woman: she was healthy and there was generally a balance in the forces around her. The *Mosadi wa Modimo*, a lion's claw in this case, usually gave indications of witchcraft. It was pointed away from the *Kgadietona* and thus implied that she was not a *moloi*. Likewise, the *More Mogolo wa Modimo*, here a bone from a hippopotamus' foot that gave information about witchcraft or deadly serious misfortune, was furthest away from the *Kgadietona*. Letlonkana continued scanning and noticed that both *Kgatshane*, a polished river stone from Angola, and *Silume*, part of a bull's hoof, had both landed upside down and were pointing to the woman. In this situation, they represented the community around the woman. The fact that *Mosadi wa Modimo* pointed to *Kgatshane* indicated possible use of witchcraft by someone other than Seitseng. Letlonkana could not be sure. He mumbled to the bones, and passed his *kgokong* over them. He asked Seitseng whether she had experienced any health problems recently. She said no. He asked about last year's winter crop. It had been good, she told him. Letlonkana rubbed his head.

He then cast the bones for the husband and asked him several questions. Then he had Seitseng throw the bones for a second time. He mumbled over them, tapped them with his *kgokong*, and asked her more questions about her neighbors and her relatives. Letlonkana looked over the bones and sighed. It was clear from all three readings that the woman was not a *moloi*. Moreover, he could not find a single transgression against the *badimo* nor the infringement of any taboo. This was simply a good, hard-working woman. The spectators were waiting for a response. He knew they would never accept the unadorned truth in this case. "The bones have told me many interesting things," he spoke up suddenly, startling some of those sitting nearby. "And time and again they have told me one thing—this woman is not a *moloi*."

Several of the bystanders jumped up instantly. "What do you mean she is not a *moloi*?" they shouted. "Have you not seen our fields? Is it not obvious she is using wicked evil powers to oppress us?" So many yelled at once that Letlonkana could not hear anything they had to say. Not that it mattered, though, for it was unavoidably clear to him that these people were profoundly angry with jealousy. He realized that he would have to tread carefully in the next few minutes if he was to avoid a bloodletting. He tried to calm them and hush them into silence so that he could talk reason into them. They remained incensed, however, complaining amongst themselves, a very dangerous prospect since it meant that fire was now feeding fire. Soon they would be out of control.

Letlonkana closed his eyes and chanted in verses that none present could comprehend. He continued to do so, repeating them rhythmically and swaying his body gently from side to side. Where reason and appeal had failed, the fear of unknown forces succeeded. The throng grew quiet, in awe of the spectacle before them. He kept on chanting until every single voice had fallen silent. Then he stopped and opened his eyes.

"*Bagaetsho*, you are wondering, then, how it is that she can have such good crops while yours are sickly and so few."

"Because she is *moloi*," cried one.

"She used magic, of course," said another.

Letlonkana raised his hand, and then spat out in anger, "Let me tell you, you ignorant ones: it is not her crops that are made better through witchcraft, rather it is yours that have suffered because you have abused the *badimo*." He saw the shadow of guilt and hate mix sourly in their faces. Be careful, he told himself. "I have even seen in the bones that two of you hired an *ngaka* to cast a spell on this woman so that she might have misfortune. You wanted her crops to wither. Because of this abuse of powers, the *badimo* are angry with you and have thought it right that you should be the ones to find misfortune." The assembled islanders looked suspiciously at their neighbors. Letlonkana had absolved each person by throwing blame onto two anonymous, and nonexistent, members of the group.

"You will not solve your problems by harming her," he continued. "In actual fact, I say to you that only the offering of one she-goat from each of your families will satisfy the *badimo* and stop them from bringing greater evil down on you. Yes, only two arranged for the curse, but your anger and support have made you all guilty in the eyes of the *badimo*." Letlonkana willed the sweat not to flow down his face. He did not need to look to see the twisted expressions that the onlookers wore. "You will bring the goats here tomorrow morning. Let me say that I cannot protect those who fail to comply. That is the remedy I see for you." He paused briefly and looked around. "I am finished."

Their anger had now been turned inward. They wanted to know: who had hired the *ngaka*? He slipped his divination bones into their bag and stuffed everything into his satchel. The group gaped at him dumbly. Rising, he beckoned for Mukambe to help him, and then asked him to take him back down the river. He could feel a burning look of embarrassed rage on his back as he walked off, but he acted like it was no more than the comforting rays of the winter sun.

Soon, he and Mukambe were back in the *mokoro* and drifting down the river. They were silent for some time, Mukambe standing aft with pole in hand and Letlonkana sitting forward, watching as the grassy banks gave way to tall reeds and then papyrus. Finally, Mukambe cleared his throat and said, "*Tate*, a goat for each family . . . that will make six goats! I have never heard of such a large offering to the *badimo*."

Letlonkana did not answer for a moment. Sighing he said, "Mukambe, you are still young. There are many things you have not seen. Besides, the *badimo* work in ways we cannot begin to understand. Who are we, after all? *Re batho fela, rena.* We're only people." He looked at the circular wake where a bream had just nabbed an insect from the surface of the river. He scratched his ear. "But you are right, this is not a common offering. Count yourself lucky to be seeing something so rare tomorrow." Letlonkana tried not to smile.

"Yes, of course," replied Mukambe in all seriousness. "I hadn't thought of it that way."

As they rounded a large bend, Letlonkana noticed a pied kingfisher hovering above the river downstream from them. Ah, you clever one, he thought, there are so many things you see as you hang in the air. Some fish waits unsuspecting below. Perhaps it, too, is waiting motionless to pounce on a smaller fish or snatch an insect from the surface. We are all waiting and devouring, all part of the balance of things. How strange. Yes, Mukambe, he said to himself, it is a lot of goats. The owners will miss them dearly, especially she-goats that could have begotten many kids in the years to come. But then they will also think twice next time about screaming *moloi* so easily. At least the next few times. After that they will probably have to be reminded again. Unreflecting as they were, he knew they would not understand that they were sacrificing precisely for the purpose of purging themselves for that lack of insight and as a spur to reflection. Perhaps the price paid would make some think further on their pettiness. Probably not. He normally disliked the bloody chore of butchering goats, but tomorrow he thought he might just enjoy it.

Mukambe woke him out of his reverie. "What was that?" Letlonkana asked.

"I said I was wondering why you were laughing just now, *tate*."

"*Ehe*. It was only that I noticed that kingfisher with the bream in its mouth and thought how odd it was that the hunter had been hunted. One can never rely on fate to tell us its intentions."

"No, I guess not." The conversation had obviously risen above Mukambe's comprehension and he chose to lapse into respectful silence.

The sun had already dropped below the trees and left the sky brilliantly red and purple. Small trails of curling mist rose from the surface of the water in the rapidly cooling air. There was very little sound save the growing tinkle of tree frogs, the far-off sound of an ibis seeking its mate, and the barking of a dog on one of the islands. A few minutes later, Letlonkana heard a soft buzzing. He listened carefully and then looked down at his arm. A mosquito made ready to plunge her long proboscis into his skin. Raising his hand, he thought with amusement, now who is the hunter and who the hunted?

Badge of Honor

(June)

Badge of Honor

THE ONLY PEOPLE Big Boy hated worse than the Hambukushu were the filthy Basarwa, the Bushmen. At least he wasn't stuck in a Basarwa settlement, he thought to himself, as he scanned the village center before him. He saw the crowded general dealer, the sky-blue paint on its concrete walls peeling, its corrugated tin overhang providing precious shade to idle villagers; the butcher shop with throngs of flies gathered at its rickety screen door waiting for a chance to enter and begin feasting; the mysterious bustling bottle shop where people wandered in and out but never loitered; the new combination bar and restaurant, which was really neither restaurant nor bar but rather more of a social hall for the more renowned villagers. To Big Boy's right were the cinder-block houses of the few affluent (relatively speaking) families of Shakawe, located along the river, and to his left stood the mass of reed and stick hovels where everyone else lived. And everywhere else there was sand, sand and more sand.

What a primitive rotten hellhole.

Leaning on an anemic chicken-wire fence, he asked himself what he, Moikakasi "Big Boy" Kwanyana, was doing in this godforsaken pit of ignorance. After all, he was the son of Okotse Kwanyana and third cousin of Sechele III, chief of the Bakwena. What had he done to deserve this horrible punishment? Why couldn't he have been posted somewhere down south with civilized people, particularly in his home village of Molepolole? He knew why. Because those stinking Bamangwato in the government had put all their family and friends into the good positions, that's why. They and their party, the Botswana Democratic Party, had been in control of the government since independence twenty-five years ago. But soon, the opposition Botswana National Front, his party and the party of those fed up with the tyranny of the Bamangwato, would change all that. Well, maybe not this election, he thought, but the certainly next one or the one after that.

Contempt. That's what he felt for these primitive villagers in Shakawe. Look at them: going around in rags, living in drafty reed houses without pit latrines, fetching their water from the river even when there was a borehole and water could be drawn from nearby modern standpipes. And their dark black skin. That just proved how backward they really were.

And now one of these miserable little hyenas had stolen his badge.

Undoubtedly to try and humiliate him. Perhaps even to try and get him reprimanded. Reprimanded! He laughed. What worse punishment could they inflict on him than the posting here? He knew the answer and shuddered: they could send him to the middle of the Kgalagadi where there was nothing—nothing but Basarwa and Bakgalagadi. Oh yes, he forgot. He also hated the Bakgalagadi worse than the Hambukushu.

One of these scheming bastards has taken my badge, he thought again. Maybe it was the thin, red-eyed one with the baseball cap who was wobbling out of the bottle store right at this moment. Or even the old man shuffling tenaciously through the sand over by the butcher's shop. Porridge Pot drove by in his imaginary *bakkie*, his arms flailing at the wheel and his tongue vicariously ringing out the rumble of his engine. No, it couldn't be him. Whoever it was, he was going to find out, though. He had nearly panicked when he first found it missing yesterday, and although fuming within, he had wisely kept his cool on the outside. He had gone out of the police station a few times on the pretext of making routine rounds and had proceeded to search explosively through random huts like a wild man. He had even searched the village shops on the pretext of checking for safety violations.

"*Wareng*, Big Boy. *Le kae?*"

Big Boy had been concentrating so hard on revenge that he hadn't noticed Jackson Sedumedi walk up beside him. He turned and leered at Jackson, who was as smartly dressed and suave as ever.

"*Waii, monna*, is that how you greet an officer of the law, you good-for-nothing?" His mien betrayed his internal anger.

Jackson was taken aback. He had drunk enough beers with Big Boy to be able to greet him casually, and besides, since no one else was around, there was no need to keep up appearances.

"*Instwarele, rra*," he mumbled in exaggerated apology. He took off his stylish driving cap and added with great politeness, "*Rra lepodise, o tsogile jang?*" And how is the honorable policeman feeling today?

Big Boy almost committed the cardinal sin of telling him to go screw himself, but caught himself in time. Yes, he'd love to say *vuitsak* to this pitiful dandy. Careful, he thought. He felt like strangling the fool, but it suddenly came to him that it would be wiser to make use of him. Actually, he realized that he had been going about this all wrong. The thief either had to be someone who had it out for him or else someone who had been around his house during the weekend and had decided to take it on a whim. He had to be thoughtful about this. He eased up and tried a different approach.

"*Re teng. Le wena?*" I'm fine and you.

Jackson relaxed a little. "*Ee, re teng.*"

"So, how is it?"

"Just okay. How is it?"

"*Ee.*"

"*Ee.*"

"So, you are in the village," said Big Boy stating the obvious in true Tswana fashion.

"*Ee, rra.*"

"*Bona, tsala,* I've got a problem."

"*Ehe,* life is full of problems, no?" Jackson was completely at ease now.

"*Ee.* It seems someone broke into my quarters this weekend and stole my police badge." He spoke looking into the distance and not directly at Jackson.

"*Ao! Monna,* is it true? Someone has done this? *Ja, ja, ja.*" He sighed in commiseration.

"*Ee.* Listen, I want you to be attentive and listen for any information that might help me find out who did this."

"But of course! I will let you know if I learn anything."

"And I don't need to tell you to keep this just between us . . ."

"*Monna!*"

"*Dankie. Naa,* I've got to make my rounds."

"*Ee.*"

"*Go siame.*" So long.

"*Go siame.*" Jackson was outwardly compliant, but inside he was aghast at Big Boy's rudeness. He had brought up his problem without any preparatory small talk and he had even had the nerve to end the conversation so abruptly. As if Jackson were his lackey! Let him see if he would help, he thought.

Big Boy decided to talk with Kitchener Semumu. Besides being a village elder and a moderately powerful bureaucrat, Semumu was a member of the Botswana National Front, the BNF, and thus a comrade of sorts. He could count on both Semumu's help and his discretion. Big Boy had used him before and it seemed he would have to swallow his pride and use him again. He found him at the *kgotla*, the tribal assembly areas, where he was discussing local affairs with other men from the village.

"*Ehe*, Rra Kwanyana, *o tsogile?*" Semumu greeted him with a broad smile.

"*Ke tsogile. O tsogile*, Rra Semumu?" Big Boy returned the greeting and then politely greeted the others nearby as well. He turned back to Semumu.

"*Ee*," began the rotund Semumu.

"*Ee*," replied Big Boy.

"So, you are at the *kgotla*." Semumu paused and wiped some dust off his sleeve. "You are seeking someone?"

"*Ee, rra*. I would like to speak with you for a few minutes."

"But of course." Semumu excused himself to the others, "*Intswarele, borra*, I am coming." Then he stretched his arm out to indicate their path and said, "This way, *mogaetsho*."

Semumu took Big Boy's hand and led him over to a bench beside the central cattle *kraal*. Big Boy gulped down his shame at being so deferential to this foolish Mumbukushu, then he went on to tell Semumu how several men had gone into his house while he was visiting a citizen of the village and had stolen some cash and his badge along with it.

"*Ehe*, but this is very serious," said Semumu through heavy breathing. His pudgy fingers stuck out of his sleeves like swollen cow teats.

"*Ee*. At first, I thought it must only be some children out for some easy money. But the more I thought about it, the more I became convinced of another explanation." The air was very dry and Big Boy could feel his lips chapping. He pulled out a small round jar of Carmex lip balm and opened it, then twirled his finger around the inside gathering up a film of the gel and applied it to his lips. He offered some to Semumu, who hesitated, being torn between wanting to hear Big Boy's conclusion and a chance to assuage his own dry lips. As always, his vanity won out. He dipped his finger in and then rubbed the balm onto his lips while gesturing for Big Boy to continue.

"I think it must have been Motsholathebe and his gang of an-archo-syndicalists. I saw them over in my ward a couple of times last weekend. I didn't think anything of it at the time, but it seems strange to me now why he should have been there. Neither he nor his friends live there, and as far as I know none of them visit a girl in that area." He scratched his chin. "I think they came to scout the place out and then broke in while I was away. Most likely they were seeking money for their thieving capitalist enterprises." Big Boy had completed his secondary school education and was always pleased to hear the way such weighty terms rolled smoothly from his tongue. He knew that Semumu had heard such words at BNF meetings, but he also knew that Semumu had very little idea what they meant and as usual would be impressed at hearing them.

"But . . . but why your badge?"

Big Boy leaned a bit closer. "To have me disgraced and then transferred, of course." He fixed his eyes on Semumu. "Without me to control their greed, they would be able to buy up the whole village and make everyone workers for them."

Semumu reflected on this. Not that he had enough intelligence to reflect; it merely seemed the proper thing to do, the kind of thing a village elder and a respected member of the community would do. Even more so, the thought of bringing down Motsholathebe made his mouth water: finally, he could get back at that pig for not marrying his daughter. He smiled noncommittally to Big Boy. "I'll talk to my colleagues and see what we can do. I have expected those hooligans to do something like this for a long time. I don't mind saying that it would please me to see those rich good-for-nothings get what's coming to them."

Big Boy glowed inwardly at his success. "You are always so clever in these matters, Rra Semumu. That is why I came to you for advice and support. I am so happy. I knew I could rely on you."

Semumu's bloated head soaked in the flattery. "*Waii, ke motho fela. It is nothing. I am simply assisting the institutions of our country, in this case, the police force." Mistaking a moment of reflection by Big Boy for anxious concern, he dropped the facade briefly and patted Big Boy's hand. "I'll let you know what I learn."

Big Boy bowed his head quickly and pressed his hands together before him to express his gratitude.

"*Go siame,*" he said.

"*Go siame.*"

Big Boy was uncommonly happy with himself. He was so clever! How he had ever thought to come up with that story about

Motsholathebe was beyond him. He was so immensely clever. Surely, it was his superior Motswana breeding. It was clear that these Hambukushu were no match for him. Now, whether he found his badge or not, he could make life miserable for Motsholathebe, which would bring him immense pleasure. Motsholathebe was good-looking, clever, hard-working, popular and considerate. All the things Big Boy was not. This naturally made Motsholathebe an object of his hatred, and as an object of his hatred he was automatically an anarcho-syndicalistic capitalist as well. Yes, he could give Motsholathebe what he deserved at last—that wretched hyena! Humming to himself, he decided he would take the rest of the day off and go visit his girlfriend Boiketlo.

He found her leaning over the washbasin in the open area in the front of her compound. Her arms rose and fell as she scrubbed clothing on a corrugated washboard, her elbows splaying each time like a butterfly at rest gently rocking its wings.

"Hey, Boiketlo, what are you doing, huh?" demanded Big Boy imperiously.

"What do you think? I am washing your clothes," she mumbled in response.

"*Gao! Mosadi*, aren't you done with those yet? Why are you so slow? Perhaps you are thinking that if you don't finish until late, then you won't have to get my dinner. Is that what you are planning?" His earlier triumphs with Jackson and Semumu had made him cockier than normal. He wanted to reassert his dominant position in their relationship by putting Boiketlo in her proper place.

She did not respond to his last taunts.

"Don't you know enough to answer me when I ask you a question? *Ao*, what are you thinking? That you are some kind of proud royal *mongwato* who doesn't have to answer to anybody, huh? You know I'm worried about my missing badge. Why do you cause me even more grief, huh, *mosadi*?"

She sighed while she wrung the soapy water out of a shirt and then laid it aside to be put in the rinse water later.

Big Boy grabbed her arm, "*Waii*, what do you say?"

She jerked her arm free. "*Xx! O a ntena, wena!*" she said—argh, you're a real pain in the ass. "Don't punish me for your lost badge. It's your fault, not mine." Then she marched into the hut.

Big Boy stood dumbfounded. This was not like Boiketlo, for her to be so forward in her irritation. He followed her into the hut and softened his approach enough to placate her but not so much as to admit any wrongdoing.

"*Naa*, it doesn't matter about the clothes. I don't need them until the day after tomorrow."

She drained a pot of *dikgobe*, sugar beans mixed with whole maize kernels, that had been sitting on the table to cool. She said nothing, and when she finished she set the pot down and began to walk outside.

Big Boy moved in her way. "Where are you going?"

"To get the *motogo*. It's finished."

"*Motogo* and *dikgobe* in the same meal?" he asked suspiciously. That was too many treats at once to be ordinary.

"Don't be a fool," she replied, "I'm letting the sorghum sit so it will turn sour." *Motogo* was a sorghum porridge that was allowed to ferment for a short period and produced a slightly sour taste that was well liked. Looking at the floor, she went around him and out the door.

Although Boiketlo was not a particularly meek person, Big Boy felt she generally knew her place as a woman and this impertinent behavior of hers baffled him. She wasn't simply trying to assert her independence or her identity. She was pissed. But why? He walked outside to find out what the problem was. She had gone around back and wasn't to be seen, so Big Boy sighed and stood looking out at the other huts in the ward. His eyes wandered up to the cool azure sky of winter. Not a cloud in sight. Nothing save a fish eagle soaring some ways off over by the river. It didn't seem to be hunting. No doubt heading back to its nest, he thought.

Kgathlego, an old girlfriend of his, shuffled around the corner and passed by. She greeted him and he grunted in return as a man would do, then watched her walk away as she swung her large shapely thighs. He scratched his crotch absentmindedly and moved to go find Boiketlo in the back. All of a sudden a cold fear and realization hit him. Serapha! That was why she was angry; she must have found out that he had been sleeping with Serapha. Damn, he thought, you never could trust women to keep their mouths shut, especially with other women. He knew he was in a real mess.

Boiketlo came around the corner with a three-legged pot of *motogo*, which she held out in front of her. "*Retsa*, Boiketlo," he said sheepishly, "I just came by to tell you that I have to work late tonight, so you needn't worry about dinner. I'll stop in later, *go siame*?"

She did not reply and he decided that he had guessed correctly. Yes, a hasty retreat was the best thing he could do now. He opened the gate and stepped into the deep sand. He found it easier to breathe in the open, but not easier to think. He really needed a beer.

The local bar, *Ema Re Nwe*, was already quite busy when Big Boy walked in. It was late June, the middle of winter, and most men began their drinking earlier so as not to have to deal more than was necessary with the early darkness and the unwelcome night chill. He noticed Kitchener Semumu at the end of the bar furthest from the door. He was talking to a small group, his large gut hanging unashamedly out like a festering boil. Big Boy went over, greeted everyone and ordered a beer.

"*Waii, mosadi*," he shouted to the woman behind the bar, "give me a Hansa, will you? A nice cold one."

"What makes you think there are any cold ones left, huh? I've been here for some time already," Semumu said swaying slightly from side to side. Both his eyes and his smile were out of focus.

Big Boy saw this and immediately sensed the advantage he held. He grinned widely and tapped Semumu on the arm, "Yeah, sho'," he said jovially in English, "I know *monna*, you are the drinking man's drinking man."

The others chuckled in glee. Big Boy entered the conversation good-naturedly and felt for the flow of discussion, hoping to pull himself into the group while maintaining as low a profile as possible. They talked first about cattle. Old Nyambe reminisced about the years long gone when bulls stood as tall as eland, he said, and were as fat as rhinoceros. Some men, like old man Kutuvanjira, would have herds of several thousand head at a time.

An agitated Kuvumbira, who was related by marriage to the chief, spoke up. "*Ao, monna*, you talk rubbish! What is this nonsense? Everyone knows that the new breeds that have come to us are stronger and have much longer horns. The cattle of our youth were thinner than the branches of spindly *mopane* trees. Tall as eland. *Gao!* I think maybe some *ngaka* has been working his magic on you."

"What is this you say, you young good-for-nothing?" replied Nyambe. "I was being initiated into manhood while you were still suckling at your mother's breast. You dare question me? What do you know about cattle? You who have only seventy head. Tsk, tsk, such foolishness."

Kuvumbira was correct in what he said, but he had been imprudent in stating it so openly. Nyambe's last comment had put him in his place and silenced him thoroughly. Old Nyambe had four hundred head of cattle, and therefore carried a lot of weight in the community. With his much smaller herd, Kuvumbira was no match for Nyambe, even with his connection to the *kgosi*, the headman.

"Now, now," Semumu tried to broker a peace between them, "you are both right. Kuvumbira is right when he says that the cattle of today have longer horns. That is so. And truly, there were many diseases that afflicted the cattle in years past. By the grace of *Modimo*, we rarely see this now. But I also remember the years of good rains long ago when the cattle were truly very big as Nyambe says. Some almost as high as a man. Kuvumbira spoke a little hastily, that is all."

This seemed to give both parties face and to calm them to some extent. Big Boy, who was following the discussion with growing pleasure, ordered his third beer. Semumu moved the conversation away from the controversial subject of cattle and turned instead to local business affairs. Kuvumbira was angry that the price of paraffin had risen ten percent in the last month. All agreed and someone suggested that this was a scheme by the *Makgoa*, the Whites, to get more money out of them.

"*Ehe*, this is true," said Mothsithsi, the village gossip, wagging his finger. "My brother's son was down in Maun last week and he talked with some fellows from the South who had been working in the mines in South Africa. They said the Americans had raised the price of petrol and oil to get more money so that they could give more help to the South African government."

"*Ao*, is this so?" asked Semumu.

"Indeed, it is. In actual fact, everyone knows that the American missionaries in Samochima are all spies for the CIA."

"Samochima? But that is only half a morning's walk from here!" cried Old Nyambe. Then, after a pause, "What is this C-I-A?"

"How should I know?" replied Mothsithsi. "It is so secret even the Americans do not know it exists. But I can tell you this . . . it is evil."

There were hushed expressions of disapproving surprise from everyone. The word 'secret' had damned the organization long before Mothsithsi had uttered the terrible word 'evil.'

Big Boy saw his chance. "*Ee*, it is true what he says. And what is more disturbing is that," he paused, looked around and then leaning closer continued in a whisper, "they have recruited some from among us to help them out in return for money."

There were mutual glances of anxiety and suspicion from one face to the other.

He continued, "I have even heard it said that they are working together with the BDP in hopes of destroying any opposition in this region." The BDP or Botswana Democratic Party was the ruling party in the government.

"What proof do you have for this," questioned Kuvumbira, ever the skeptical one. "Are you certain?"

Big Boy stuck out his chest. "*Waii, monna*, are you doubting my word? I am the chief of police here after all. Besides, can you doubt it if even Mothsithsi has heard about it?"

Semumu, who considered himself indispensable to the management of the community and a senior member of its leadership, was horrified at the thought that he might not be aware of something as important as this. Big Boy is well educated and has high connections in the South, he thought. He must know what he is talking about. "*Ee.* I have heard something about this myself," he added casually, "but I have not brought it up so as not to alarm people."

"*Ehe*, so it really is true," said Kuvumbira putting his finger to his lower lip pensively.

Big Boy let the falsehood settle in for a moment. Making it appear that he had briefly considered the group's trustworthiness and found it acceptable, he moved closer once more and said, "Indeed, I even have some names."

"*Ruri, a o bua nnete, monna?*" gasped Kuvumbira. Was he really telling the truth? Big Boy nodded.

"But who? Who would do such things?" asked Nyambe.

Big Boy looked slowly around the room, then into the faces of each man in the group. "Motsholathebe. He and his friends."

"*Ija*, but this can't be so," exclaimed Kuvumbira. "He is a fine boy!"

"Oh yeah? Have you not thought about all the money he seems to have suddenly," Big Boy hissed.

"But he works hard. His plumbing business has been very busy since last summer."

"Come now, you expect us to believe that? Has he not been making large additions to his compound? Didn't he give away a lot of money for his aunt's funeral? Doesn't he have many new clothes all at once? You think he made this from a plumbing business in our small village?" Big Boy's voice rose to an unsavory level.

"He is making additions to his compound because he plans to marry Sethunya Dishero," offered Kuvumbira.

Semumu winced at this embarrassing reminder.

"Marriage?" asked Big Boy. "Yes, he says so. But tell me, how many cattle does he have?"

"Why, two or three, I believe."

"Two or three!" laughed Big Boy. "Does that sound like a man who is looking to get married? And why doesn't he buy cattle with all this money he is making from his business? I'll tell you why, because he wants to live the good life and he knows that more money will come in if he helps the Americans. He can always buy cattle when he wants to. Yeah, sho', maybe he does want to get married, but you can believe me that it won't be money from his business that gets him his bride price of cattle. Sethunya is worth ten head at least."

Semumu calculated his losses and sighed.

"You know, come to think of it," said Mothsithsi, "I have seen Motsholathebe down by the Americans in Samochima several times. He said he had to repair some pipes and what-what. I thought nothing of it before, but now it makes sense."

Old Nyambe and Kuvumbira were not completely convinced but the seed of doubt and mistrust had been sown and that was all that was necessary. Big Boy knew that time would do the rest. A moment later he noticed out of the corner of his eye that Jackson had just walked into the bar. He excused himself from the group under the pretext of going to the toilet and walked over to Jackson.

"*Naa, monna, wareng?*" he greeted Jackson.

"*Ehe*, Big Boy, *ga ke bue sepe.*"

"So, you have come to the bar."

"*Ee.*"

"You must let me buy you a beer, *tsala*. Come on."

They went up to the other side of the bar and Big Boy ordered two Hansas. He engaged Jackson in some small talk for a few minutes, and then when he thought the moment was ripe, he changed the subject nonchalantly. "By the way, *monna*, have you heard anything about that matter we discussed today?"

"No, nothing, Big Boy. No one knows a thing."

"*Ehe.* Well, it doesn't surprise me. But, you know what? I did hear something."

"Yeah?"

"Yeah." Big Boy dropped his voice to a whisper. "Someone has heard that Motsholathebe probably had something to do with it."

"Motsholathebe? Impossible." Jackson took a drink of his beer and leaned on the bar. He looked at Big Boy. "You really think so?"

"*Waii, monna*, this is just what I heard. But why not? He never liked me. It's because of that girl of his, Sethunya. She was too hot for me, you know, and I couldn't say no forever. Between you and me, I have slept with her already. So, now he wants to marry her and he is jealous of me." Big Boy leaned back on the bar resting on both arms. He continued while looking ahead of him and not at Jackson, "I don't see the girl any longer. I have moved on to better things, but . . . who knows? Anyway, just see what you can find out, okay?" Lies were coming easier than breaths tonight for Big Boy.

"Yeah, sho'. No *mathata*."

"*Naa, tsala*, I knew I could count on you. Let me get you another beer and then I've got to get back to Semumu and his friends." When the beers came, Big Boy clapped Jackson on the back and made his way over to the others, who were now discussing rumors that the coming year would bring a lot of rain. Now on his sixth beer, Big Boy had trouble understanding much more than the general out-lines of the conversation. He stood wavering, a mute partner in the proceedings. Kuvumbira and Old Nyambe had finally agreed, based on omens they had heard, that it would indeed be a good year.

At that moment, Motsholathebe walked into the bar with his friends Twamanine and Kubula. "*Wareng*, Motsholathebe!" shouted someone from a table by the window. "What, drinking so late? Don't tell me you couldn't find your way in the dark. Or did that Sethunya of yours keep you busy, eh?"

"*Heela*, Phakalane, maybe your wallet is as big as your mouth and you can buy me a beer, huh?" Motsholathebe teased him back.

"*Nna?* Me? I am a poor man. But you are right, I will match my mouth with my wallet and keep it closed," he laughed.

Motsholathebe and his two friends went up to the center of the bar and ordered three Ohlssons. Twamanine noticed Jackson and smiled, "*Waii, monna, o kae?*" Jackson moved his hand grudgingly in recognition and then walked away from them to one of the tables at the far end of the room.

"What's gotten into him?" wondered Twamanine aloud.

Motsholathebe simply shrugged his shoulders. He took a sip of his beer and turned to lean sideways on the bar in the direction of Big Boy and his group.

"*Dumelang, borra!* How is it, father Nyambe? Rra Kuvumbira? And you Rra Semumu, *go ntse jang?*"

Good manners dictated that they return his salutations and they did so. Embarrassed, they were undecided as to how far they should go in ostracizing him. Nyambe and Kuvumbira cast their eyes on the floor, while Semumu looked away towards the tables on the other side of the room. Only Big Boy held his gaze steadily fixed on Motsholathebe.

"*Dumela*, Big Boy. *O thlotse?*" asked Motsholathebe deliberately in greeting. Big Boy did not respond. Motsholathebe grinned widely in embarrassment and then turned away.

"What's the matter, Big Boy," demanded Kubula, "are you too important that you can't answer when you are greeted?"

"Was I greeted?" Big Boy did not move a muscle of his body. "I always reply when greeted by people, sometimes to children. But to animals . . . never." The words came out slowly.

The three of them stiffened at hearing this. "Are you calling us animals, Big Boy?" Twamanine's eyes narrowed.

"I didn't call you anything. I just answered a question."

The three young men were puzzled. Motsholathebe knew that Big Boy did not like him, but for what reason he didn't know. He certainly didn't have any idea why he should be so hostile tonight. Motsholathebe hadn't even seen him in over a week. How could he have given him cause to be upset? He decided it would be best to let things drop. Motsholathebe and his friends had no quarrel with Big Boy—if he was in a bad mood that was his problem. Motsholathebe put his hand on Twamanine's arm and gestured with his head. They grabbed their beers and headed for the porch outside.

Big Boy would not be put off so easily, however. "Whazz the problem, *ditsssala?* You don' like our comp'ny in here?"

None of them looked around and they continued on outside. Even Semumu, who had been drinking all evening and was hardly sober, recognized the folly of such antagonism. He told Big Boy to let them go, that they were not worth bothering about. Old Nyambe and Kuvumbira were already ashamed and had turned to the bar to dissociate themselves from Big Boy, who was nevertheless insensible to it all. He was too full of rage at the loss of his badge, at his girlfriend's sulking, at his posting on the edge of the world, at the sanctity of this honorable Motsholathebe. He was too drunk.

He lumbered out the door and found the three friends in the dark sitting to his right against the porch wall. They saw him and froze in expectancy, their eyes fixed firmly on his shadowy bulk. Big Boy came up and stood before them swaying and trying to focus his eyes on them. Nothing was said for a moment.

Then finally Big Boy spoke up, "So, you jus' ignore me, huh? Think you can jus' walk out here and ignore us 's if we were ants? Well?"

The said nothing in return nor did they move. They just sat mutely regarding the figure before them. To have even implied that Big Boy was drunk could have been construed as an insult. They wanted neither to insult him nor to incite him, and so they remained silent. A group of four other men sitting at a table on the porch broke off their conversation and turned to watch. Big Boy was in an uncomfortable spot. He had forgotten exactly why he had come out to the verandah in the first place and he had absolutely no idea what he should say next. He couldn't very well just walk away now that he had taunted them, and the predicament of the situation only served to anger him more.

He exploded in rage, "Who do you think you are Mo-tsho-la-the-be? A *kgosi*? Huh? How is it you think you're better 'n everyone else?" Inside his stone expression, Motsholathebe's eyes glowed like lava. "Why? I'll tell you. Because you're a selfish cap'lis' pig and an . . . an . . . an . . . anarcho-syn'calis'. You're a money-grubbing dog and a thief!"

Motsholathebe jumped up quickly and moved as if to strike Big Boy. But he had no intention of doing so. Instead, his arm rose to make a point as he spoke, "You have insulted me, Big Boy. I have witnesses to the awful things you have just said. I will take you to the *kgotla*!"

His arm came down and all at once Big Boy seemed to awaken out of his frenzy. The mention of witnesses brought back to him the reality of his surroundings, and to his horror he realized what he had done. To apologize would do no good since the words were already out and as painful as the consequences might be if he didn't, he refused to lower himself before this man Motsholathebe. Embarrassed and yet trying to remain outwardly nonplussed, he grinned broadly and walked slowly out into the deep sand and the moonlit night.

He trudged along calmly at first, but the shifting mire of the sand beneath his feet and the biting cold of night irritated him and ate away at the last membrane of self-control that held his anger back. He could not shout, he could not curse. Someone might recognize him and it would be very unseemly for a police officer to be caught behaving in such a way. In frustration, he lifted his knees higher and increased his speed. To Boiketlo's, he thought, to Boiketlo's. He would expunge his hatred in her bed as he had done so many times before. The thought of imminent release warmed him and excited him further.

She was asleep when he arrived and he had to scratch at her door for ten minutes before he got her to open up. "What took you so long, you lazy woman? I could have frozen to death of cold."

She was holding a paraffin lamp in her hand and in the soft light thrown over her face he could see she was still pouting. In her hurt eyes and expressionless mouth, he saw the embodiment of all the scorn he felt had been heaped on him and caused his current troubles. "You're not going to make a fool of me like that Motsholathebe did tonight! You hear me?" The thought of seeing abject pain her face only fed his desire. He grabbed her by the wrist and dragged her into the bedroom. She resisted until he threw her against a wall post and then onto the bed. She knew him well enough to perceive he was in no mood to be challenged; she would have to give in. Her many attempts to fight back in the past had only brought harsh beatings upon her. She had run away from him, too, several times, but where could one go in a small village like this? And what would she run to? A life in her village of Ncamasere caring for her daughter and being a servant to the rest of the family—cooking, cleaning, washing, sewing, chopping wood until she dropped of exhaustion? No, the best solution was to quietly submit to him and make him pay for it later.

He took his clothes off and blew out the lamp. Then he pulled her under the covers with him and pushed up her nightgown. He was already excited from anticipation, and she stiffly acquiesced as he forced her legs open and entered her. She was unwilling and winced with pain, but he didn't notice. He only lunged and lunged with forceful thrusts, in his mind each being a blow to the face of those he hated. Images swam through his head of bruised faces crying for mercy, and only when the stinging hand in his mind had drawn blood and had become red to the elbow did he find release.

He collapsed panting on Boiketlo, his body rising and falling above her body. She waited motionless.

Finally at peace, his fury spent, he rolled off her to the side of the bed next to the wall. His mind and his body were thankfully relaxed and he wallowed in the comforting warmth created in the bed by his exertions. He flicked away a mosquito from his ear, scratched and then let his hand rest on his cheek. Exhaustion came over him and he began to sleep, and as he did so his hand fell slowly away from his face and dropped between the bed and wall awakening him with a start. He shook his head. When he put his weight on his left hand to turn himself in bed, he felt something hard and cold on the floor. Releasing his weight, he grabbed at the object and ran it through his fingers. He held it up to the moonlight and gasped.

"My badge! It's here. I've found it!" He sat upright in bed and screamed with happy relief. The shock was then all the greater as his joy instantly plummeted into an abyss of despair when he remembered the grief he had stirred up over the badge and realized that its return in this way was far from a blessing. "Oh, no. Oh, no. They'll ruin me if they find out!" He covered his face and sank into the bed, crushed by the vision of newly rising woes. How would he get out of this, he thought? He would have to plant the badge somewhere in Motsholathebe's compound. He couldn't admit the truth. He must think of something, he told himself, but he was too tired. Soon he was lost in his own thoughts, gradually floating away towards sleep. He had long forgotten about Boiketlo at his side.

It was very dark in the hut, but a small strip of moonlight came in through the upper window and fell across the upper part of the bed like a swath of silver cloth. Big Boy threw his arm across his eyes and turned on his side toward the wall.

Silence returned, the silence of darkness; but the silver strip of moonlight seemed a loud ringing song for Boiketlo. Had Big Boy thought to look over, he would have noticed that she was smiling.

Go Hithla Motho

(July)

Go Hithla Motho

"She will have to go, there is nothing else to be said about it."

"But you must give me more time. Please, I beg you. I have nowhere I can take her."

Nurse Keatlaretse looked sternly down her nose at him. There were regulations to follow and rules to abide by. These were made to be obeyed. Why couldn't these people understand that? And now this man. She tried once again, "But you must take her out. We are overcrowded as it is and after three days the bodies start to stick together. It is most unpleasant."

"*Ke a itse*," I know, said the old man, "you have told me this already, and you are kind to explain it to me again. Still, I need some time to solve my problems."

"*Nyaa*. The answer is the same. I'm sorry." She sighed deeply, more out of exhaustion than frustration. She stiffened in preparation for another attempt by the man to break down her resistance. But it did not come. He sat immobile, his eyes lowered in shame and his trembling hands grasping his woolen balaclava between his knees.

She softened her stance and looking closer she realized why he had failed to beg her another time. He was crying; the old man had broken down in tears. To be sure, Nurse Keatlaretse was renowned for her sense of duty and her firmness, and there were many who had made protracted and emotional supplications to her before—all in vain. And yet, even her heart could not withstand the misery of this poor old man. She could see that his anguish was genuine. She ground her teeth together for a moment and then told herself that she supposed it wouldn't hurt to bend the rules a little this once.

"All right," she said kindly, "I'll give you an extra day. It's all I dare to do. Really, you must have her out the day after tomorrow, okay?"

The old man slowly raised his head and forced a quivering smile through the tears on his face. "*Dankie, mma, ke itumetse thata, dankie, dankie.*" Thank you, miss, I'm very grateful, thank you, thank you, he said falling to his knees and bowing with clasped hands before him.

Nurse Keatlaretse told him to get up, that everything would be okay. She was a little embarrassed, but also happy to see him so moved. Yes, she thought, life is sometimes hard, very hard.

The old man shuffled down the main hospital drive. It was lined with tall syringa trees, leafless this time of year, their light gray bark peeling like sycamores and echoing his withered age. His back was hunched slightly and his long driftwood fingers clutched desperately at the head of his cane with each step. The warm winter sun felt good and helped to take the chill out of his bones. He had been too long indoors this morning. Near the end of the drive, he looked around absently, expecting to see his son Joshua there to meet him, but then he remembered that Joshua was in Francistown and that he had come down to Maun from Shakawe by himself. He sat on a log that lay just inside the front gate of the hospital compound. There was sunlight here to warm him and he decided it wouldn't hurt to rest a few minutes and get his thoughts together. The brittle cold in his joints made it difficult to walk.

Moikokobetsi Ramphisi was as near to being a broken man as one could get. Three months before, his sister Seobo had been viciously mauled and killed by some unknown *ngaka* who evidently had needed parts of her body for his mysterious potions. This incident had left him deeply saddened for many weeks afterward, and no sooner had he raised his spirits high enough to bring himself out of his depression than word came from his cattle post to the northwest of Shakawe that twelve of his nineteen head had contracted hoof-and-mouth disease. They would have to be destroyed and there was little likelihood of any compensation. This most recent blow had been almost too much for him to endure.

His wife had come down to Maun last week to visit a cousin of hers whom she hadn't seen in three years. She had suddenly been stricken with a heart attack the day before yesterday. The staff there had notified the police in Maun who in turn radioed the police in Shakawe. Moikokobetsi had immediately set out on the road, catching lifts wherever he could, only to arrive late this morning. It didn't matter, for his wife had died yesterday afternoon. Although she had passed away under the care of the hospital, because she had not come down from Shakawe in hospital transport, they were neither compelled nor authorized to return the body. Moikokobetsi must see to that and he had no money.

He sat numbly on the log and wished beyond hope that he would soon awaken from this horrible dream. He debated unconsciously the merits of going on—of going anywhere. Why leave this warm spot in the sun and this moment of peace? He had no relatives in Maun, and any acquaintances he had known had died or left years ago. There was his wife's cousin. She was a reasonable starting point, but all he knew was her name and a vague recollection of which ward she lived in. It was all he had. It would have to do.

He sat with his forehead lowered onto his hands, which rested on his desiccated walking stick. This was Moikokobetsi: a lanky old man with deep furrowed lines in his face; a gray wispy three-day growth of beard; worn and tattered clothing stained from years of use that had long ago lost any claim to color; dusty leather shoes split along the outer seams, no socks, and a ragged and dearly-loved maroon balaclava on his head. He had labored long in life to build a family, to gather some security and to survive the lean years of drought; he had done rather well. But all of that held very little meaning for him at present, for all of it was in the past and he could see nothing in the future. That was for his son to deal with.

There was one last task to be attended to: he must bury his wife. To accomplish this he would need to use every last grain of energy and cunning remaining to him, for he had no money. Thus resolved, he pushed on the walking stick, stood up, and, after allowing a minute for fresh blood to flow through his veins again, he set out walking for the only source of help he knew of.

His wife Separe's cousin, Olebile, lived in the northwestern part of the village, and so Moikokobetsi walked up the hundred meters to the tarmac road and followed this to the right towards the village center. He had only been to Maun a dozen times in his lifetime, and it had always made him feel uncomfortable. The last four or five, he had been terrified. There were so many people to be seen here, walking rapidly in one direction or another, and vehicles thundering down the road. There was noise and movement every-where. He never could understand how humans could live in such perverse confusion, how they could live in villages that were so big it took almost an hour to walk from one end to the next. He stopped to rest for a minute at the junction to the Francistown road. Four-by-fours and *bakkies* and tractors and donkey carts and even some modern passenger cars buzzed about like mosquitoes: some passing through, some stopping for petrol at the filling station, some going to the building supplies store on the other side of the road, some turning off on to the sandy tracks that led to the interior wards of the village. Standing there was more exhausting than walking for Moikokobetsi. He looked down the Francistown road, which crossed the river and disappeared over the hill on the other side. He tried to imagine what that faraway town was like where his son now lived and worked. It was larger than Maun. Was it possible for a place to be more disturbing than this village?

His eyes caught sight of a huge spiral mass turning slowly like a corkscrew into the arid blue sky. He squinted and shaded his eyes, and soon he could make out that it was a flock of marabou storks lazily drifting on a thermal updraft. He thought with envy how marvelous it must be to be such a creature, able to rise above the clamorous bustle of humanity. With a sigh, he marched onward keeping to the firm shoulder of the tarred road. He would have to do a good deal of walking in the enervating sand, and it was best to take advantage of anything that would save wear and tear on his ancient legs.

He was very tired by the time he reached Olebile's ward and extremely thirsty, for his body had used up every drop of moisture during his march through the dry air. Nevertheless, he was consoled by the tranquility of the neighborhoods away from the main road. To his right he saw a compound in which two men chatted beneath the shade of a large *morula* tree. There were also three women weaving baskets sitting near the doorway of a spacious *rondavel*. Moikokobetsi walked up to their gate and greeted them, his hands clasped deferentially in front of him.

"*Dumelang, borra. Dumelang, bomma.*"

"*Dumela, rra,*" they answered in unison.

"*Ee, le tsogile jang?*"

One woman replied for all, "*Re tsogile. Le wena?*"

"*Ee.*" He paused momentarily so as not to seem in a hurry and cause any rudeness. "*Naa, bagaetsho, ke kopa metsi.*" Brothers and sisters, I would like some water. "I have had a long walk from the hospital and I am greatly in need of something to drink."

"But, of course," said one of the men this time. "Come in, come in."

Moikokobetsi lifted the rusty wire that held the gate shut and entered the compound. One of the women shouted to her daughter, and when she came out, told her to get a cup of water for the visitor.

The girl returned before long with a yellow tin cup, the enamel of which was chipped and scratched with wear. Moikokobetsi gestured his thanks and gratefully drank in the water, feeling it soothe his chapped lips. Finishing, he returned the cup to the little girl who accepted it respectfully with both hands and then disappeared around back.

"So," began one of the men by the tree, "you are visiting Maun?"

"*Ee*. I am from Shakawe. My wife was visiting her cousin here and became ill. I came down to see her, but she was already late when I arrived." He paused for a moment as if nurturing the next thought to come forth. "Now I am arranging to take her back home. To do this, I must find her cousin. In this, *bagaetsho*, maybe you can help me. Her name is Olebile. I believe she lives in this ward."

The largest of the women turned to what appeared the eldest and remarked, "Could that be the Olebile who lives over by Ontlharetse? She comes from Sepopa." She looked to Moikokobetsi. "Your wife's cousin, is she from Sepopa?"

"*Ee*. I believe so."

"*Ehe*, that must be her," she said slapping her thigh.

"So, you can tell me where she lives?"

"I will take you myself," rasped the man who had not yet spoken. "It is not right that you should have trouble finding your way at a time like this." He waved to one of the women, "Tell Ntede to bring my walking stick."

They were only five minutes in reaching Olebile's house. All the same, Moikokobetsi was thankful for having a guide, since he was sure he would have lost his way otherwise. They parted at the gate to Olebile's. Moikokobetsi shook the old man's hand and told him to visit him next time he came to Shakawe so that he could return the kindness. The other tipped his hat and walked away with slow, deliberate steps. Moikokobetsi could see no one in the compound, and yet the door to the *rondavel* was open and it appeared that someone was at home.

"*Koko*," he called out tentatively. "*Koko*."

No one answered and he called again. At last a woman came around from the back wringing her hands in her dress. Evidently, she had been washing clothes.

"*Dumela*," said Moikokobetsi. "*O tsogile jang?*"

"*Ke tsogile, rra. Wena, o tsogile?*"

"*Ee.*" He licked his lips unhurriedly. "*Ke kopa thusa.*" Could you help me? "I am looking for a Miss Olebile. Is this her house?"

"*Ee, rra.* I am Olebile," she said with a hint of suspicion.

"*Ehe.* I am Moikokobetsi Ramphisi."

At these words, her face sagged in comprehension and pity. She came to the gate and dragged it open through the sand.

"I have come to ask your help," stated Moikokobetsi simply, not knowing what else to say. He remained before the gate.

"I know," was all she replied. "Come inside now."

She motioned for him to sit on a wooden stool outside the entrance to the *rondavel*. The night's winter cold had not yet left the interior of the hut and he would be more comfortable sitting in the sun. She then walked around to the back of the compound and into a small corrugated tin hut where she did her cooking. She returned with a bowl of mealie porridge.

"Ah, *bogobe*! That is very kind of you." He reached out both hands and took the plate. He ate ravenously, surprised at his own hunger. When he had finished and had drunk another cup of water, he felt much stronger. But with the new vigor there also came vivid reminders of the awful predicament he faced.

He began speaking quite suddenly, "The nurse at the hospital says I must take Separe away by the day after tomorrow. At first she wanted her out today, but she had pity in the end and gave me another day. What am I to do? I have no money here and no family either. Somehow I must get together enough for a coffin and for transport back to Shakawe."

"Won't the hospital help?"

"*Nyaa.* They say that because she was not brought down using hospital transport, they cannot help me bring her back."

"And you don't want to bury her here in Maun?"

Her question had been the logical one, really less a question than a statement. He shook his head, however, and said aloud what they both understood, namely, that it wouldn't be the proper thing to do. "*Nyaa. O itse sent'e, ga e siame jalo.*" Moikokobetsi was so lost in thought he did not feel a fly that ran up the side of his face. "Besides, she begged me many times that if she should pass away before me, I was to bury her in her mother's home compound at Xanekwa."

"*Ee*, you are right," she sighed. "I can borrow you one hundred pula, but that is all I have to spare."

"*Ke itumetse, mma.*" Although he truly was thankful, the amount hardly came close to solving his problem. He began turning his bala-clava in his hands. "I still have seven head of cattle outside Shakawe. Once I return I can sell some of them to pay back my debts." He was silent for a while, and appeared to be falling asleep. Olebile saw that he was actually crying, and she said nothing nor did she move so as not to embarrass him. After a few minutes, he raised his head and asked, "Is there anyone else you know who might help me? I do not even know where to begin."

"I will ask my brother Moitshepi whether he can help. Otherwise, your only choice is to see Mophiri, the moneylender. He will charge a lot to borrow you money, but at least you will have what you need." She exhaled slowly in contemplation. "The only other way is to go to Barclays bank and ask for a loan."

"*Ee,* I will do all of these things. I will also wire my son in Francistown. Maybe he can send some money." He did not appear reassured. "I must also arrange for a coffin to be made. Where should I go for that?"

"John Gaolekwe is the cheapest, but he will take weeks to finish one for you. Go to the brigades on the other side of the river. They can have a coffin made in a day, no *mathata.*"

"Okay. I will go there first and find out the price, then to the bank and the post office. *Naa,* where can I arrange transport for the coffin?"

She told him.

"I am going." He stood up and held his cap in both hands. He hesitated seemingly oppressed by some thought. "*Mma . . .*"

"*Rra?*"

"I am wondering . . . I have no place to stay, no relatives here . . ."

"You will stay here." His glance in her direction was his painful thanks. Olebile smiled compassionately, "Now, go. You have much to do."

"*Ee. Go siame.*"

"*Go siame.*"

The people at the brigades were very polite and helpful. They said they could make the coffin in one day, but not faster than that, so Moikokobetsi must let them know by the next morning whether he wanted them to begin if they were to have it ready in time. Unfortunately, they were asking five hundred pula for a coffin, which was more than Moikokobetsi had expected. He scratched his head in confusion and wondered how he could manage to borrow that much money. After all, five hundred pula was more than two months salary for those lucky enough to have jobs in Shakawe. He sighed and began to get up.

"*Bona, monna mogolo,* you say this is for your wife?" asked the carpentry manager.

"*Ee, rra.*"

"As for myself, I come from Gumare."

"*Ehe,* so you come from the same area!"

"*Ee, rra.* And my father came from Sepopa. I know what life is like up there. Sometimes it is very good, but, well, at other times . . . *Retsa,* if you can bring me cash for the coffin, *monna mogolo,* I will let you have it for four hundred and twenty-five pula. Okay?"

"*Dankie, rra, ke itumetse.*" Moikokobetsi expressed his deep gratitude by bowing slightly several times. He must still find a great deal of money, but the savings of seventy-five pula was a lot. It might make all the difference in the end. He then walked the ten kilometers back across the river to the center of Maun. His first stop was the post office where he sent a telegram to Joshua in Francistown explaining the situation and asking him to send as much money as possible. Next he walked down a few buildings to Barclays bank.

The interior of Barclays was densely crowded with people, most of whom were waiting in line. Moikokobetsi had often stood in line for hours when the bank plane came to Shakawe once a month, so the half an hour he would spend here did not bother him in the least. On the other hand, in Shakawe he waited in the open air, and it was very oppressive for him to be among so many people crowded into such a small closed space. He eventually moved up to the counter of the 'enquiries' line. When he asked about applying for a loan, he was told that he must see the manager.

"*Ee, mma.* I will speak to the manager." He stood expectantly smiling.

"But you must have an appointment," said the clerk.

"*Ehe,* that's all right. I will wait right over there," he indicated a bench built into the wall.

"*Waii, monna mogolo,* you don't understand. You must sign up for an appointment to see him. A person does not just 'wait' for the manager." Poor Moikokobetsi could not understand that he had struck a tender bureaucratic nerve in the clerk.

"*Naa,* let me sign up, then. When can he see me?"

The clerk pulled out a large black leather-bound book and imperiously ran her fingers up and down the pages. "Not until two o'clock p.m. on Monday," she said with some satisfaction in her voice, her nose raised slightly.

"But today is Wednesday," he cried, "I can't wait that long."

With her nose still in the air and her eyes turned to the side, the clerk added finally, "That is the earliest you may see him. Do you want an appointment or not?"

Moikokobetsi did not own a watch, what good was an appointment to him? Besides, Monday would be too late. This was all too confusing for him. No, thank you, he told the clerk, he would not need an appointment.

He was no more successful with Mophiri, the moneylender. Moikokobetsi was desperate enough to be willing to accept the exorbitant rates of interest demanded and Mophiri's nose smelled the weakness of that desperation. However, Moikokobetsi could not come up with any substantial local references; he was not gainfully employed with a registered company and Shakawe was too far away for Mophiri to want to worry about how he might collect in case of default. Mophiri let business sense be his guide and refused to lend him anything.

Doggedly, Moikokobetsi moved on to look up the names Olebile had given him for transport of the coffin. Both gentlemen were very polite and willing to undertake the journey, but their prices were too high. The cheapest rate offered was one hundred and fifty pula—about the price of four goats and many times the normal fare for passenger lifts.

"But it is only sixteen pula if one takes the transport truck!" Moikokobetsi remonstrated to the second man Moremi.

"*Waii, monna*, that is true, but it carries many people—you are only one. Anyway, that road, it is too bumpy. Every time I drive it, something comes loose. It is not just a matter of petrol and my time, there is also the serious abuse that will be done to the vehicle. No, I am sorry, but it is not worth doing for anything less."

Moikokobetsi hung his head from fatigue and told Moremi that he would return tomorrow to confirm. The cool evening air was already beginning to move in, and that meant it would soon be dark. He set out for Olebile's, his legs tired from the walking he had done that day, and he wondered to himself whether he would be able to arrange everything as he hoped. It was not looking good. He would need almost seven hundred pula, and that meant selling two healthy cows. The funeral alone would cost another two cows and he would have to slaughter a bull for the ceremonies. That would leave him with only two cows to see him through the rest of his old age.

He arrived at Olebile's just after nightfall, the cold having already clawed its way into his joints. She opened the door and he greeted her with a smile. There was no reason to let her know of his troubled day.

She brought him a plate with some bread and jam for dinner. "How did it go?"

"I think it will be okay, but I haven't received any money yet. I will go back and finish matters tomorrow. The brigades were most helpful."

"What about your son?"

"*Ija*, I was so busy visiting others that I did not have a chance to check at the post office for a reply. I will do that first thing tomorrow morning."

"Well, anyway, here is the hundred pula I promised you. At least you know you have that." She pressed five red twenty-pula notes into his hand. He said nothing, but she knew he was grateful. He released a small sigh and she sensed that he did not wish to talk any more. She prepared bedding on the floor for him while he drank a cup of tea with milk and copious amounts of sugar. When she was finished, she turned her back while he modestly disrobed and climbed inside. He was quickly asleep.

The sun rose the next morning to a ground covered in frost. Moikokobetsi had great difficulty getting out of bed even though he had awakened with the roosters before it had become light. The long walk the day before and the gnawing cold had both weakened his body such that he hardly felt he could ever move again. He murmured to himself that he had a duty to fulfill and he must complete all arrangements by the end of the day; so he got up off of the floor and dressed. He lingered over a cup of hot tea that Olebile had prepared, enjoying the soothing comfort of the warmth on his hands and the hot liquid running down his throat.

At seven o'clock, Moikokobetsi made for the door. Olebile stopped him, "By the way, I forgot to tell you last night that I heard of someone who was driving his *bakkie* up to Ncamasere. Perhaps you can make arrangements for him to drive you on to Shakawe. It's not that much further up the road."

"*Heela*, that would be helpful."

She explained where to find the man and then he left for the post office.

The air was crisp and clean, and it stung his cheeks as he walked. He labored through the sand and soon heavy puffs of mist came from his lungs. *Waii*, he thought, there goes my soul from my body even as I walk. Not that it alarmed him: he knew that his remaining time was short. Realizing that and watching his white breath dissipate into the frigid air, he wondered if it was cold where the dead resided. Did the spirit of his wife feel the same stinging sensation? Probably not. After all, that was life was it not: the ability to feel and sense, to suffer and enjoy? And what was death? He grimaced as he jostled his cracking, dry, frozen bones over the sandy path and he thought: death is release from torment like this. He stopped to catch his breath and felt the cool air rushing through his lungs. You lived each moment of life only once, he thought, and to say that one was better than another was pointless because no moment could ever be lived again. Each brief flash of existence was as it was, and then it was not, another moment was. That's all. So what did it all matter? Look at me, he laughed, I'm suddenly some kind of wise *kgosi* or *ngaka*. Clear your mind of such thoughts and get about your business!

He continued on to the post office. The doors had not yet opened when he arrived and so he sat down with his back to the wall together with all the others who were waiting. The peeling walls were painted dark blue above and aqua below, and surrounded as he was by them he couldn't help feeling himself back in Shakawe sitting instead on the banks of the Okavango. To be cradled in its abundance, to be embraced by its seasonal ebbs and flows, its love and its wrath, where death and life were often jumbled, but where he was always somebody who existed, who counted. In Maun he felt himself to be so much of a nuisance or an inconvenience. He was a source of income or a source of trouble. Very seldom, though, had he felt like a human being here. He thought of Joshua in Francistown—what was such a place like? How did he endure it there? Moikokobetsi thought he now understood and he discovered that his small spark of interest in such places had now fallen cold and inert into the corners of his soul, never to be re-ignited.

The post office opened and he shuffled in with the others. With so many service windows in this branch, it took him several minutes to identify the one he should go to. There was only one small counter in Shakawe. The clerk rummaged around in back for several minutes before returning with his telegram. Unfortunately, it had been sent back with the explanation that no one by Joshua's name lived at that address. He asked the clerk to check the telegram against a slip of paper he had with his son's address on it. She did and found it correct. What could have happened? Of course, he remembered, Joshua had mentioned in his last letter that he had a chance of a better position in Selebi-Phikwe. Perhaps he had taken it. He knew that Joshua would write him before long with his new address, but that certainly didn't help him with his present problem. He could track him down through his employer, but that would take several more days. Such time was not available to him. In fact, few options seemed to remain for him once he reviewed his situation. No, the coffin was now out of the question, but he might still arrange for transport of the body to Shakawe. He would go and talk to the man mentioned by Olebile.

Mokgwebi Dihatsa was in his compound when Moikokobetsi arrived. They greeted each other and Mokgwebi invited his visitor to sit down with him in the morning sun. They talked leisurely of the weather and of general news about Maun. Moikokobetsi knew none of the names that Dihatsa referred to and he soon felt overwhelmed by the number of things that seemed to occur in the village. He often had a difficult enough time keeping track of who was who and what was what in Shakawe; truly, a person must be very smart if he was going to live in such a busy place as Maun. The complexity of this village of twenty-five thousand people swamped Moikokobetsi's senses and he suddenly felt the compelling need to go back home.

He was impatient to settle matters and, besides, they had talked long enough of local gossip. After a short pause, he broached the reason for his visit, "I hear that you are going to Ncamasere tomorrow."

"*Ee, rra.*"

"I am asking for a lift. There are two—my wife and myself."

"That can be done. I have already promised lifts to five other people, but, really, I think we can fit in two more. The price is fifteen pula per person."

Five other riders! This did not sound good. There was no way the others would accept a lift with a corpse, and yet it was also unlikely that Dihatsa would agree to turn away the others and reserve the trip for Moikokobetsi and the body of his wife. He dared not bring up the subject. Then he had an idea.

"Good," said Moikokobetsi. "However, I am going to Shakawe and I am wondering if you could take me there. I will pay an extra twenty pula for the two of us. You see, my wife, she is very weak and it would not do for us to wait for another lift from Ncamasere to Shakawe. You know how difficult it is up there."

Dihatsa thought this over for moment, then slapped Moikokobetsi's knee. "I'll do it, *monna mogolo*. I need to be back in Ncamasere by nightfall, but then Shakawe is only twenty minutes further. It will not be a problem."

Moikokobetsi thanked him and turned the subject back to small talk. After a few minutes, he said he had some business to attend to and must leave. Dihatsa walked him to the gate.

"*Waii*, I nearly forgot to ask," Moikokobetsi turned around in the road, "where shall I meet you and when?"

"I have to buy some supplies first and then fetch the other people . . . Where do you live?"

"I am staying in the Mathiba ward, but I must pick up some medicine for my wife tomorrow morning at the hospital. Maybe it would be best if we met you where the hospital road and the main road meet."

"*Ee, rra.* I will be there mid-morning."

"*Go siame.*"

"*Go siame.*"

There was little else Moikokobetsi could do. Before he went back to Olebile's, though, he would try to send word to Joshua by way of his company. It was too late to contact him for the money, but at least he would know of his mother's death so that he could come back for the funeral.

Fatigue set in on the way back. He had walked very far again today; more than his old limbs were used to doing. The pliant sand seemed deeper than usual, perhaps because a little sense of purpose was lost in each step as if stolen by the vague indentations left in his wake. He sat down on an old fallen combretum tree to rest and watched as the sun fell behind the trees and huts in front of him. The end of another day, he thought. And then what? Darkness and cold and nothing until the morning. And then the same process over and over. He shook his head. Slightly to his right and down below in a dry wash, a horse was grazing noisily on the few remaining tufts of edible grass. An oxpecker was perched on its back and nipped occasionally at unseen insects. Moikokobetsi thought back humorously to the time he had been scolded as a boy by his father for trying to knock oxpeckers off the backs of the family's cattle with small sticks. The sticks were too small to do the cattle any harm, only annoy them at worst, but there was too much wealth and status tied up in those large lumbering creatures for his father to feel comfortable with such games. More importantly, it showed a certain lack of respect and consideration. His father had beaten him; not very hard, only enough to make his point. Ever after that, Moikokobetsi had taken to tossing a stick at oxpeckers whenever he was sure no one was watching. If nothing else, it was a way of keeping the memory alive. But that had been long, long ago—still within the time of the Mumbukushu king, Dibebe II, before the Hambukushu had been wholly subjugated by the Batawana. There had been no lorries or *bakkies* or airplanes or any such machines then. How many lifetimes ago was that?

The sun had now sunk below the horizon and all that lingered was a deep orange glow merging upwards into a darker and darker blue. The grazing horse was becoming difficult to see and Moikokobetsi was surprised to realize that he had had no inclination to throw a stick at the oxpecker on its back. There was just too much time now between that little boy and his present self. There was no need to refresh the memory any longer. That was already a different existence.

He stood up and walked on. He arrived at Olebile's shortly after dark. She was sewing a hem when he entered and he sat down on a chair across from her. The repetitive motions of her hands soothed him and he watched as if mesmerized. All at once, he recognized that she had been speaking to him.

"Sorry, what did you say?"

"I said how did it go today? Did the money from your son come? Did you arrange a lift?" She looked intently at him as she asked these questions.

He hesitated briefly. "The money did not come. It seems my son is no longer living at the same address. But I did arrange for transport."

She stopped sewing and looked up. "But what will you do about the coffin?"

He did not answer. He was lost in thought. Finally, he sighed and said, "Don't worry. Everything has been arranged. *Mme, ke botsa gape, tota ke kopa thusa*—but I have to ask you again, I really need your help." His eyes grasped at hers beseechingly. "Do you think your son could come with me tomorrow morning? Please ask him. I will only need him for a short time."

She began sewing again. "Of course, I will ask him. I don't think there will be a problem." She was curious, but thought better of being so forward as to try and pull any answers from him. After all, he looked utterly exhausted.

"And may I borrow two of your blankets?"

"*Ee, rra.*"

She got up and went to the kitchen to get him a cup of tea and some biscuits. When she returned she found him staring forlornly at the chair she had been sitting in. He looked at her as she set the tea and plate of biscuits beside him.

"*Iyoo, go hithla motho go senkadi tota,*" he said softly: my God, it is truly difficult to bury someone.

"*Naa, ja dijo tse,*" she said—come on, eat some food.

She stooped down and pushed the plate toward him. He simply gazed at her and shook his head with a smile to say that he didn't want any. The he stood up and walked to his bed. He fell asleep almost immediately and soon fell under the swirling gust of a troubled dream. He turned his head from side to side and kept mumbling '*go hithla motho*' over and over. Olebile went back to her sewing and thought of her husband's death. Yes, she thought, it really can be difficult to bury someone.

The next morning, Moikokobetsi rose early and packed his small bag. There was very little, only some spare clothes and his two-year-old toothbrush. Olebile heard him and also got out of her bed. She covered herself in a coat, went outside to make a fire and put some water on to boil. She returned shortly with an egg in her hand.

"It will be a long day for you. I got this egg from my neighbor. It will give you the strength to do what you must today. I also sent her boy with a message to my son. He is to meet you at the hospital. If he can't come, he is to find a friend who will. Someone will be there to help you. My son's name is Tumelo. Wait for him by the main gate so that he can find you. I'll be back in a few minutes." She went to the door.

"Olebile," Moikokobetsi was patting his arms to shake the cold out of him. "I am grateful for the help you have given me."

She barely smiled. "*Ee, rra.*" Then she turned and went out back to the cooking hut.

Moikokobetsi was at the hospital before its opening time of half past seven. He waited in the cold by the main gate for Olebile's son, but Tumelo still hadn't come ten minutes after opening. He told the gatekeeper his name and said that someone would be meeting him there soon, but that he had important business to attend to inside. He asked him to tell whoever came to meet him that he would be back in a short while. He then sought out Nurse Keatlaretse. It was some time before he could finally see her. She had morning staff meetings to deal with and was not yet on duty for patients. Moikokobetsi had no watch but he knew it was getting late. Nonetheless, he showed no signs of impatience outwardly. A quarter of an hour later, Nurse Keatlaretse came down the walkway to her office. She recognized Moikokobetsi at once and called him into her office. He took off his hat and held it respectfully in his hands before him.

"I have come to take my wife, Mma Keatlaretse."

"*Ee, rra.* Wait right here."

She went out and was away for several minutes. Moikokobetsi looked around the white sterile room with its bare walls and its smell of the modern world. Yes, that smell summed up Maun for him. He could only imagine how horrid and noisy the capital Gaborone must be. Nurse Keatlaretse came back into the room briskly.

"I have arranged for her to be released to you." She sat down at her desk. "If you will sign these papers, please."

He went over to the desk and took the pen offered to him. He searched helplessly across all parts of the paper with its squiggly lines. She finally realized that he could not read and pointed to a line at the bottom. "Make your mark . . . here."

He made a wobbly 'x' with painstaking concentration, and then carefully laid the pen down and stepped away from the desk.

"Go to the morgue ward," she said, "and ask for Rra Bamphusi. He will be expecting you."

"*Dankie, mma, dankie.*" He bowed nervously.

"*Go siame,*" she replied. She seemed to want to say more but instead went back to the papers on her desk.

"*Go siame.*"

Moikokobetsi then walked to the front gate and found Tumelo. "I'm sorry to keep you waiting. I had to sign the papers for my wife."

"No *mathata*," said Tumelo. "How can I help you?"

He was slightly taken aback when Moikokobetsi told him, but he made no protest and followed Moikokobetsi silently to the morgue nevertheless. The attendant, Rra Bamphusi, was busy when they entered and they had to wait for ten more minutes. When he called them, Moikokobetsi explained his business.

"Why, of course," intoned Rra Bamphusi sympathetically. "Please come this way." He led them down an open corridor and into the cadaver storage room. "And where is the coffin?"

"It is at my sister's house," Moikokobetsi answered. "I could not arrange for transport to bring it here. My nephew has agreed to help me carry her back."

"No coffin? This is rather unusual." His concern was now that of a bureaucrat and he thought momentarily while rubbing his chin. He then waved his hand casually and said, "But that is no matter. As long as you have signed the papers and everything is in order."

Ten minutes later, Moikokobetsi was walking down the short drive to the tarred road. Tumelo walked beside him with Separe's body, which Moikokobetsi had clothed and then wrapped in blankets. They soon reached the road and Moikokobetsi pointed to a tree about fifty meters further down away from the village center.

"Over there," he said.

Tumelo heaved a sigh and walked on. Once at the tree he leaned the body against the trunk. Moikokobetsi sat down beside it, but Tumelo found it more comfortable to remain standing on the other side of the tree. He began to wonder what his mother had gotten him into. They waited as the sun climbed higher in the sky. The sharp chill was gradually vanishing from the air. After an hour, Moikokobetsi saw Dihatsa's sky-blue *bakkie* approach.

"*Bona*, my lift, it is coming."

Tumelo could only stare incredulously at him. Dihatsa pulled over to the side of the road in front of the tree. Moikokobetsi walked up to the cab, and, leaning his head in, greeted Dihatsa and the passengers sitting next to him.

"So," said Dihatsa, "are you ready to go, *monna mogolo*?"

"*Ee, rra*. As soon as my nephew and I get my sick wife into the back, we can go."

"Do you need help?"

"*Nyaa, nyaa, rra.* We will manage."

He and Tumelo then carried Separe's body over to the *bakkie* and set it gently in the back. Moikokobetsi had already instructed Tumelo to place her upright in a sitting position and to be careful not to let any of the blankets come loose. This he did. Moikokobetsi then grabbed Tumelo's hand and looking up at him thanked him for his help. He climbed awkwardly into the back and sat himself next to his wife, tightly wedged into one of the corners in the far back.

"*A re tsamaya!*" he cried. Let's go!

The vehicle spun its wheels in the dirt of the shoulder and then bounced onto the tarmac. Moikokobetsi greeted everyone in the back. Some of the riders were trying to catch a glimpse of his wife's face, but he had covered it with a veil as a precaution.

"I apologize that my wife doesn't greet you," he added, "but she is very sick. She had her throat operated on at the hospital and is still very weak. In actual fact, she has been sedated for this trip."

The others nodded in understanding and sympathy. Soon they were lost in their own thoughts, huddling against the wind and bracing themselves for the bumpy ride that would begin in a few minutes when the tarmac ended. Moikokobetsi looked back and watched as an astonished Tumelo grew smaller and smaller.

"That man there, he is too sorry to see you go, I think," said an old man diagonally across the truck bed.

"It is certainly a shock to him," replied Moikokobetsi, "that much I can say."

He wondered what the others in the back would do if they knew they were riding with a corpse. His anxiety about their response was tempered by the fact that he was too tired to care. There was no law against dead people catching lifts was there? Anyway, it was the only way he knew to do what was right by his wife. He could think of nothing else. In seven or eight hours he would be in Shakawe, and he could prepare his wife for burial in her mother's compound as was proper. And then he could rest.

The obese woman to Moikokobetsi's right hollered over the passing wind, "So, you are going to Shakawe?"

"*Ee, mma.*"

"That is your home?"

"*Ee, mma.*"

"I think it will be good for your wife. She will be much happier there, don't you think?"

"*Ee, mma, o bua nnete.* As for myself, I will be happy, too."

The woman nodded knowingly—although one couldn't be sure through her triple chin—and then she turned to settle into her riding position. The man diagonally across started to ask a question, but was interrupted by the slowing of the vehicle and a jolting bump. They were now on the dirt road. The man gave up his inquiry, knowing he would never be heard over the constant shaking and thumping.

Moikokobetsi was glad. He lowered his head forward and closed his eyes. Petting his wife's shoulder he muttered, "We'll soon be there, you'll see," and soon fell asleep with his head on her shoulder.

Eggshells Are for Drinking

(August)

Eggshells Are for Drinking

ISAAC always liked the late winter mornings best. With the biting edge of coldness smoothed away, they were bearable and the air was somehow insubstantial and brilliant like moonlight reflecting off water. Clean, sharp and strong. On such mornings the world was being born again and rested in the peaceful calm between winter and summer, between the harsh disappointments that had been and the ordeals yet to be suffered. A sense of life and death filled one's nostrils: not with turbulence as when two streams flow together forming eddies and swirls, but quietly like the full moon when it climbs into the world to greet the fading sun.

It was on such a morning that Isaac heard the old clanking Land Cruiser of Joost Du Villiers driving up. Isaac had been expecting him, although to be truthful expectation had very little meaning in this part of the world. Expecting someone meant feeling neither vexation when they were late nor satisfaction when they were punctual: one arrived when one arrived, that was all there was to it. Joost had sent word to Isaac a week earlier, asking him to make arrangements to have three Bushmen ready for a group of *Makgoa* who would fly in that day. He had come out early to make sure everything was prepared as requested and to spend a few minutes idly chatting before the outsiders came and shattered the tranquility with their demanding ways.

Isaac was a Mumbukushu, originally from the village of Shakawe. He had lived for the last fifteen years out in the small settlement at Tsodilo Hills, having originally come out to help tend his brother's cattle. Eventually, he could think of no reason to return to the closed world of the village. Maybe it was simply a life chosen for him by his ancestors. His grandmother had been a Bushman and he himself had had two children by a Bushman girl. The Bushman spirit flowed strongly in his veins in spite of his physical appearance and his name. Perhaps it was fate. Or nature. Or chance. Who knows? Whatever the reason, he was happy out in the bush. He sometimes missed the company of the villagers; but then, he used to say, they always wagged their tongues so—and to what purpose? At least out here, he was a kind of a king. The Hambukushu people had long been the talented traders of the region, so it was natural that Isaac, as the eldest and most knowledgeable Mumbukushu in the settlement, should assume the role of social navigator and negotiator in the region between the Bushmen of Tsodilo Hills and the outside world.

The weathered Land Cruiser pulled up beside Isaac, its white paint contrasting with Joost's deeply tanned skin. He shut off the engine and stepped out, wobbling and bending to stretch his legs, which had grown stiff after two hours of slogging and bumping through a sandy track. The two of them exchanged pleasantries and news. The children, all of mixed Bushman and Hambukushu parentage, stood around them, transfixed momentarily; but they quickly grew bored and began chasing each other around the newly arrived vehicle. The two men who faced each other were very much alike, all physical differences aside. Joost was very tan with sandy-colored hair, medium in height, and had the Germanic body features of sinewy musculature with forearms like clubs and upper arms that seemed rather too short for the body. A slight paunch and long thin legs helped give the deceptive impression that he lacked significant strength, but this was a mistake one was wise not to make at the wrong moment. Isaac, on the other hand, was tall and lanky and very dark. His eyes burned brightly like exploding stars, and his diffidence deceptively masked a character of great depth and confidence. Although he did not carry the physical strength of Joost, his stamina and his ability to withstand the hardships of life in the bush were superior. In temperament they were both calm and steadfast as the hills that stood at their backs.

As they spoke, one of the Bushmen from the settlement, /Gashay, led out old Gumtsa past the thornbrush fence that encircled the compound like a dry prickly moat. Gumtsa, his eyes clouded over with the dark night of blindness and his body encased in a hide withered and wrinkled by an age in the desert, was the eldest member of the settlement. He had been greatly respected as a hunter in his youth, something he still prided himself on to the detriment of his more worthy faculty, the wisdom of his experience. As such, he came off as a somewhat comic figure that turned more tragic as one came to know him better. He and /Gashay came up and greeted Joost. Joost had grown up in the Ghanzi area to the South and knew how to speak passable Nharo and /Gwi Bushman, but he didn't know the !Kung dialect spoken by the Tsodilo Hills people, and so they conversed in Setswana, native to none of them but the universal language of the region.

After a polite stretch of banter, Joost walked into the compound area to greet the others. He began with the eldest and worked his way down, asking them all how they were doing and what news they had. Joost likewise brought them up-to-date on village gossip. Everyone had a good laugh when Joost told them the story about "Big Boy" Kwanyana and how he had turned the village upside down looking for his badge, which he thought someone had stolen when in fact it had been underneath his girlfriend's bed all the time. Old Xama, the matriarch of the settlement, chuckled and said that Big Boy was foolish to worry about something so worthless after having enjoyed something so valuable. They all laughed and Joost said that he agreed.

He then called to several of the boys and told them to go to his Land Cruiser where there were gifts for everyone: sacks of mealie meal, *samp*, sorghum, rice and sugar. There was also tobacco for the adults and sweets for the children. Gumtsa, Xama, /Gashay and the others beamed inwardly but did not openly express their gratitude as this would have been rude. Although these Bushmen in the settlement (actually only four were pure Bushmen, most were of mixed parentage and some were even full-blooded Hambukushu) were used to receiving handouts, either from the government or from tourists, nevertheless they were grateful for food under any circumstances. This was particularly true of the older ones, as many youths had grown spoiled, but in general all were thankful. How could a people so used to living on the borders of existence ever take the essentials of life for granted?

A soft low drone, barely louder than a mosquito, announced the coming of the airplane bringing the *Makgoa*. There was no rush to get to the airfield since the plane wouldn't arrive for another five minutes yet. All the same, Joost and Isaac began winding up their conversation and made themselves ready to drive off.

Gumtsa, /Gashay and ≠Toma were three of the four purebred Bushmen in the settlement. It would be their job to act 'authentic' during the day. They stood around dressed in a wild mixture of clothing that was at once destitute and fashionable: Gumtsa wore a faded UCLA sweatshirt and torn polyester slacks; /Gashay sported a New York Yankees baseball cap, faded designer jeans two sizes too large for him and a white cotton oxford shirt with a large blue stain on the left breast; ≠Toma had no shirt, he wore only on an Yves Saint Laurent vest and red Manchester United shorts. Joost smiled to himself and then kindly asked if they could now change into their loincloths since this is what the *Makgoa* had come to see. The protested that it was still too cold, that it made no sense to strip down so early on a late-winter morning. Joost thought about it and agreed, suggesting that they compromise by putting on their loincloths and then putting their other clothes back on top. In that way they could keep warm until they were needed in traditional dress and perhaps the sun would have warmed things up enough by then anyway. Reluctantly, they set about changing while Joost and Isaac got into the Land Cruiser and set off.

They drove to the northern fringe of the airstrip and swung the Cruiser around to face the east, the direction from which the airplane would approach. An overwhelming silence emerged as he switched off the engine. Gradually the intermittent and eerie sound of faraway birds became audible. An ancient world of profound peace lay around Isaac and Joost, also one of unpredictable violence and lurking mystery where human existence was always precarious but rarely meaningless. They still breathed enough of nature not to think too highly of themselves, to inflate their worth and significance out of proportion. They and the others in the settlement knew that they were a passing phenomenon on whom a moment of magic had been bestowed and nothing more. Joost looked beyond the ponderous shadows of the 'male' and 'female' hills of Tsodilo. Somewhere out there was the plane whose metal groans were growing ever louder, erasing that primeval world with its approach. He had a hard time seeing it as the bright morning sun, only recently free of the horizon, washed out everything in the eastern sky. Curiously, he suddenly recalled that the dazzling light also obscured a new moon, which bided its time ever so patiently.

The plane appeared and came in low, barely clearing the trees. It then dropped precipitously and just caught the leading edge of the runway: undoubtedly, the ebullient Portuguese Paulo was piloting. The aircraft kicked up puffs of fine sand and then braked down gradually to the far south of the runway after which it turned and taxied back to the northern end. It had barely come to a halt when the door opened and out stepped a tall aristocratic man with thinning blond hair. He stood very erect, clothed from head to foot in olive-brown. His hat, safari suit, cravat, socks, shoes—all were the same color. Only his wristwatch, his skin and the soles of his shoes were shaded differently. And his eyes, which were a sun-bleached blue.

Joost nodded to Isaac to indicate that this was the great Connell Britchford, self-proclaimed master of many disciplines: African folklore, Bushman painting, fencing, ornithology and a river-full of others that Joost had never heard of. Joost had met him several times at his fishing camp outside Shakawe, resulting in an intimacy that had grown emptier with each meeting.

Down stepped the magnificent Mr. Britchford, his eyes never once lowering from a far distant horizon unseen to others. "Good day, Joost," he said, "splendid day to view rock paintings, don't you think?" He looked blankly down at Joost.

Joost nodded.

"You do have the Bushmen ready, don't you? This gentleman most certainly does not appear to be of Bushman stock."

Joost squinted and looked away towards a large camelthorn tree. "They're waiting at the settlement. They'll be ready when we get there. Isaac here has made the arrangements and will help us to translate if necessary." He turned his gaze back to Britchford. "My !Kung Bushman isn't very good."

"Splendid. Capital. Let's get the filming equipment loaded into the Cruiser."

Other men climbed out behind them. Britchford introduced them as a German film crew making a documentary on rock paintings in southern Africa. Gunther, the director, was very tall with dark hair, a large bushy beard and piercing gray eyes. The cameraman Hans and Juergen the soundman were of a more moderate stature. Only Juergen had the light blond hair and fair features that one expected in Germans. They carried a lot of equipment with them, each piece being carefully packed in aluminum cases that revealed long use and countless kilometers traveled. Once everything was out of the plane, Paulo started up the motors, went through his checklist, waved briskly from the cockpit and taxied down to the other end of the runway, after which he took off into the cloudless porcelain sky. He had another run to make and would return later in the day.

The group stopped briefly at the settlement to pick up /Gashay, Gumtsa and ≠Toma, and Connell used the opportunity to get out and walk around the compound. Tucked beneath his arm was what appeared to be a riding crop but was actually an old worn walking stick, called a *molamu*, like the ones old Batswana men often affected. These canes were shortened to accommodate the bearer's diminished stature and towering Connell would have looked ridiculous even contemplating the use of it as a walking stick. All the same, his attempt at looking rakish was only comic to all but himself.

While walking through the compound, he smiled broadly with forced bravado as if bestowing gifts on impoverished subjects. Outwardly he appeared to be delighting in the activities of this colorful people and expressing a keen interest in every detail of their lives. In fact, he was in the process what he called 'imbibing the atmosphere' in anticipation of the filming later on. It was a thespian trick he employed whenever on location in exotic locales.

Joost came up. "We're ready to begin if you want."

"Good." Connell shivered. "My but it's damned cold."

"We're in the shadow of the male hill," replied Joost. "It'll be warmer when we get back in the sun."

"Splendid. Listen, I've planned out a little itinerary for us to follow so that we can cover some of the important paintings I know of. If you've any others you want to recommend, however, I'd be happy to entertain them." As usual, Connell was treading a fine line between omnipotent lord and humble student with respected individuals he spoke to.

He and Joost discussed possibilities for several minutes and tried to compromise between Connell's romantic inclinations to hit the most dramatic paintings and the simple demands of logistical reality. Finally, they had what seemed a workable plan that would produce the best visual results in one day's viewing. They called everyone together. With all of the filming equipment, there really wasn't enough room to fit everything and everyone comfortably in the vehicle, so Joost decided to make two trips. The film crew would need a few minutes to set up, anyway; he could use that time to fetch the others.

They first stopped at the famous Laurens Van der Post panel, which was located off the main track running around the western side of the female hill. The paintings were on a large vertical rock face about twenty meters up on a promontory. It seemed best to begin here since this site offered the most scenic view, was closest to the Bushman settlement and had the most tortuous access of all the panels they would visit today.

The German crew had a difficult time getting their equipment up the rocks, but it was Connell who emerged at the top puffing the most dramatically. "I say, I rather feel like Sir Edmund on Everest." There was no irony in the corner of his eyes.

"Ja, dat vas some climb," panted Juergen.

Joost, Isaac and the Bushman said nothing since such idle chatter was normally considered extravagant to those accustomed to living in the bush.

"Why, it's splendid up here," said Connell, "these rocks, the paintings . . . and the view! This will make a marvelous shot, but I'm afraid the light isn't right. How long until the sun comes over the hill?"

"Not long," said Joost wincing inside. He knew it would actually be another twenty minutes or so yet and he could see that the poor Bushmen were freezing. It had been quite an ordeal getting the film equipment up the hill to say nothing of old Gumtsa. No, they would have to stay, miserable as the wait would be. It would be foolish to climb down again only to return later in the day. Connell became quickly absorbed in designing camera angles and blocking for his narration of the panel. He paced out distances and tested timings for his movement like a child preoccupied with an imaginary friend. Joost called Gumtsa, /Gashay and ≠Toma to him over near the ledge on the pretext of discussing what they were to do. He knew that it would be the first place the sun would hit and thus give them a head start in warming up. Talking idly, he offered each one a cigarette. At least the tobacco would keep their minds and bodies occupied for a few minutes longer.

"*Tshikhi! Ke a sitwa thata! Makgoa otlhe a a tsenwa, o a itse, monna?*" Isaac said he was freezing from the cold and teased Joost that all Whites were crazy.

"*Didimala lesilo! A o tla tshabisa diphuduhudu, wena?*" Hush you fool, replied Joost jokingly, do you want to scare away the steenbok?

The oblique reference to Connell as game was not lost on Isaac. He grinned. "*O bua nnete, monna. Phiri e mpe e e nang le dijo e itumela go feta tau e tona e e nang le tlala.*" You're right: the ugly hyena that has food is happier than the mighty lion that is hungry. Joost and the others laughed.

Fifteen minutes later, the sun crept over the rest of the hill and Connell began rehearsing his scene in earnest.

"Ze contrast is now too much, Connell," said Gunther. "You vill not be able to mufe away from ze panel as you vanted. I sink you always must stand in ze same place."

"Well, we don't have much time to wait around for ideal lighting, do we? So much to film today. Very well. Let me just edit my script a bit."

This he did, and when he was ready, he had /Gashay stand in the scene with him. The cameras rolled and Connell spoke eloquently of the mysteries locked in these rocks, how the numerous paintings scattered all over the hills were, so to speak, gateways to those mysteries. The Van der Post panel with its images of eland, giraffe, wildebeest and handprints was especially unique in its juxtaposition of man and nature. Of course, most Bushman paintings revealed the hallowed place that game animals held in their universe, and these drawings were examples of the homage Bushmen paid to their well-respected magical powers. But on this panel one also found human handprints: signatures of the artists. At this point, Connell had /Gashay place his hand dramatically over the imprint on the rock face. This grossly obvious comparison held no meaning for the confused Bushman and so Connell had to physically grasp /Gashay's hesitant wrist and guide his open hand to the desired spot. That the *Lekgoa* wanted him to put his hand in this way on the side of the hill seemed particularly insane to /Gashay. He reminded himself, though, that he was to be paid handsomely in tobacco and beer for this. Besides, everyone knew that the *Makgoa* were a bit crazed in the head. That was part of the magic powers that enabled them to generate such large sums of money wherever they went and to conquer peoples the way a dust storm strips the earth of its fertile garment. At last /Gashay's hand lay spread out over the painted handprint and Connell expounded on the propinquity of the Bushman and the world around him, of their relationship that was often problematic but never truly adversarial. /Gashay smiled fatuously. Then Connell closed the scene with something about the paintings shouting their message loudly over the parched plains, and as he said this he slowly swept his arm across his body and outwards toward the open veldt down below while the camera panned to follow, ending with a portrait of the stark vastness of the Kgalagadi.

The scene was now finished and the group packed up and clambered down the rocks to the track, finding it somewhat harder to get Gumtsa down than it had been to get him up. Intricate plans were drawn up by the three Germans at each stage as they considered how to get him from one ledge down to the next. After twenty minutes, they had succeeded in bringing all the people and equipment back to the Cruiser. This time they managed to squeeze everyone into the vehicle so they would only have to make one trip, and soon they were on their way.

Cameras and lights were set up once more at the next painting and again Connell went through his ritual of rehearsing. Already baffled as they were by this strange man, the Bushmen were even more so when he made repeated thrusts of the hand across the painting during his monologue. In this scene, ≠Toma was to lead old Gumtsa up through the trees, which were thick in this area, and up to the rock face where they would pretend to have accidentally happened onto the paintings. Connell would then step mysteriously on camera from some unseen dimension and appear to listen intelligently to their conversation about these mystic figures. It goes without saying that he spoke not one word of Bushman and what he was doing in the middle of nowhere at just the moment these luckless Bushmen stumbled along was anybody's guess. Anybody's but Connell's, that is, since such stretches of the imagination never seemed to strike him as even the least bit absurd.

And so, this thrusting of his hand across the painting, which displayed two rhino facing to the right, pushed ≠Toma's curiosity to the point where he just had to ask Isaac: what the hell was Connell doing? Isaac had only caught about a third of what Connell had said and so asked Joost for a full translation. It seemed that Mr. Britchford was indicating that the artist had intended the rhino to be heading across the rock face out of the merciless sun and into the cool darkness of a cleft in the rock several inches ahead of them formed by a narrow shadow cast onto the panel from a tiny upraised ledge. To any white person, this might appear to be a reasonable explanation, but to the Bushmen? Indeed, the Bushmen of Tsodilo Hills had no idea who had made these paintings or even how far back in time. No tales or traditions relating to them had been passed down over the years and until the *Makgoa* had come to enlighten them, they had not even believed them to have been done by any of their ancestors at all. Thus, they were briefly impressed by Connell's explanation, that is, until their intuition told them otherwise. Lacking knowledge about these paintings as they did, they still knew enough from their culture to sense the aura of the figures and to recognize that such a prosaic intention was certainly trivial at best. Surely, the yearning for shade was irrelevant for magical spirits such as these. As before, Connell finished his scene in fine melodramatic style and he continued to glow for some time while the film crew busied themselves with packing up and the others gossiped. Joost saw that Connell was lost in his own world, and he knew that the only way to break into it was to be gently rude.

"You don't mind if I give them a couple of beers, do you?"

Connell looked thoroughly bewildered by the question as if Joost had asked the best way to Mars using a bicycle. "Pardon?" he replied absently.

"For them," said Joost indicating the Bushmen patiently. "They've been working pretty hard. I think they deserve a beer."

"Why, yes, go on and give them each a beer," said Connell as if shooing an annoying mosquito off.

"No, no, no," said Joost emphatically. "Not a beer each. They won't be any good later. I'll let them share." Joost sometimes found outsiders nearly intolerable in their total lack of common sense.

"Yes, yes, go ahead. And could you get me a cool drink while you're at it?"

He brought Connell a cold soft drink and then handed the beers to Isaac, /Gashay, Gumtsa and ≠Toma. They took turns voraciously gulping from their can and were finished in less than a minute. Joost considered giving them another cigarette to smoke but thought it better to hold some incentive in reserve.

At the next filming spot, there were paintings depicting an ostrich and a whale and Connell had the Bushmen talk in their own language as if they were in deep intellectual discussion about their mythological attributes or their colorful history. He then broke in and drew the audience into the marvel of the drawing of a whale nearly fifteen hundred kilometers from the nearest ocean shore. However, this was no wonder, he explained, when one considered the Bushmen's vast wanderings and their likely contact with other Bushmen, some of whom probably had in fact seen the cold Atlantic of the Skeleton Coast to the west. Then he went on to point out the graceful lines of the ostrich, its almost picaresque presence, and remarked that the ostrich was an important bird for the Bushman since the meat provided food, the feathers soft insulation and the eggs were made into jewelry to adorn their bodies. Some of these paintings were possibly twenty to thirty thousand years old. These were proof that man's artistic talents lie deep within his very being.

When Connell finished, old Gumtsa asked Joost what the tall *Lekgoa* had said. He already knew that these paintings had been done by an ancient people from ancient times who were now long dead and it did not surprise him to hear that they were very old; but when Joost told him what Connell had said about the ostrich, he seemed perplexed and he asked Joost to repeat exactly what Connell had said. Still not satisfied, he asked Isaac if this was also his understanding. From what he had understood, Isaac agreed that this is what he had said. Gumtsa shook his head and walked away.

As they moved on to a nearby site, Joost noticed that Connell was still nursing his soft drink. "I reckon you'd better finish your drink, Connell."

"When I'm ready," answered Connell slightly annoyed.

Joost nearly sighed out loud. "The bees will be after it very soon."

"The bees?"

"Ja. It's the middle of the dry season and there's very little moisture for them to drink. A sweet liquid like the one in your hand is almost as good as a ton of nectar for them. Once one of them finds it, there will be hundreds of them around in no time."

"Really?"

"Yes. They're even attracted by our sweat. They go after any moisture. That's one reason I insisted on not trying to do too many panels today."

Reluctantly, Connell downed his drink in one long swallow. And then, muttering to himself, "Bees! Of all things. In the middle of a desert, no less!"

Joost ignored him and drove on. They soon came to the next painting, which portrayed a Bushman trance dance. A group of male silhouettes with erect penises were pictured strutting across the flat rock face in transcendent ecstasy. In this instance, the erect penises are not so much a sign of eroticism, fertility or power as merely a symbol for human beings, for it is a physiological fact that all Bushman men have continuous erections. Connell, in typical fashion, began with a long-winded introduction regarding the mysteries of the trance dance and its importance in the culture of the Bushman. In hushed tones, Joost translated the gist of his speech for the benefit of Isaac and the Bushmen. They were amazed to hear what he had to say; not that any of it was necessarily wrong, but the trance dance was a mystery, a part of one's life, that one grew up doing and understanding only through intuition. They had never analyzed it in this way nor heard it explained in this categorical manner, especially as the whole purpose of the dance was precisely to let the spirit run free of the body and of the rational mind. It was unfathomable, but here was Connell blithely labeling it like fresh produce. Overall, this was becoming a very instructive, and very confusing, day for the Bushmen. This bizarre *Lekgoa*, who was intensely animated whenever the cameras pointed at him and who was in his own peevish sort of trance at all other times, was explaining the cause for everything they did in life. What they had always done naturally and without forethought all seemed to be the product of some intricate design. /Gashay thought of the *Makgoa*'s machinery when he heard all of this and grew more puzzled. It was like madness or a severe case of sunstroke.

The point came when Connell, having finished his oration on the trance dance, wanted the Bushmen to perform it before the cameras. The trance dance was not a routine that one called upon like a vaudeville act, and this certainly was not the time the Bushmen would have normally chosen to do one. Embarrassed, they stood mutely. To dance now would be ludicrous, and yet, to refuse openly would be impolite. They compromised and just grinned.

"Come on," prodded Connell, "right up here on this ledge. That way we can get a shot of the painting in the background to compare it with. It'll be jolly good fun. Do come on."

They didn't move.

"What's the matter?" Connell asked Joost. "Tell them that we're not mocking them; on the contrary, we are celebrating their wonderful way of life. This is their chance to let the world know what it is like to be a Bushman."

They don't even know themselves any longer, thought Joost. Poor devils, first it was the black Bantu peoples pushing them into the desert, and then the Whites came, eventually finishing the job with their relentless technology and intensive way of life. Joost made no attempt to argue. What was the point? Instead, he turned to the Bushmen and explained that the tall *Lekgoa* still wanted them to dance. They demurred.

"Look," said Connell with a hint of anger, "we're paying them to do a job after all, aren't we? I don't mean to force the issue . . ." Of course, he *was* forcing the issue.

Joost and Isaac talked at length with them in what seemed to Connell to be a rather leisurely pace. After some time, they made headway.

"They'll dance. But they each want a cigarette first."

"Oh, all right. I suppose it's just another . . . as long as they don't take too much time."

They didn't. /Gashay and ≠Toma had smoked theirs down to the butt in under a minute and ancient Gumtsa was only twenty seconds behind. Beaming widely from the nicotine rush, the three of them stepped up onto the rock ledge below the painting. They shuffled clumsily for a few seconds and then all at once old Gumtsa began singing. He grew hoarse and started to cough. Then he began again and the others joined him. There was no fire to dance around as was usual, indeed there was no space at all in which to dance in a circle, so they shifted their weight back and forth between their legs and jogged in place. What should have been a pathetic and embarrassing scene was rendered noble by their rhythmic *a capella* singing. It drifted out into the canyons of the hills and seemed to hang like a mist. Even the birds seemed to stop their twittering, and for a few magical seconds all attention was focused on the haunting chant coming from the throats of these three wrinkled men.

Gumtsa stopped and then the others. He tried to begin again but the spell was broken. The middle of the day in front of these *Makgoa* was not the proper occasion to arouse the powerful *n/um* energy. The bathos of their actions shamed them and caused them to stop singing. They gingerly climbed down from the ledge and stood listlessly. They would sing no more.

It didn't matter to Connell because he already had what he wanted on tape. "Very good. Splendid." He smiled, "Shall we break for lunch now?"

Joost had been looking behind them at the ridgeline of the male hill and thinking of his childhood when he used to help his father gather cattle for a drive to the abattoir in Lobatse. They would camp out in the remote veldt at night, and as they lay on the soft Kgalagadi sand beneath warm wool blankets, they could sometimes hear the reverberations of the trance dance as it wafted across to their sleepy ears. It had always seemed to him like a glimpse of heaven, the nearest one came to uniting with the infinite where all things came together as one. That was gone now, gone forever.

"Yes," said Joost turning, "I think we should."

They ate lunch in a clearing near the spot where they had parked the Land Cruiser. The group took advantage of the warm sun to chase away the cold that had crept into their bones from the morning's filming, much of which had been done in the shade. Joost set out the meal that his wife had prepared: sliced-beef sandwiches, coleslaw with beets mixed in, hard-boiled eggs, *nartjies* and *biltong*. The lunch was meant primarily for the clients, the *Makgoa*, but once they had been served their portions, Joost brought some over to Isaac and the others. Overjoyed at the generous meal, they thanked him and then ravenously devoured the food in a matter of minutes, punctuating their feast from time to time with satisfied belches.

Joost walked back to where Connell and the film crew were eating and took a seat. Eager for news from the outside, he asked them how things were going in Europe. He listened regularly to the radio news from South Africa, but having dealt with foreign tourists for many years, he knew that he wasn't getting the full story from their broadcasts. Still, his was a disinterested curiosity; much like local gossip, it was something that was compelling when offered but not missed when absent. The actions of large foreign governments were far removed from the daily life of Northern Ngamiland. For someone like Isaac, they were meaningless—obscure fables about faraway kingdoms. Joost was slightly more educated and widely traveled. While he understood the concrete importance they held, even for him such happenings had little more significance than a puppet show.

"Ach, this is good. Vat do you call this dried beef?" asked Juergen while waving a bee away from his drink.

"It's called *biltong*. *Lekker*, isn't it. I made it myself last week."

"You made this yourself?" Hans was incredulous.

"Ja, it's quite easy," said Joost. "We usually make it in the winter time. It's cool and dry enough in the daytime and the meat cures quickly without spoiling. And being the dry season, it's also the best time of year to make it since the farmers have very little to do. So, you see a lot of it around. Soon it'll be too hot to make it."

"A hunting party I was with in Kenya survived on nothing but *biltong* for three days," reminisced Connell. "We were three days from the nearest town in the middle of a safari. A troop of baboons had come into camp while we were out tracking lion and cleaned us out of all the food we had. All that remained to us was the beef jerky we had taken along with us into the bush."

The German crew was impressed and their regard for Connell swelled. This man even lived from hand to mouth on wild hunting excursions. Joost just drew circles in the sand with a stick and said nothing. ≠Toma and /Gashay had been watching the *Makgoa* all this time, Connell in particular. They asked Isaac what Connell had said and he complied as best he could. They snorted in disgust when they heard about Connell, the great White hunter, and exchanged derogatory epithets among themselves. Then /Gashay had an idea. He pulled out his small bone pipe, walked over to the foot of the hill and found some small stones, and lastly picked up a small strip of bark from a statuesque knobthorn tree. With these in hand he went over by the *Makgoa* and spoke to Joost.

"*Rra yoo, mo bolelela gore ke tla laola ka bola.*"

Joost turned to Connell. "He says he wants to tell your fortune."

Connell was somewhat taken aback at first, but then he realized the opportunity it presented and he brightened visibly. "Why, that's an excellent idea." He shook a bee from his half-eaten apple, and continued in a velvety voice. "I would like that very much. Gunther, do you think we could get this on film?" Hans smiled hollowly and rose to get his camera out of the Cruiser while Juergen set up his sound equipment. When all was ready Connell looked complacently at /Gashay and said to Joost, "Tell him we may begin."

Joost translated. /Gashay explained that he had five divining pieces: the bone pipe which was called the Brown Hyena, three oddly shaped stones which he described as Earth, Water and Wind, and lastly there was Eland, the piece of bark. These he placed in his white shirt, wrapped them up, and shook them rhythmically while humming an incantation. He let go of his shirt and the pieces tumbled out onto the sand. With mock concentration he gazed on the scattered markers and pretended to see portentous signs. Then he mumbled in a mysterious monotone for a full minute, then broke off and looked up. He spoke to Connell.

"He says," interpreted Joost, "that the bones bow down before you in humble respect. They recognize the presence of a great man."

Connell's chest heaved and he held his breath for a moment while his spine stiffened.

"The Wind stone has fallen and is leaning on the Earth stone. This means that like the swift wind, you will travel great distances over the land in days to come. The Brown Hyena has landed on its side. This is not a good sign."

Connell leaned forward and his brows came together in tense concentration.

"There will be sickness or, perhaps, a loss of money. This will cause you great distress, but he says not to worry: the Water piece has fallen nearby and so . . . uh . . . recovery, yes, a recovery will follow closely. There will then be a great success and much fame."

A sigh came from Connell.

"Lastly, he says that Eland's position facing the Water stone means that you will find great success within the next year and its, uh, firmness in the ground shows your kindness and generosity. This is usually the sign of a man who is not stingy with his food or drink. He says you should be proud."

Joost laughed inwardly, for although the names that /Gashay had given the divining pieces were authentic, /Gashay was no shaman or caster of bones. The ceremony had been concocted. As intended, the comment about success had especially pleased Connell, and now he beamed broadly.

"Remarkable," he said. "Their talents are astounding. One only wishes that we could be so close to nature and so privy to the mysteries of existence." He walked into the middle of the clearing to view the side of the male hill across the small valley and stood there for a minute lost in thought. Then he turned back and made as if to speak pompously when his eyes grew large and his jaw dropped.

"My God, they're everywhere! Bees!"

Indeed, they were everywhere. Unfinished drinks and small bits of fruit left uneaten had attracted them and now there were hundreds buzzing around the lunch site. The others had already noticed this and had begun picking up the refuse and leftovers. They put everything in plastic bags and then into empty cardboard boxes hoping to lessen some of the scent that drew the bees to them.

Connell spoke in halting tones, "I think we'd best get on to the next site." He was out of breath from watching.

"Ja," agreed Joost.

Attempting to regain some composure and authority in his voice, Connell cleared his throat and then said deeply, "While we pack up the equipment and prepare for the next scene, why don't you give /Gashay and the others a couple of beers. No, a beer for each of them," he added magnanimously. "I'm sure it won't hurt much." Joost did not mind the barb at his former remark and even winked at /Gashay by way of congratulations. He then went to get beers for them out of the cooler.

They spent the rest of the day at several paintings on the male hill. The falling sun began to shed an orange glow on the sheer western face of the hill, and the film crew used the opportunity to take some spectacular shots for fillers. The Bushmen were no longer needed and so they walked back to the compound while Connell and the film crew wrapped up their final shots. An hour before sunset, they packed up all the equipment and climbed into the Cruiser.

"I've had a most splendid day, Joost," said Connell expansively. "I thank you heartily for your guidance and your preparation."

The Germans, nursing nascent sunburns, joined in with their appreciation. Joost just smiled and drove on. The Cruiser rocked and bounced on the rugged dirt track and stirred up a thick cloud of dust in its wake.

"You know," added Connell, "the pilot won't be here for another half hour yet. Let's stop at the Bushmen's compound. I want to have a look around."

"Okay," said Joost. They had to drop off Isaac anyway.

There was a lot of activity at the compound when they arrived. The children were taking advantage of the last warm rays of the sun to play in. The boys had interesting toys called *djani*, which consisted of hollow reeds with a feather on the end and another on the side. This shaft was in turn attached to thin leather straps with weights on the end. Using sticks, they would toss these up high into the air from where they would glide downwards with a vigorous twirling motion.

The women had gotten up from their midday gossip and were preparing dinner, which was to be cooked in a three-legged Dutch oven provided last year by the government. Gumtsa, ≠Toma and /Gashay, the only men in camp, were already drinking their day's earnings and well on their way to being extravagantly drunk. Connell strode directly into the compound area, heedless of any sense of privacy or decorum that might prevail, and began a thorough examination of anything that interested him. Sensing a potential customer, some of the women fetched the crafts that they had made for visiting tourists. These they shoved towards Connell's face, each one vying with the other in true bazaar fashion.

"Buy this. This good," said one holding an ostrich-shell bracelet.

"Reka lotlawa le. Reka, reka, reka! Cheap, cheap!" shouted another with a colorful necklace of glass beads.

"How much for this one?" asked Connell of a young girl who had a leather purse adorned with red, blue and green glass beads.

"Forty pula," she replied.

"Forty pula? That's too much." Connell frowned. "How about twenty-five?"

"No, forty pula," she insisted.

Connell hesitated. "No, I'm afraid that's too much."

The girl pouted for a few seconds and then insolently said, "Thirty pula!"

Connell grinned. Evidently the girl sensed she was losing her customer. "It's a deal," he said graciously. He dug out the money from his wallet thinking all the while what a bargain he had made. The purse would surely go for sixty pula in Gaborone.

Still pouting, the girl accepted the money and walked away. She was laughing inside. Crazy *Lekgoa*! The purse had only cost her four pula to make and she would have been happy to have sold it for ten. Bless the gods for stupid *Makgoa*.

Connell made several more bargain deals and then began to walk back to the Land Cruiser. Suddenly, old blind Xama tugged at his elbow and accosted him. She seemed to have something to say to him, but what it was he couldn't make out. He excused himself and said he didn't understand Bushman or Setswana. He tried to pull away politely but she persisted. Looking up he spotted Isaac a few paces away talking to the Bushmen who had come along with them today. Catching his attention, Connell beckoned him over.

"I say, Isaac, I'm having a frightful time with this old woman. She keeps jumping around and muttering some sort of gibberish. What the devil's she saying? She's been pestering me for several minutes now!"

Isaac exchanged a few words with Xama. Then he turned hesitantly to Connell and stood quietly with hands folded behind him. He seemed to have difficulty forming the words. Eventually he summoned up the necessary courage along with the language.

"She says that eggshells are for drinking."

"Eggshells are for drinking?"

"Yes. The ostrich eggshells . . . they . . ." He finally found the right words, "They use them to carry the water."

"Well, of course, everyone knows that! What's her point?" Connell was irritatingly confounded.

The men had come back to the compound and reported all the happenings of the day including all of Connell's narration that had been translated for them. Their annoyance at Connell's behavior had somehow become focused on his comments about the ostrich painting and Xama was now trying to let him know this by pointing out his basic flaw of observation concerning that painting.

"They are for drinking—for holding water." Isaac stumbled for the words to express this, but his command of English was not sufficient. Besides, how could one explain in a sentence, especially a foreign sentence, the primal role of water in the lives of people like the Bushmen? Connell knew this, but he knew it as only one fact among many other facts for him that related to the Bushmen. His mind saw it as data, known data. Had Isaac known the words, 'vital,' 'central' or 'quintessential' he still couldn't have made Connell grasp the true depth and significance of that precious commodity and the importance of the vessels that carried it. The meaning, but not the significance. Water wasn't simply a vocabulary word for the Bushman, it was synonymous with life itself.

Hearing the low buzz of the approaching plane, Connell sought a speedy exit from the discussion and so he changed tack. "I see, yes," he said smiling, "I understand now. Tell the old woman that I appreciate her pointing it out to me. Go on, thank her. That's right. Well, I'd best be off now. Good-bye." And with that he spun around and ran for the front seat of the Cruiser.

Isaac turned his head to follow the departing Connell, and noticed that Joost was standing on the other side of the thornbrush fence. He had heard the entire discussion. Isaac's face expressed embarrassed anguish for Joost, that he should belong to such an uncomprehending race: how Joost must suffer! As for Joost, he looked up at the far-off plane to avoid further embarrassing Isaac by appearing to consider the matter. Then he too walked over to the Cruiser and started it up.

The incident was quickly gone from Connell's mind. As they drove over the dusty track to the airstrip, his thoughts grew rapidly distant: he was imagining the enthusiastic reception he would receive back home when his breathtaking documentary of the rock paintings of Tsodilo Hills was broadcast. Why, Connell, they would say, what courage you had, what daring, and the way in which you got to the very heart of those people!

Part III

Phefo (Wind)

Fa Ele Jalo

(September)

Fa Ele Jalo

Dr. Birgit Sveinnson stood by the edge of the river and watched the wind caress the face of the dark blue water. It wrinkled the surface and threw forward small rocking waves that moved upstream, seeming to reverse the river's flow. There was something very disorienting in all of this for her.

Winter was gone. For all practical purposes summer was here; it was hot, very hot. Those accustomed to the northern temperate zones, like Dr. Sveinnson, found this transition abrupt and illogical, almost rude. If there was a springtime in this part of the world, then it would have to be defined as the time of the winds, for in late August and most of September it was just that—profoundly windy. But hot as it was, any pretense to spring remained purely semantic. Dr. Sveinnson watched in consternation as a bobbing clump of papyrus floated slowly against an illusory current caused by the wind. She sought signs of life in the river and in the swaying papyrus and reeds along the shoreline, but all she could perceive was confusion. In the end, she had to look once more toward the cloudless sky above. Nothing but the same thin pale blue canopy that had hung there in haunting purity for over four months now. The same blue emptiness. That uncomfortable reminder of primeval chaos, of the beginning of all things and of their end, of eternity and change.

She turned around and began walking through the gray-brown sand. The goats had eaten most of the grass by this time and only scattered small brown humps survived to hold some firmness in the ground. The overgrazing would continue until the rains brought new growth or until nothing was left. More often, it was the latter.

Senyema was dying.

To Mokgara Maeze, Dr. Sveinnson was a small blue and red dot. He sat in his *kgotla* chair within his compound and watched the dot wobble in the spaces between the many fence reeds in his compound. The dot moved to the left and disappeared behind a green smudge and then emerged in the next reed-space to the left. Up and down the dot bobbed, becoming gradually larger. Mokgara focused for a moment on the light brown reds, their smooth shiny texture: the sparse dark brown flecks stayed fixed while the fuzzy blob of red and blue flitted vertically in the background. He switched his focus back to the dot again. It moved to the left and this time disappeared into and then reappeared from several green splotches until it finally vanished into a part of the fence to the left where the angle of view closed the remaining gaps. He tried briefly to focus intently on the fence as if his effort alone might make the dot reappear, but it did not. He took another drink of *kgadi* and made no attempt to wipe the small amount that dribbled down his chin.

Mogorogorwane, or monkey oranges as they were called, were now in season. The empty half-globe of one, its wood-hard shell, lay on the ground to his left with the white inside facing up to the sky and the orange rind reflected in the sand. Many of the dark brown seeds, about three centimeters long and tear-shaped, lay scattered around him, particularly to his front. *Mogorogorwane* were eaten by sucking the flesh, which combined the tartness of orange and the burnt sweetness of brown sugar, until all the juices were gone and only a slippery sinewy pulp remained around the seed. These were then spat out and a new one taken into the mouth. Some of the sticky orange-colored juice had fallen onto Mokgara's white cotton T-shirt. Many older stains had already claimed their victories on it, and what was not stained was taken up by two large holes, one on the lower right front and the other on the left shoulder. This was the only shirt he owned and it was three years old. He looked down at the lower hole, which showed his jet-black skin and the waistband of his gray polyester slacks. His only pair. He wore no shoes, only calluses.

He might have been thinking about his daughter, who was mortally ill, or he might have been thinking about the pain in his aching stomach. They had plenty of mealie meal to eat, but little of anything else. Meat was too expensive, and fresh vegetables and eggs were rarely found in the village. Tinned vegetables cost too much anyway and were too heavy to carry the six kilometers from the shops in Shakawe. Perhaps he was just thinking about where that red and blue dot had gone. Or it could have been that he was having so much trouble keeping anything in his head that he wasn't thinking at all.

And Senyema was dying.

Birgit watched her blue canvas pumps move forward and backward below her. In the beginning she could not walk in the pliant sand without looking down, but over the past year she had developed a feel for walking in its shifting ambiguity and could, if she wished, keep her eyes raised. However, she had stepped solidly on a long camel thorn several weeks ago and had no desire to repeat the painful experience, so she maintained a careful watch. Besides, she had been warned that with the coming of warmer weather snakes would be more numerous.

Out of the corner of her eye, she could see the blurred shape of a solitary compound about one hundred meters to her left. It was surrounded by a high reed fence and a dense cluster of trees, while bushes rose up from the earth behind it. A lack of rain and an overabundance of grazing goats and cattle had combined to take away nearly all of the green from the landscape except for the higher branches of the trees and the poisonous thornapple plants scattered haphazardly over the gray-brown sand. Nearly everything else was beige and merged imperceptibly with the high reed fence. Only the sky above, hugely blue, sat indifferently apart.

Enervated by the dry heat, she stopped to sit on a large tree trunk lying prone on the ground. It had been felled by lightning only last summer but looked as if it had lain exposed to the elements for much longer than that. Any portion of it that had been reasonably easy to remove had been detached long ago for firewood; the bark too had been burnt or had been digested by hungry goats or donkeys; the pale inner wood displayed the long shallow winding carved trails of beetles, and a crusty residue around the base betrayed the presence of termites.

Birgit shielded her eyes from a sudden gust of wind and looked at the compound across the open space of mottled green and beige. She knew that Mokgara and his wife Morolana lived there. She knew that Senyema was living there, too, although she could just as easily say that Senyema was dying there. Words could be so strange at times.

Living, dying, existing.

Mokgara, Morolana, Senyema, her brother Letia and her younger sister Mweowa were all residents in that compound, they had a physical presence there and certain legal rights united them with that particular location. But Birgit could not say that they all lived there. Perhaps Letia and Mweowa, yes; but Senyema was dying; as for Mokgara and Morolana—they merely existed.

Birgit knew that Senyema was dying because she was a doctor. She had learned of Senyema's illness nine months before and had immediately driven down from the village clinic to have a look at her. She found Senyema sitting on the ground in the family compound, a thin bony figure leaning in abject exhaustion against the fence. She had had a generally non-productive cough, but no bloody sputum had evidently been noticed. The presence of hemoptysis was not a good sign and Birgit was not surprised to find, on examination of the armpits and back of the jaw, tender swollen nodes and the onset of lymphadenopathy. Given these symptoms and her generally emaciated appearance, there was little doubt that Senyema had acute pulmonary tuberculosis. To be certain of her diagnosis, Birgit used multiple-puncture tines to administer three TUs of a purified protein derivative stabilized with a polysorbate detergent in the diluent as a means of obtaining a definitive diagnosis. The presence of palpable induration of eleven millimeters two days later confirmed Birgit's supposition.

Senyema was dying.

Mokgara could see the red and blue dot again through the reeds; this time to his left. He turned his chair to face in that direction. The dot seemed to have stopped some distance away. Probably by the large *mokutshumo* tree that had come down in a storm during the rainy season some years ago. It had been a good tree for firewood and he was glad that the *badimo* had favored him by felling it. Many things came and went in life and he knew that he liked it better when things came. His wife Morolana came out of their reed hut and also gazed at the red and blue dot.

"*Naa, gape oa tsile,*" she said languidly—So, she's come back. Mokgara did not answer. He continued to fix one eye on the dot.

The two of them also knew that Senyema was dying. At the first signs of her illness, they had consulted a local *ngaka*, Lewanika Marovu. He had come at once with his *kgokong* and his *moraba*, and he had cast his bones several times. In the end he had concluded that Senyema was suffering from *lebejana*. This, they were told, had been brought about by *meila* on the part of both parents, that is, transgressions against sexual taboos. Mokgara had been at fault for having repeatedly slept with other women, even while his wife was giving birth. Worst of all, however, and the reason why Senyema was sick and not the other two children, was that both parents had failed to respect the forty-two day confinement period following her birth. Morolana had left the house to pay social calls as early as the twenty-ninth day and had even gone to buy food in the village on the thirty-fourth day. Mokgara had slept with his mistress many times during the confinement period and had even forced himself on Morolana twice before it was over. Marovu perceived a great anger by the *badimo* in his divination bones. They had decreed that Senyema must die.

Overcome with shame and horror, Morolana had begged the *ngaka* to do something, anything, to save Senyema. These matters were rarely reversed, said Marovu, but he would try. He prepared Senyema for *go lomega*, or "sucking," by making three parallel cuts on either side of her chest. He then applied the wide end of a kudu horn to each set of cuts and sucked on the narrow end. From the left side he pulled out a small piece of flesh, which he claimed to be a piece of the liver. This was an ominous sign, he said. He then prepared an herbal mixture and told Morolana to make a broth from it every day and to have Senyema drink it in the morning. She followed his advice closely and called him back on several occasions. Finally, however, Marovu said that there had been no change in her condition and that there was nothing that could be done. He would not return.

Senyema was dying.

The next day Birgit was again sitting on the tree trunk. These last two weeks, whenever she had had free time, she had driven down to Xauga, a group of compounds outside of Shakawe in which Senyema's family lived. Birgit didn't really know why she did it. Possibly because she wanted to catch a glimpse of Senyema, unlikely as that was in her bedridden condition. It could be that she had spent so much time in the Maezes' hut that she now found it hard to break away from them once and for all. It could be that she was so debilitated by the illogical act of waiting for a child to die whom she knew modern medicine could save. She was always angered by the inability of Senyema's parents, and of the people in this place in general, to understand that an ebbing life like Senyema's could be brought back from the hands of death. The constant thought of this unreasonableness wouldn't allow her to forget or stay away.

After all, she thought, she had ameliorated Senyema's condition immensely in the space of three months, hadn't she? When she first diagnosed Senyema, she had immediately instituted a regimen of curative drugs that would inhibit the dispersal of the viral infection and the harmful effects of pulmonary excavation, thus allowing the body to perform its proper tasks in repairing and revitalizing the damaged tissues. An initial combination of isoniazid and ethambutol had dampened the excess production of niacin and catalase, and had instantly halted the processes of caseous necrosis, liquefaction and cavity formation.

At first, Morolana and Mokgara were indifferent to Birgit's treatment. At best, they felt that no harm would result. However, suspicions in them had been fostered by gradually persistent questioning from neighbors and a growing rumor mill. They grew hostile to the intrusions of a *Lekgoa*. Recognizing the imminent crisis, Birgit sought another approach. She understood the financial and emotional strains on the family and suggested what she thought would be a palatable solution: she would take the child for three months and provide medical care for her; she would also feed, clothe and school the child. The parents argued that they would lose her labor if she were to leave. Furious inside, Birgit offered to buy them one bag of maize meal a week. They acted offended with that proposal, but quickly accepted when Birgit augmented the deal with two kilos of beef.

Senyema was taken to physician friends of Birgit's in Maun where she was given a new set of clothing and enrolled in a nearby elementary school. She was immediately put on a program of isoniazid, rifampin and, initially at least, streptomycin and pyrazinamide to accelerate the suppression of the virus and lead towards its eventual annihilation. For three months, each morning before she had breakfast, Senyema was given 250 milligrams of isoniazid, 300 milligrams of ethambutol, and 250 milligrams of streptomycin. For the first two months, she also took 1.5 grams of pyrazinamide. This regimen could have brought about a total cure in as little as nine months. A healthy daily diet with three meals of balanced food groups would accelerate the repair of damaged tissue and strengthen her body's resistance to relapse leading to further infection.

The results were astounding. When Senyema returned to her family three months later, she was six kilos heavier, her skin had a resilient sheen to it, she was energetic and there was no cough. Moreover, she was smiling and laughing.

But Senyema was dying.

Mokgara took a drink of *kgadi* and refocused on the yellow and white dot sitting beyond his fence. Yesterday it had been red and blue, today yellow and white. How crazy of that *Lekgoa* to try and defy the *badimo*, he thought. Did she really think she could fool them by taking Senyema away and having foreign *dingaka* work their magic on her? They would only make her seem to be better. It was only one of many tricks from their magic bag. That she had looked better did not change her fate as foretold by Marovu. Everyone, even a village idiot or the youngest child, knew that when an *ngaka* said that a person would die, there was no hope, no possibility for deliverance. That was fate and it was a fate conjured by powers much greater than those of feeble mortals—even those of a foreign *moloi*. Still, that never stopped these *Makgoa* from believing they knew the answer to everything.

Mokgara picked a long dried-out reed from the ground and brought it down between his feet. He slowly raised it in the air and brought it down, then up and down with supple consistency. He stopped, looked at the far end of the reed, which lay in the sand and said aloud, "*Ija!* This *Lekgoa*, if she wants to help so much, why doesn't she buy me some cattle?" His wife Morolana did not answer.

A wrenching series of coughs came from inside the hut where Senyema lay. They were husky and very guttural at first, trailing off afterwards in a tremulous wheezing. Morolana turned towards the doorway, but she did not move from where she stood. She soon turned her attention back to the yellow dot on the other side of the fence. Her face was haggard and drawn with exhaustion. Where had life gone, she often wondered. She really had had no particular expectations from it, but somehow she sensed that what she most cherished earlier had become only a thin wisp of a dream. She looked down at her husband who sat slumped in the *kgotla* chair, his chin resting on his chest, the reed in his right hand and his left arm hanging limply at his side. She felt nothing. She only knew that she was tired.

Senyema was dying.

Birgit heard the coughing and hacking from where she sat and for a moment she got up as if about to rush over to the hut. But she quickly sat back down and continued to stare blankly across the stark open area.

Birgit had hardly moved today in all the time she had been sitting on the log, and now, for no apparent reason, she drew her right foot back to the base of the log. Most likely, it was to make her more comfortable; the ground being slightly higher at the base of the trunk, her right leg was elevated marginally higher thus causing her weight to shift onto her left buttock. The rising incline at the base of the fallen trunk came from the brittle wood and sand mixture that had been left by termites consuming the decaying timber.

Birgit did not know that the residue came from termites, in this case, termites of the species *macrotermes natalensis*, which were among the largest termites in the world. That they were *macrotermes natalensis* was indisputable to any specialist who could see their orange-yellow bodies and rounded heads. They were well known as a species that constructed the largest aboveground mounds in the world, the mound of this colony being 2.25 meters high with an average diameter at the base of 3.12 meters. Had Dr. Sveinnson closely surveyed the area around her, she would have seen the mound only 32.45 meters behind, slightly to her left. Connecting tunnels, excavated in the ground below, extended for many tens of meters away from the center, one of which led up to the fallen *mokutshumo* tree. Interestingly enough, *macrotermes natalensis* do not digest wood using protozoa such as *trichonympha campanula* or certain other species do. Instead, they feed on the fungus and fungus by-products that grow from fermentation of the wood. The termites carry small pieces of wood to their nest where they are stored and cared for until they produce the desired fungus. The residue left behind does not result from the ingestion process but is used by the termites to camouflage the wood that has been removed.

Dr. Sveinnson was not aware of these facts as she looked down at the hard residue while shifting her weight onto her right hand so as to lighten the pressure somewhat on her retracted right foot. She was recalling Senyema's return to her family. Within three weeks, Senyema had once again become consumptive and emaciated. She wore her old tattered dress and her smile had disappeared. Outraged, Birgit had demanded why the parents had done this, why had they allowed her to relapse? They refused to reply. Through the *Motswana* nurse that she had brought along, Birgit strived to communicate to the Maezes the critical nature of Senyema's condition. They were unreceptive. Then Birgit had begged them to give Senyema to her; she would take care of Senyema at her own expense. They would not comply. Birgit had demanded to know the reason, to which Mrs. Maeze had shrugged her shoulders and simply replied, "*Fa ele jalo . . .*" The nurse had translated for her: if it be so. That was all. If it be so.

The Maezes had had nothing more to say.

Senyema was dying.

Letia brought plates of *bogobe* from around back of the hut to her parents. Mokgara still sat in his *kgotla* chair, and Morolana was now seated on the ground. They ate their dinner to the faint background wheezing of Senyema. It was something they had grown used to, having heard it for many months. So much so that her more frequent coughing attacks and more labored breathing had gone unnoticed by them.

They eagerly scooped up spoonfuls of the steamed mealie meal and pushed it roughly into their mouths. There was no light banter, no savoring of tasteful nuances, only the occasional glance over at the yellow dot in the distance, grown brilliant now with the late afternoon sun. In their haste, small chunks of the *bogobe* fell to the ground. They did not care, their three chickens would scavenge them tomorrow morning. Morolana called for Letia to come collect the enamel dishes. As was custom, she indicated that now that the parents had finished, the children could have whatever scraps were left. There wasn't much, but that was how it had been when they were children. Why should it be any different now?

"*Ija*," said Mokgara smacking his lips, "if that woman is always hanging about, why can't she be useful and bring us some nice meat?"

"*Waii*, who understand *Makgoa*? They have more money than there is water in the river and all they do is hold on to it. They never give us anything."

"*O bua nnete*. At least we got some money out of that dress that Senyema was wearing when she returned."

Morolana nodded her head. They had promptly sold the dress and used the cash to buy several kilos of meat for the family and several liters of *kgadi* for Mokgara.

Morolana sighed. "She has tried very hard to help her, but, after all, she is only a *Lekgoa*. How can you expect her to understand the ways of the *badimo*?"

"That's just it. They can't know such things." Mokgara picked up the cup beside him. "*Ao*, my *kgadi* is all gone. Letia! *Tla kwano! Mpha kgadi!*" he said, yelling for his daughter to get him some more *kgadi*. But Letia did not come. Mokgara sensed that something was wrong. It was suddenly much too quiet. Mokgara shouted again, as if the jarring sound of his voice might shake the world back to normal, might bring back the security of routine.

"Mokgara! *Tla kwano!*" Morolana was calling for him to come inside.

He got himself awkwardly out from his chair, the oppressive heat seeming to weigh him in. He cursed his wife and daughter for making him move. Women. Girls. They never showed any consideration or respect. He entered the hut and blared, "What do you want? What do I have to help you with now? Can't a man sit . . ." Inside Letia was standing against the wall to one side, staring across at Senyema's bed. Mokgara followed her gaze and saw Morolana kneeling with her head in her hands.

Senyema is dead.

Birgit sees a young girl in a very short torn dress come out of the compound and begin walking toward her. The girl is looking at the ground, not at her, but there is no question she is headed for Birgit. She senses this and lets out a protracted sigh. The little girl walks up with dusty legs, and while picking her nose tells Birgit what she has already guessed.

She feels an impulsive need to go instantly to the reed hut and see for herself, to express her sorrow; but she does not move. Her right foot is still drawn up against the *mokhutsumo* trunk and rests on the hard mix of sand, wood and enzymes. The little girl stands glancing to the side of Birgit, her left index finger hanging onto her lower teeth, her weight on her right leg.

Birgit stands up, smiles at Letia and then begins walking to the river. A mild wind blows against her back and pushes all the calf-high thornapple in the same direction that she is heading, as if leading the way. Her long shadow follows perpendicularly at her side, its outline jostled by the contours of the ground as she walks. She looks up and seems momentarily to have lost her way, then realizes that it is simply the change in lighting, which she has failed to take notice of. She marvels at the golden green of the trees against a deepening violet sky. When she looks down again she realizes she has forgotten to watch for snakes.

The river is calmer than when she had been there the day before and now the current appears to flow in its natural direction. She stands on the low bank, on brown close-cropped tufts of grass, and surveys the Okavango from left to right letting her eyes unconsciously follow the current downstream. The sandy banks are etched with horizontal lines formed by the receding water, which has been going down for nearly five months as if it were exhaling in a long drawn-out sigh.

Several sandpipers tiptoe lightly on the further shore, and a tiny iridescent malachite kingfisher skims the water at her feet. Her squinting eyes have scanned every inch of exposed sand for ominous dark gray shapes, but there are no crocodiles to be seen this late in the day. Her face is completely unexpressive and her eyes take on the sheen of a daydreamer. After what seems to her many minutes but has only been several seconds, she snaps out of this listlessness at the sight of something clinging to a reed on the far shore. She focuses and all at once her tense eyes spread out in recognition. It is a carmine bee-eater. Her surprise grows as she realizes that there are more than just one in the reeds; there are twenty or thirty!

She has seen some of these birds in the last few weeks. They are beautiful with bright maroon and turquoise plumage, long thin tails and long hooked beaks, but she has been too busy to go see their nesting area. She remembers being told that each year in late August, they migrate from the north on their way south and stop to make their nests in places such as the steep banks along the Okavango. Within long narrow tunnels, they raise their young until the chicks are ready to fly on their own in late October. The empty expression is gone from her face and she begins walking northward along the riverbank. She knows that another kilometer up toward the village there is a steep bank where she will find more bee-eaters.

The terrain is difficult. There is either deep sand or jutting mounds of grass roots; sometimes she must go around a dense stretch of thicket. She stops for a moment to watch two African skimmers fly past almost at water level, their wings beating with grace and power. They, too, are building nests. The sun is low and there is not much time; she must decide whether to go on or turn back. She decides to continue. Her steps become mechanical, compelled by inertia. Maybe she is thinking of nothing and merely relishes the invigorating physical exercise.

Engrossed in her thoughts, she has reached the sheer sandy bank where the bee-eaters are nesting. Quite suddenly, there is a clamor and a darkening of the sky. Hundreds of them have risen up from the trees and from the bank, startled by her arrival, and have formed a huge scarlet and purple disk that wheels languorously through the air overhead with her as its axis. The air resonates with their sharp guttural caw so very like that of a sea gull. Although not sonorous, it is nonetheless pleasing. In a single instant, Birgit seems pulled into a churning whirlpool of life that is both wondrous and confusing; and soon she, too, is wheeling around, turning and turning and turning until she falls onto the sandy earth below. She lies on the ground and tries to catch her breath.

The sun has set. All shadows gently vanish and a cool dusting of blue settles over everything. Birgit stares into the dark purple-orange sky that hangs overhead, infinite and empty, and repeats over and over to herself, *"Fa ele jalo."*

A Burning White Sky

(October)

A Burning White Sky

MOITSE wipes away a fly from his nostril only to have it persistently return. He has to swat at it diligently for several minutes until it wanders off for good. He closes his eyes from time to time as if drifting in and out of sleep. Most likely he stays awake because it is too hot or maybe because he is watching over his father's cattle, which are grazing in the small meadow to his right. Other than these occasional eye movements—the closing and opening of eyelids, the glance to the right—he remains motionless in the parsimonious shade of the tall russet bush-willow tree against which he is sitting. There is very little sound. Only a fly or dung beetle passing now and then. In the background, one hears the intermittent muffled ripping of grass from cattle feeding on the last remaining blades.

Moitse glances at the solitary man who is lying on the ground about fifty meters to his left. The man's head is propped up against the vinous base of a poison-pod albizia tree, and his bare feet stick out beyond the borders of the tree's dark blue shade. A pair of scuffed black dress shoes, their seams split, lie neatly together beside the man's left thigh. He, too, is motionless save for the picking and sucking in his mouth on what appears to be a toothpick or wood sliver that he holds casually between his thumb and index finger. It seems that the man has not noticed Moitse, probably because two sour-plum bushes beside Moitse largely obscure him from the man's sight. For his part, Moitse has not spent much time regarding the man: it may be that he offers little in the way of interest or it may be that it is simply too hot. Outside their small islands of shade, the world is bleached of color by a burning white sky.

❧

Jackson Sedumedi walks energetically towards the main road. The air is cool and feels good in his nostrils. He looks forward to an enjoyable day. He is not on his way to work, for he has no job; rather, he is leaving the compound of Boiketlo, a woman with whom he has spent the night. Since her boyfriend, Big Boy Kwanyana, is away on business down in Gumare, Jackson has little fear of being caught. All the same, he would prefer not to have anyone know that he was at her house.

The crowing of roosters and barking of dogs grows louder as he passes reed huts lying at the southwestern edge of Shakawe. Boiketlo's house is now several hundred meters behind and Jackson no longer worries about being seen by any of the women in the compounds who are busy chopping wood, making fires and preparing food. The smell of *bogobe* circulates through the air and draws at the strings of hunger in his stomach. He thinks of his sister's family with whom he lives, and especially of her daughters who are most probably preparing *bogobe* at this very moment back in their compound. He feels he will particularly enjoy eating it today.

He comes to the main road near where it forks, one branch of which runs through the village center and the other onward to the border to the north. The going is easier in the deep furrows of the road, which have been created by passing vehicles, as the stone aggregate base below provides more solid footing. Normally, he would not have had to move to the side so early in the morning, but a huge truck rumbles down the road toward him coming from the heart of the village and he has to step onto the sandy shoulder to let it pass. As it approaches, he recognizes the driver, who waves to him. The driver stops the truck for minute to chat and tells Jackson that he is going to Maun to pick up some supplies for the general dealer. Jackson asks the driver if he could get him a carton of cigarettes from the wholesaler while he is there; he will pay the driver back when he returns. The driver agrees and says good-bye. Watching the truck pass by on its way southward, Jackson notices a young man sitting in the back with a kind of starved look in his face. He has seen the man before and tries to recall who he is. Just as the vehicle passes out of view around a distant bend in the road he remembers that the man is an *ngaka* from across the river.

∾

Bom-ta-da-bom-ta-da-bom-ta-da-bom-bom. The drums beat their relentless rhythm in the black night and the reverberations of their pounding seem to crawl out from the trees, the ground and the air like feverish termites during their yearly night of mating. The drums have sounded since sundown without pause and without change in the rhythm. One's eye is drawn by the beat and eventually notices the far-off flicker of a wood fire. Moving closer, the pulsing beats become louder and louder, as if coming from inside one's own skull. Their energy is so dominating that even the stars in the sky seem to dance in time with them. The fire can be clearly seen now, its orange glow highlighting a large verdant tree to the right and a reed hut inside a fenced compound to the left. Three men stand around the fire and play long narrow drums that extend from their chests down to their ankles. The brown-black bodies of the drums are supported by leather straps that run over the left shoulder of each man. They play them with the forearms almost caressing the sides and the wrists bent in lithely over the drumheads.

In front of the three drummers, between them and the fire, a man dances wildly. He wears only a loincloth, rattling ankle bands made of leather and old dried-out bean pods, a tall narrow headdress of dark feathers, and flowing shoulder coverlets made of guinea fowl feathers and wildebeest tail-hairs that flare up and out from his arms as he dances. Soft smudges of red cascade from his inner eyes in downward arcs across his cheeks. There are long curved scratches running in an arc from his left shoulder to his right midriff. When he moves he violently shakes his shoulders and makes rapid, almost mechanical, jerks of the head, while his hips and legs appear almost static. Closer examination shows that the entire body moves in a fluid, tightly woven mass like a swarm of ants following the terrain. *Bom-ta-da-bom-ta-da-bom-ta-da-bom-bom.*

એ

Mohengi Nyangana, the chief's representative, his brother Kuvumbira, Nyambe Tuvumbudara and Sarambo Dishero sit on their folding *kgotla* chairs while Pelontle and her mother Pono talk to them. They listen closely with cocked ears and pursed lips. They are concerned by what they are hearing, and when the two women have finished, they agree formally to investigate the matter thoroughly. There is no clear case of transgressing the laws of the state, but there has certainly been a cultural infringement of some kind. This is the function of the tribal assembly, the *kgotla*, and it is the duty of all adults, especially elders who regularly attend it, to hear complaints of any sort and pass judgment based on the available evidence.

Pelontle looks down and sees her shadow, a squat bumpy oval that really doesn't seem to belong to her. The relative comfort of the early morning is gone, now replaced by oven-dry heat. There is still a tinge of blue to the sky and a sense of color still remains in everything. Very soon, though, the land will cower under the burning white sky. The gentlemen feel that it is time to seek shelter, but stay on briefly to learn more. They want to know, for instance, when the women first heard of the accusation made against Pelontle. Only shortly before they came to the *kgotla*, they say. Mothsithsi the rumormonger had told a neighbor who then came and told them. They were shocked, of course, but when Pelontle explained afterwards what had happened, they immediately understood why.

☙

Bom-ta-da-bom-ta-da-bom-ta-da-bom-bom. The drums play all through the warm night; their groans mingling with the murmuring of locusts.

☙

Pelontle Kutupura runs lamely under the burning white sun. Although her arms and legs are slightly scratched, she is not injured. She is exhausted, though, and has great difficulty raising her legs and maintaining forward momentum. She is sweating profusely; her breathing is deep and heavy. As she approaches the parallel ruts of a vehicle track, she spots someone approaching from her left, and, at that very moment, she steps on a stray camel thorn in the sand. In an effort to take off some weight from her right foot, the one pierced by the thorn, she disrupts her stride and trips. The soft sand has cushioned her fall, but she is shaken and the thorn in her foot is causing her pain. She begins to cry. The stranger approaches and she sees that it is only the village idiot Porridge Pot, who is driving his 'bakkie' out on this track for a purpose known only to himself. He stands above her, visibly distraught at her condition. She pulls the thorn out of her foot and he helps her to stand up. Why is she crying, he asks he, why is she crying? She will not answer, and instead begs him to go get the water container she has dropped by the water hole. He does so cheerfully while she waits in the naked light of the seething white sky.

154

ᘓ

Bom-ta-da-bom-ta-da-bom-ta-da-bom-bom. The man with the headdress is dancing frenetically, has been for hours. There is a diffuse look of animation in his glaring eyes, the only part of his body that appears truly motionless. A moderate-sized crowd, which has gathered around the drummers and the fire, is clapping along. From time to time a woman will release a chilling ululation that pierces and then is swallowed by the black night.

The dancer is Nkgwedi Haujipindu, an *ngaka* from the other side of the river, and he and his assistants are performing the *mendengure,* a ritual dance used for healing, driving away malevolent *badimo,* and identifying *moloi.* The Ndara family who live in the nearby compound have experienced a series of misfortunes—stolen cattle, a daughter dead of illness, withered crops, a brother ill with malaria—and are convinced that some *moloi* has put a curse on them. They have hired Haujipindu to find the *moloi* for them. He shakes his shoulders rapidly back and forth, and the shoulder feathers flutter in disembodied weightlessness. *Bom-tadabom-tadabom-tada-bom-bom.*

ᘓ

Pelontle is sweating in the intense heat as she approaches the slope down to the water hole. The decline is gentle and wide at this point and fans out towards steeper banks on either side. She squints in the harsh sun at the pale green flood plain. There is no wind and the white light of day sits limply on the surface of the water. Walking down, she notices a man lying under the shade of the poison-pod albizia tree to her right. She pretends, however, not to have seen him and continues on into the water, where she first splashes her face and neck and then fills the plastic water jug that she has brought with her.

As she leaves the water hole, the man greets her and remarks how hot it is. She agrees and begins to continue on her way, but he calls for her to stop and demands that she come over to him. *Tla kwano,* he says, *tla kwano.* She tells him she must be going, but he jumps up and walks over to block her path. She is very beautiful, he says, and she blushes. He asks her name and after briefly hesitating she tells him. He says that he loves her, loves her more than any other woman he has known. Although a part of her feels these words to be pleasing, her main impression is one of alarm. He then says he wants her to have his children. These are words she has heard from men many times before and it only deepens her feeling of apprehension. It is hot and she wishes to get back to the compound; but she does not move. She waits tensely under the heat of the white sky, hoping, like one who has come across a black mamba snake in the bush, that if she freezes and patiently bides her time, the dangerous beast will pass on its way. He asks where she lives, but she will not tell him. He runs his hand over her breasts and buttocks, and when she attempts to leave, he grabs her roughly by the arm and pulls her toward him.

ℰⅅ

Abel Sirumbu is the first to see Pelontle come staggering up to the compound supported by Porridge Pot. He calls to Kotlo who, when she sees Pelontle's condition, runs to help her. She guides Pelontle into her sister's hut, which stands just to the back of hers. Soon she and Pono are washing the scratches and scrapes on Pelontle's arms and legs.

The men at the shebeen are intensely curious about what has happened and call Porridge Pot over. Since he rarely speaks in anything larger than monosyllables, they are stumped as to how they should get anything sensible out of him. He is frightened by all the attention and lowers his head. They ask him if he saw what happened and he shakes his head in the negative. They ask if she was behaving wildly or strangely when he found her, and this time he does not answer. They are perplexed and begin suppositions among themselves as to what she could have been doing to have brought her to such a state.

When Kotlo comes back they question her repeatedly, but she steadfastly refuses to answer. She has become stern and irritable, and when finally she feels they have asked one question too many, she nearly explodes and suggests that if they don't like her *kgadi* then they can all leave, otherwise, they should all hold their tongues.

They will learn nothing more for the moment. Realizing this, Mothsithsi gets up and walks off. He will go out into the village to begin spreading the word that Pelontle has been possessed by a *moloi*, either through a spell or through the injection of *sejeso* into her body. This is obvious to him from the frenzied state in which she returned.

&

Batada-batada-batadabombom batada-batada-batadabombom. Exhaustion has been conquered long ago. The drummers and the dancer Nkgwedi move tirelessly in a single rhythm; they are one organism pulsing simultaneously. Their energy is pungent and it emanates outward. It has drawn in the bystanders, who move in a kind of secondary wave mirroring the possessed Nkgwedi; for just as a night fire casts a diminishing circle of light that illumines more ambiguously the farther it moves from the fire, so too the power of Nkgwedi's dance spreads outward, dangerously potent at the center but weaker at the fringes. To invoke the cooperation of many of nature's spirits, he mimics the movements and characteristics of a host of animals: the lion, the duiker, the wildebeest, the zebra, the elephant, the eagle and the leopard. He seemingly embodies the very essence of each of these creatures to the onlookers. His heart and theirs are one tonight and with their help he will discover the *moloi* he has been called to find. *Batada-batada-batadabombom batada-batada-batadabombom.*

&

The lengthening shadows offer relief to the men and women gathered at the open-air *kgotla*. It has been an exhausting day of debate about the Pelontle matter, in which judgments have been repeatedly derailed by the occasional injection of new gossip throughout the proceedings. A consensus has formed, at least based on the views of those villagers who have chosen to speak in the last couple of hours, and it looks as if the assembly can part ways: the old men to drink *kgadi* at Kotlo's, the younger ones to revel at *Ema Re Nwe*, and the women to begin preparing supper. To all present, the long blue parallel strips on the sand herald the approach of evening's relative cool, which will supplant the hot furnace of day.

While Mokgwasho Nkape, who owns the butchery, is finishing his speech, Gaotsielwa Haindongo leads his son Moitse into the covered oval of the *kgotla* where they sit down on the low foundation wall of bricks that house the roofing posts. No one stirs, but all attention falls incidentally on them.

Nkape concludes and Mohengi stands to address the assembly. He says that it is now time to take a vote on the issue and he thanks all those who are present for attending. He welcomes Haindongo to the meeting and asks if there is something he would like to add before they take the vote. Although those gathered are weary and ready to leave, they are also intensely curious about Haindongo's late entrance. Mohengi's offer to Haindongo is mandatory and a matter of good manners. Still, there is no one who groans or whines about it. It is the quiet of the eye of a violent storm.

Haindongo stands up and removes his hat. He thanks the chief's representative for recognizing him and says that, yes, he does have important business for the assembled members and he hopes they will bear with him for a few minutes. He explains that he has heard the gossip today about Pelontle and he has also heard about the charges being discussed at the *kgotla*. The reason he has come so late, he says, is that because of the gossip his son Moitse has told him something that otherwise he would not have considered so important. Haindongo asks his son to stand and recount for the people what he has seen. Moitse does so and when he is finished there is much mumbling and discussion. Mohengi thanks Haindongo and the boy, whose account, he says, supports what they have already concluded based on their investigations and deliberations. Nonetheless, he asks if anyone wishes to comment before they take a vote. Naturally, many do want to add something, although the remarks are, on the whole, reiterations of everything already expressed.

Mohengi, Kuvumbira and Kitchener Semumu all sit impassively as if the proceedings interest them very little. In fact, they already met together at midday and decided on the best outcome. They are members of the Botswana National Front and happen to be in controlling positions in a village that lies in the only district in Botswana to have elected a BNF representative to parliament, and they are particularly concerned to maintain the image of leaders who are in control and who look out for the people's interests first. To lend legitimacy to the charge made by Nkgwedi and not to take heed of Pelontle's explanation would be to present themselves as a backward people. The views of the people assembled at the *kgotla* have been falling in line with their preferred result, and they are inwardly ecstatic about the corroborating testimony of Haindongo's son.

Consequently, it is with great satisfaction that Mohengi stands up after the last speaker has made his remarks and calls for a vote. It

is unanimously against Nkgwedi for slander and assault. He will be
fined two hundred pula and given three lashes the following day.

ↄ

Bomdadabomdadabomdadabomdadabomdadabomdadabombom.
The drummers, Nkgwedi and the onlookers all gyrate in a flowing unison that seems to transcend time and space. For those who
have attended the gathering from the beginning—yesterday after
sundown—there is a sense of disembodiment and communion. The
beat of the drums continues on relentlessly as the eastern sky grows
pale and the stars are driven under the western horizon. Nkgwedi,
showing no signs of exhaustion, hops and shakes around the fire
with even more vehemence than when he started, and with the dis-
solution of night he begins an unintelligible chant. It, too, develops
an inertial power of its own, and his chanting swells in volume until
the first rays of the morning sun strike the treetops. Then Nkgwedi
begins to shout out words, almost in a scream, and just as the sun
rises over the trees and completely clears the horizon to stand freely
in the sky, he collapses onto the ground.

The drums stop; the ensuing silence is oppressive. After a minute
or two, he rises to his feet and calls out to the gathering: *ke phoromile moloi*, I have found the witch. To which the group responds
in unison: *ke mang?* who is it? Five times this is repeated:

Ke phoromile moloi! Ke mang?
Ke phoromile moloi! Ke mang?
Ke phoromile moloi! Ke mang?
Ke phoromile moloi! Ke mang?
Ke phoromile moloi! Ke mang?

Nkgwedi slowly turns around and scans each person in succession.
He looks up in the sky and then brings his eyes down full of burning fire. They are bloodshot and ferocious as he cries out: "There is
a woman called Pelontle who lives not far from here; find her and
you have found the root of your problems, your *moloi*!"

ↄ

Moitse can sense the tension in the air as the girl dips her plastic
container into the water. The man under the tree is sitting up now

and watching her bent figure. His left leg is extended straight out in front of him and, while resting his right arm on the other drawn-up leg, he continues to suck at the toothpick as if in a trance. Moitse has completely forgotten about the debilitating heat in his interest, and he watches as the girl puts the cap on the container and then walks out of the water. His eyes shift back and forth between the girl and the man, mesmerized by the invisible path that is to bring them ineluctably together. The man says something to her about it being hot and she agrees nervously. With head bowed down, she moves on her way, but the man calls for her to come over to him. She shakes her head and says she must get going. The man gets up and walks calmly over to her. Moitse can no longer make out what they are saying, but he sees the girl turn her head in disgust. The man starts fondling her body while she remains rigid with fear. He says something else to her and she again shakes her head. Then he grabs her by the arm and drags her towards some bushes. She drops the water container and tries to pull away from the man with both arms. The man reaches back with his left hand to grab on to a low-lying tree branch. He draws her closer to him, and she scratches him viciously across the chest and stomach. He throws her on the ground, looks at his stomach and mutters some curses at her, then sits on top of her and slaps her several times. She sobs in seeming submission and the man pulls her up to her feet to take her to a more secluded area, but just as he gets her up she pushes wildly and catches him by surprise. He stumbles backward into the branch he held onto only a moment before, hits his head and falls to the ground. Moitse stands up and watches as the girl runs away. He is about to go see if the man is okay, then notices him get up and rub his neck. The man begins to chase after the girl, apparently changes his mind, and returns instead to the poison-pod albizia tree, where he grabs his shoes. Still rubbing his neck, he walks off into the bleached-out landscape.

❧

Shahatsa Kotetuka gears down the truck he is driving. He sees his friend Jackson up ahead on the road and wonders what he is doing out at this end of the village so early in the morning. It would be impolite to drive past, and, besides, it would be interesting to see what he can get out of Jackson. They talk for a few minutes, but Jackson won't give away anything about what he has been up to. He says that he has come out to see about buying some cabbages from Alexander Karapo, but Shahatsa knows he wouldn't be so eager for cabbage as to venture out at this hour. It must be a woman, he thinks. He suddenly remembers his passenger, Nkgwedi, who has paid him good money to get him to Sepopa without delay. Personally, Shahatsa wouldn't mind turning him over to the *kgotla*, but payment of one hundred pula to take him forty kilometers on a route he already has to take is too good an offer to refuse. He says good-bye to Jackson, promising to buy him some cigarettes in Maun, and then crunches the transmission into gear. He is thinking that it's always best to get as much driving done as possible in the cool of morning, for soon the earth will succumb to the choking heat of the white burning sky.

Part IV

Mbu   (Earth)

Black Papyrus

(November)

Black Papyrus

THERE IS a kind of silence usually found only in the desert on a warm windless night, and it is strangely present today.

To the left, right and front, there is uncompromising devastation. Black and gray. The area seems oddly flat, low and empty, save for the charred strands of tall palm trees, which stand arbitrarily in stunned confusion. Where once grass, reeds and bushes grew, there is now only a soft blanket of black ash. The banks of the river are mostly bare except for the occasional shriveled clump of black papyrus. Everywhere there is the dark crisp smell of charcoal.

Some green can be seen behind to the north where the flood plain narrows. The firmer soil and abundance of trees has helped to dampen the fire's advance. As if the smoldering earth were not enough, the sun now moves towards its zenith making the area an unbearable furnace. The first clouds of the season are beginning to form, but they are too small, too scattered, too immature to provide any relief.

"*Wat vir 'n domheid is dit? Wat makeer sulke mense wat moet so 'n aangenaam olifant doomak? Slagters. Niks sonder slagters.*" Game Warden Piet Oosterhuis shakes his head in disgust while looking down at the large carcass of a female elephant. She had not died directly from contact with the flames of the brush fire, but as a result of complications from severe burns to the undersides of her feet. Elephant feet are highly complex structures that must bear a great amount of weight. On firm land, their feet spread out to help distribute the enormous weight they bear; likewise in soft muddy soils they must contract when lifted so as to prevent the elephant from becoming stuck. When the bottoms are burned and have grown sensitive and swollen, there is no reasonable means to support the heavy weight of the body, a mass which must range widely to ingest upwards of two hundred and twenty-five kilograms of vegetation a day to survive. This particular elephant could not make it out of the burnt wasteland because of its painful feet and so it collapsed here and died of dehydration, exhaustion and shock.

"*Heu, baas, did is nie lang dood nie,*" says Teaspoon Divundu, one of Piet's Hambukushu assistant game wardens. "*Sekerlik nie meer as 'n paar uure nie.*" He thinks the elephant has only been dead a few hours.

"*Ja, so dink ek ook,*" says Piet in agreement.

"*Kyk, baas, daar is die anders! Daar, agter daardie bome.*" Matteus Sadimba, Piet's other assistant, has spotted some of the herd members lingering anxiously behind some trees on the fringe of the charred plain.

"*Ja, hulle is ungelukkig want hulle s'n vriend is dood. Hulle wil na dit kyk.*" Teaspoon thinks they are sad at the loss of one of their own and that they want to look after her even in death.

"*Wat sal ons doen?*" What'll we do, asks Matteus.

Warden Oosterhuis sighs resignedly. "*Niks vir die Olifant. Daarvan moet ons die natuur handel. Maar ons sal moet ondersoek alle feuers en die doodmaak.*" Let nature take its course, he says, and otherwise put out all the remaining fires.

Oosterhuis looks towards the south. About two kilometers in that direction is the border with Botswana, and somewhere a handful of kilometers beyond that is where the fire started. He rubs the day-old stubble on his face and wonders whether he shouldn't go talk to someone over on the other side. It probably won't do much good given the approaching independence of his country; both governments are eager to leave the days of South African rule behind as quickly as possible and they are loath for the time being to engender any friction, no matter how small.

He and his assistants turn and head toward the river where their vehicle is parked. The ground crunches delicately under their feet and small black clouds of ash rise up and circle their legs. When they reach the vehicle, they begin loading their equipment into the back. While turning to pick up a box, Oosterhuis notices a silvery object floating in a small backwash of the river down below him. He walks to the bank and sees that it is the bloated carcass of a large tiger fish, one that probably weighed a good seven or eight kilos when alive. He rubs his chin thoughtfully again and then walks back up the sooty embankment.

જી

It is the previous day and tall broad flames are swirling about the papyrus and reeds. There is an incessant crackling caused by the explosion of swollen gasses in the stalks. The long dry season has left everything vulnerable; there is nothing to slow the flames down, only the wind to spur them on. The yellow wall of flame has been consuming the flood plain at a rate of some three to five meters a minute. Black smoke rises high in the air and then bends compliantly to follow the prevailing northeasterly breeze.

Two hundred meters to the north, a herd of elephant crosses the river to the western side of the flood plain from the eastern side where most of the fire is. The matron of the herd is experienced and has remained calm, suppressing the urge to panic that permeates the others. A large bull contributes to the order by remaining on the eastern bank and guiding the younger ones into the river. Unknown to this group, a cow has stayed behind to look for her calf, which became separated in the rush from catastrophe. She is not aware that the matron has already found it and seen to its safety. The lone cow will eventually try to cross the smoldering plain tomorrow in an effort to rejoin the herd, but in the process she will burn her foot pads severely, a wound that will prove mortal.

The elephants have stirred up a lot of debris in the riverbed and loosened a great deal of reed stems and papyrus. Moving downstream with the current, the debris serves to disorient some of the fish in the river. A particularly massive bunch of debris has caused one large tiger fish, exactly seven and eight-tenths kilograms in weight, to plunge into a shallow patch of water in one of the side channels off the main river. It soon becomes lodged in the abundant growth of reeds and only manages to wedge itself in more tightly with each new attempt at escape. Before long, the conflagration creeps up and devours the plant life around it; within minutes the surrounding water is churning with bubbles. The tiger fish still flops from side to side, though less vigorously now. It is growing weak from the diminishing oxygen in the water. Moreover, the high temperature of the water combined with panic has caused it to overwork its internal metabolism. Another few minutes and the water is visibly boiling. The tiger fish opens and closes its mouth rhythmically as if singing a final dirge. At last it gapes open widely revealing its sharp and menacing teeth. Seconds later it is dead.

 C/3

Earlier the same morning on the Botswana side of the border, a gaunt man trots towards the riverbank several kilometers north of Shakawe. He precariously clutches a jumble of objects in his two arms, trying to carry as much as is possible at one time. There are several articles of clothing, a blanket, a cooking pot, a kerosene lamp and a gun. Not far behind him there comes a woman and a young girl. The woman carries a baby on her back and in her arms holds more clothing, some cooking utensils, an axe, and a large canvas bag. The girl holds a bag of maize meal in her arms and balances a large woven basket full of sorghum on her head.

In the background, one can see a reed hut with thatched roofing, which apparently belongs to the man and woman. Behind the hut is a wide sheet of red flame, so high that it hides all evidence of land, trees and horizon behind it, as if it were slowly becoming the universe itself. The man, woman and girl drop their belongings on the sand by the river, begin hastily loading everything into a *mokoro*. There is so much that they nearly forget to leave room to sit. The man runs back several meters as if intending to return to the hut and fetch more things, but he gives up almost immediately, realizing that the fire will get there before he does. Instead, he watches silently as the sky rains down embers, some of which have already fallen onto the grass thatching of their hut. It is consumed with flames in a matter of seconds, its dry reed walls and grass-thatch roof providing a ready supply of easily combustible material. The man returns to the *mokoro*. They have little time to leave the island if they are to get away safely. As it is, the fire is moving in the upstream direction, which means they must float past it, for the *mokoro* is too heavily laden for the man to pole it against the current. He pushes off the sandy shoreline and gently sweeps the long oar in such a way as to cross over with speed to the other side while maintaining balance. So intent on this is he, that it is almost a minute before he senses the intense heat. Looking up, he sees a red and yellow demon gyrating into black smoke. He is momentarily distracted by this fearful presence, its dancing red, yellow and blue screams mesmerizing in their intensity. But he quickly forces himself to focus on keeping the *mokoro* next to the far bank. Ten minutes later, they pass the last gasps of flame into the relative coolness of the day's usual heat. Ahead they see the smoldering ruins of a black desert.

හ

For those unfortunate enough to live near the river, the only sound heard is a persistent muffled crackling; for those who are closest, there is also the hushed sigh of a warm breeze that gusts from time to time; for those farther away, there is a only a dull red glow in the blackness of night.

People downstream walk back to their compounds, exhausted and yet relieved that the fire did not spread to their side of the river. One occasionally sees a family balefully scanning a bed of pale red ash that once was their home. Across from the fire, there is more activity as people brave the darkness and the abundant snakes to watch for floating embers that might set their thatching alight. Some get pails of water from the river while others huddle expectantly in blankets. Everyone shouts, for the rumbling of the fire makes it difficult to be heard.

Upstream in Shakawe, there is an uneasy stillness. They are all in bed pretending to sleep and hoping that a semblance of routine will dampen the fears that burn inside them. Maybe the wind will shift and blow the fire away from them to the northeast. Maybe the river will be wide enough where they are to keep them safe. Maybe the fire will not reach them until morning.

Maybe.

☙

Early the previous afternoon, six and a half kilometers south of Shakawe, a female crocodile lies hidden among the tall green reeds of a sandy finger of one of the islands in the flood plain. She is large, perhaps as long as four meters, and sits languidly on a small open patch of sand. She is not basking; instead she is covering a clutch of eggs that are buried in the sand just below her belly. Under normal circumstances, a mother will only rarely venture away from the nest until the eggs have hatched. She does this partly to protect the eggs against preying birds, snakes and civets, and partly because she must maintain a constant temperature for them to incubate properly. It is difficult for her to do this at the moment, though. She senses a sharp increase in the surrounding land and air temperatures, and she is confused about what to do. She can cool the eggs by re-burying them deeper in the ground or by adding water on top of them, but the change in heat is too rapid for her to anticipate a plan of action.

She wheels around and moves off to her right in search of a cooler area. It is no different there, and when she turns to the right again, she encounters an even higher temperature. She pivots right once more and passes over her eggs and onward another ten meters. Finding the heat strong in that area and unable to sense a direction for the source, she returns to her nest in a panicked state and begins to dig up the eggs. She will carry them in her mouth through the water if she has to. She breathes heavier as she finishes exposing the eggs; the pungent smell of smoke stings the linings of her nostrils and sharpens her anxiety even more. In a rush to cradle the eggs in her mouth, she damages one of the eggs and pauses briefly to watch the vital albumen ooze out. Her mouth full, she cannot roar her sorrow. Instead, she clatters through the reeds and slips into the water and heads for the main channel, but what she doesn't know is that a long, thick arm of the fire stands between her and access to the river. It has easily jumped the narrow rivulets and side channels in the flood plain and continues to roll northward unabated. In fact, the surface water fifty meters ahead of her is already boiling. She soon feels the water begin to fester and churn. She hesitates momentarily, then quickly turns about and goes back in the direction from which she came.

The water cools as she swims and so she continues onward to the swampy marsh at the end of the side channel. The temperature is much more tolerable here and she moves up to dry land to find a new place for the eggs. Other than slivers of ash that occasionally fall from the sky, things are much calmer here. She builds a new nest and begins the process of regulating the incubation temperature again. The respite is temporary, however, as unknown to the crocodile, she has positioned herself between two forward-creeping arms of the conflagration, and, being even further from the river, she has effectively placed herself in a trap.

Crocodiles rarely make noise, but they can cry out with a power and vibrancy that makes the earth quiver around them. Within the hour, she will scream ferociously in this manner and at length. Anyone within a kilometer would easily be able to hear it. None will. No one is close enough and the bellowing of the fire will have drowned it out anyway.

♥

An hour later, Tony Atkins flies over in his Cessna single-engine plane. Don Llewellyn sits to his right in the front and Terry Williams in the back seat. Don presses his face to the glass and looks down directly at the spot where the crocodile made her last nest. Since the plane is moving quickly and he is not specifically looking for her, he does not see the smoking, charred remains of her body on the ground below. Its long powdery black shape merges imperceptibly with the sea of black ash that is the wake of the fire. The three men in the plane are tired of seeing black. They can no longer see details; they can only sense the blunt magnitude of the devastation.

"Why the bloody hell to they do it?" asks Terry, a native of Cape Town. Although he has traveled through Zimbabwe and Namibia and even been hunting once in Botswana, his knowledge of the area outside of South Africa has not really progressed beyond that of a tourist. "I mean, I can understand when it's caused by lightning; but as you say it's more often the locals that start 'em."

"There are different reasons," Don shouts above the noise of the engine. "Sometimes they start the fires to bring rain; sometimes they start them to ensure a good season of fishing; sometimes they do it to clear out wide patches for hunting, and often they do it to stimulate the rapid growth of fresh grass for their cattle. There's not much fodder left for them this late in the dry season, and they need their oxen strengthened for the planting to be done within the next month. If it hasn't rained by now, it probably won't do so until the middle or end of December and they can't wait that long to get their cattle in shape."

"It seems a bloody awful price to pay, doesn't it?" says Terry.

"Well, in better years there will be enough early rain to keep the fires from spreading wildly, but when it's this dry, the damage can be unfathomable. Still, you'd be surprised at how fast the land bounces back. A month after the rains have come, this whole area will be a solid carpet of green again. The reeds and papyrus will already be chest high by February."

"So, it isn't so devastating?"

"Well, not for the plants really; but the animals suffer terribly and fires like these can reduce local populations considerably. It may take the crocodiles, the sitatunga, the lechwe, the various birds, snakes and so on several years to recover properly."

Don is trying to be understanding and impartial. He understands that nature is sometimes cruel and there are large cycles of creation and destruction. Still, he too cannot help feeling deeply nauseous when he sees the smoking black earth below. No matter how much he explains things and puts them into their proper perspective, he knows that human ignorance and selfishness are often as much the driving force behind misfortune in this world as is the impartial hand of nature.

ೢ

There is something curiously majestic in the way a palm tree burns. The flames do not reach up all the way to where the fronds are nor is the bark flammable enough for them to climb up to the top, and so the fire defeats the tree by a process of dehydration and searing attrition. Hot waves of air rise up and the fronds bounce around as if mocking the flames below. The fire passes on and the fronds settle down, seemingly triumphant. Eventually they turn brownish-black and wither, but only after the fire is long gone and out of sight. It's as if the noble palm refused to let the fire see it vanquished.

ೢ

Kelodile Sirumbu stands looking to the southeast where a huge gray column of smoke rises in the air. She feels an uncertain change in the weather. The clouds have been building all afternoon as if it might rain, but they don't have enough of a presence about them for it to be likely. On the other hand, maybe they will get a light downpour of a few minutes, what is called a *makomakoma*. The wind has shifted and is now blowing strongly from the southeast. Kelodile can see the broad top of the plume shift and move towards her. She has just been to the river to get some water and is on her way back to her compound. She moves on. The wind picks up and whips her skirt and headscarf in waves around her body. She glances over her shoulder several times and sees the tower of smoke spread out in the sky as if ink in water. When she reaches her compound, she calls her children in from where they are playing and tells them to go inside immediately. Looking again to the southeast, she sees an enormous sheet of black-gray mist approaching. It seems to swallow everything in its path. The wind grows stronger and large chunks of ash come floating with it. She joins her children in their reed hut and they huddle in the corner. A few minutes later and the cloud has engulfed them, blotting out the sun and leaving a translucent darkness. The hut shakes in the wind and handfuls of black ash from burnt reed and papyrus slip under the door and through the cracks between the roof and walls.

By the time the windy storm has passed five minutes later, everything inside the hut, including Kelodile and her two children, is covered with a dry black layer of silt from the brush fire.

∾

The sitatunga is a kind of aquatic antelope. The long sleek legs, the powerful haunches, the broad cropped tail edged in white, the elongated muzzle, and the horns, which are wide and sweeping on the male, all give it the appearance of an antelope. You will rarely see one scampering on land, though, for they are normally found in the moist world of the flood plain. Their hooves are splayed; cleverly designed by nature to distribute the weight of the lithe legs evenly over a larger area. In this way, they can gain brief but sure footing on wads of floating reed or papyrus that would otherwise yield to most animals. It is splendid to watch them graze and then suddenly clunk off into the dense reed beds at a seemingly relaxed rate that is actually faster than any other mammal in the watery bush. Although their feet splash loudly into the water and give the impression of clumsiness, their hooves catch every time and launch them doggedly forward in a rhythmic, if only marginally graceful, manner. Primarily nocturnal, they are seldom seen.

On this night, the first night of the fire, a herd of sitatunga is browsing on the edge of a side channel of the Okavango about fifteen kilometers south of Shakawe. They move about leisurely, lifting their heads frequently to check for predators. To the inexperienced eye, they would appear to be calm and relaxed, but there is a tentativeness to their tearing at the grass, their heads are a little too still when lowered: a sign that they are pretending and are in fact on edge. A large doe raises her nose to sniff the wind coming from the south. There is a strange scent in the air that she cannot peg down. It comes and goes; it is subtle. It is not the smell of an animal nor is it even a human, and this worries her. If she sensed a lion, she could make the herd ready to move quickly away from it once she had determined its position. This is something else, though. She drops her head to the grass again to go through the motions of feeding.

All at once the wind shifts, coming from east-southeast, and she realizes immediately what the danger is. She has encountered this smell before and it signifies disaster: it is a fire. There is no time to lose. She bellows curtly twice and then jumps into the tall reeds leading the herd northward. They have been feeding in the pocket of a river bend with water to the west and south of them. The doe realizes in a fraction of a second that the flames have been moving northward to the east of them and that now, with the change in wind direction, the fire is heading straight for them. They must move without delay to the north or they will be boxed in. The herd runs into the thick reed bed with a chorus of crunching and splashing. There is confusion as the others try to determine the herd's direction. Panic-stricken fawns madly seek out their mothers. The din soon diminishes as they move away.

All is quiet except for the sound of softly thrashing water. The leg of one fawn has fallen through the papyrus and become snagged in the roots below. The tendrils have wrapped around the fetlock and hoof. The young animal tries in wild panic to fling the leg free, only to entangle herself even more tightly. Minutes pass and the fawn tires. With heaving breath and pumping heart, she stops to rest for a moment. She knows there is danger, but she has not seen any evidence of it yet. Perhaps she can take a short respite. As her heartbeat slows down and her lungs stop heaving, she begins once more to hear the world outside of herself. She does not hear the deep splashing of a lion or a leopard, nor can she hear the approach of any other animal; but she does hear a soft rustling that grows ever louder and louder. She tries to free herself one more time and again fails. She falls on her side exhausted. As her breathing returns once again to normal, she senses the imminence of something evil. The world turns gray and dark and she can hear nothing but strange cracklings, hisses and pops. Her nose and eyes begin to sting. What is it? Why is it suddenly so hot?

℮ↄ

It is a cool morning and high in the pale blue sky, the sun is churning up the first heat of the day. A lone man with a rifle slung over his back walks from the east along a narrow path in the flood plain. He is in an open field of golden grass, the edges of which are ringed with green papyrus and patches of tall green reeds.

His name, if someone were to ask and if it mattered, is Boithato Manyenga. He lives on an island on the eastern side of the flood plain where he raises some cattle. More often, he fishes and hunts. He is known to some in the village of Kaoxwe on the other side and to very few in Shakawe. He has a wife and two sons, and brothers and sisters who live in his compound on the eastern bank of the Okavango. He is a man who makes his way through life like so many others: one day at a time. Today, he is simply a lone man in the middle of the flood plain.

He stops and looks around slowly. It is unclear whether he is lost and trying to get his bearings or if he is looking for someone or something. Maybe a friend or one of his cows. Maybe he is looking for game. He holds up his hand in the air and holds it motionless for a full half-minute. There is now a look of satisfaction on his face, and he quickly drops into a squat. His arms appear to grab at something on the ground. He continues to move his arms in large rhythmic arcs. He stands up, apparently finished, and once again scans the area around him. He crouches again and reaches into his breast pocket. At that instant, it becomes clear that he has been pulling at grass and has formed a small mound of dried stalks. Boithato's hands flash with movement.

It is now sixty-seven-and-one-half hours before the moment when Warden Oosterhuis, forty-one kilometers to the north, will look southward and rub his chin in consternation. Boithato holds a lighted match in his hand, and, with solemn and studied care, he lowers it gingerly to the waiting mound below.

Pula

(December)

Pula

UNDULATING WAVES of heat already overwhelm the fading bloom of morning. The air is faintly redolent of damp expectancy. It hints at change; but almost eight months without a drop of rain, the first five without even a tiny mutant cloud to tarnish the smooth sky and the last three cursed with stern pitiless heat, one vainly tries to recall what change is like and wonders how else the world could possibly have existed. The recent heat has boiled away all memories of the chilly winter nights and all that remains is the doughy taste of dry heat and the bleached white vision of a shadowless sun. Small bulbous clouds have only recently crept back into the sky's domain cooling it down mercifully to a softer blue. And the air has also become different. It has grown heavy and the tongue now moves more easily in its cradle. Surely the harbinger of change.

Pono Kenyaditswe and her grandfather grow uncomfortable as pensive morning gives way to the full anger of day. They are waiting in the *Kgosi's* compound for the funeral mourners who will be famished and most likely on their second wind after having bitterly grieved all through yesterday and last night. Pono is stirring *motogo* in a large iron pot over an open fire while her grandfather sits quietly by her side coddling his brittle bones, which in old age are stiff from a night in bed. He too will be driven into the shade before long. Pono stops stirring and, raising her hand to protect her eyes, looks back over her shoulder into the east. She sees tiny puffs slowly building in the sky.

"*Heela*, still the same. It will never rain this year," she sighs heavily. She turns back and begins to stir again. "There will be drought again and everything will shrivel up until there is nothing but dust and skeletons." She clicks her tongue in disgust.

Her grandfather raises himself a little in his wooden *kgotla* chair causing the leather straps in the seat to creak in a short crescendo. He looks into the northeast and, having made his reconnaissance, reclines in his chair with another brisk creak. He listens briefly to the cooing of a mourning dove, then closes his eyes. "*Naa*, it will rain today," he says casually. Suddenly grunting he adds, "And about time, too!"

Pono looks at her grandfather with a loving but disbelieving smirk. "*Waii*, I know, you old people and your 'feelings.' Your feelings about cows and goats and for rain." She laughs lightly. "You need more science, that's what you need. Why, just the other day in class, Mr. MacEwan said that . . ." She does not finish. Her grandfather has opened his left eye, the glare warning her to hold her tongue. They have had such conversations before and never have they gotten anywhere. His look implies that she may tell him all about it when she reaches his age; in the meantime leave him in peace to enjoy what is left of the morning's coolness. She decides to desist, but cannot help adding, "It won't rain, though. You'll see." Her grandfather says nothing. She begins to sing a song she has heard on the radio to help pass the time while stirring.

Kgosi Motlhotlheletse Nyangana, *kgosi* of Shakawe and of many of the surrounding villages, including some on the other side of the river, has died. He passed away at a very advanced age, the exact figure of which is not known as no official records of his birth exist. He always claimed that he had been born at what the Christians call the turn of the century, and indeed there is some reason to believe that he came into the world before the deposition of Lethsolathebe II in 1906. He was born sometime around the close of the Boer war to the south; he became *kgosi* of this area while hardhearted Dr. Malan still governed in the Republic of South Africa; and he was already seasoned and wise when Botswana gained its independence in 1966. He can trace his maternal lineage back to the great Hambukushu headmen of the Andara kingdom to the north during the seventeenth and eighteenth centuries. During his regency, he cultivated the highest regard, affection and devotion among his people, and although the glory days of Andara may be gone, none can forget their legacy nor will any forget the fortitude with which Kgosi Motlhotlheletse endeavored to maintain that heritage. Indeed, he will be sorely missed.

The funeral was held yesterday at the *kgotla*. As the gathering place for the tribe, the symbol of its unity, it is the most fitting place to honor its leader both through the funeral ceremony itself and by laying him to rest under the heart of the true *kgotla*, which is the central cattle *kraal*. Last night, the local *ngaka*, Letlonkana Mokumbwanjira, led the mourners in the rite of passage for the dead soul, a rite which ensures a pleasant journey to and arrival in the new world. Dancing, drums, dirges and lamentations colored the night in hopes of easing and speeding that journey. In truth, there is another world coextensive with our own where the somber spirits of departed ancestors reside. Only the thinnest of intangible tissues separates the two, and, sad to say, those dearly beloved ones can still stick their mischievous noses into the stewing pot of our reality at their whim. In short, they can cause all manner of trouble, and as such the living are especially concerned with delivering the deceased from this world properly and respectfully. This means that rites must be scrupulously followed at the time of parting and thereafter gifts should be made from time to time by way of offering and appease-ment. This, amongst others, was the reason for the ceremonies last night, which were so eloquently accompanied by drums and wailing. And so, we say farewell, noble *Kgosi*. May you find your new world comfortable and worthy of your greatness—and may you bother us as little as possible in this one!

The heavy air of sadness and fear is absent, though. Aren't the dead at peace and freed of the gnawing worries and troubles of this world? Aren't they released from that most vexing anxiety of all, the dreaded knowledge of one's own mortality? These concerns are swept thoroughly away and a new life begins. Besides, through this mourning process, which is a time of recollection and meditation, the living who still inhabit this world are given another chance to conjure something meaningful for the time that remains to them. They too can be reborn if they so choose. And so, how can we not but conclude that death is rather a time to celebrate and not to grieve. Grieve instead for those who fritter away their span in this world by preparing for something always to come, for the end; who are so occupied accumulating and taking for themselves that they neglect the spirit, which withers like an unwatered garden and becomes dried and brittle; who immerse themselves in the passing things of this world in hopes that death, a passing thing itself, will forget them and pass them by. For life is ever changing in form but ever the same in essence. Indeed, isn't the shiny coin that will one day rust even more fleeting than the song of a nightingale? Now is a time for celebration for our friends in Shakawe. Maybe you doubt that they would allow their hearts to lighten after the death of their dear *kgosi*, thinking that instead they would prefer to weigh themselves down with dark and taciturn grief? Let's look in on them and see.

Looking below, we can see the *Kgosi's* house in his compound next to the river. It is the large fenced-off one with many people gathered inside. On the upstream corner is a tall broad jackalberry tree, and across from it a Western-style house built of cinder blocks and roofed over with corrugated tin. Its walls were once a vivid white, but they have aged to pale patchworks of faded grays, soiled beiges and aged off-whites. One of those small reed huts beside the fence on the village side of the compound is used for storage while relatives of the *kgosi* live in the other two. The ground has been cleared of all shrubs and grass; only the deep grayish-brown sand remains. This is to deprive snakes of places in which to hide. Fortunately, still many trees remain to cast some shade, such as that camelthorn, the poison-pod albizia and those two combretum trees near the hut and the tall stately patriarchs lining the bank of the river—the jackalberry, a knobthorn, a russet-bushwillow and a sausage tree.

However, it is midday now, and what few areas of shade there were in the morning have burned away. Only narrow circles near the trunks of the larger trees offer any respite from the sun. True, the huts are cool, but they are also very small. You don't even want to think of going into the main house as its corrugated tin roof turns it into an oven by day; perhaps a hackneyed description but unerringly to the point. Move slowly or the heat will quickly consume you.

You can once again see Pono hard at work over by the fence to one side of the jackalberry tree. She is now helping to prepare *bogobe* for the funeral luncheon that will be served later after the speeches. Her grandfather has returned to the cool hut in their own compound, where he can rest in more comfort. Pono's arms are very tired from stirring the thick porridge. She doesn't complain because, if the truth be told, she actually relishes the attention she is getting as one of the cooks. Certainly she will be a very sought-after person when everyone queues up later for food.

In the middle of that group of young people sitting over on the river side of the compound are the newlyweds Motsholathebe and Sethunya Modibu. They were married only a week ago in Sethunya's home village of Sepopa half an hour to the south. Not all of their friends from Shakawe were able to attend, so the couple is taking advantage of the festivities today to celebrate with them. They have been drinking for a couple of hours already and have reached a very desirable state of alcoholic bliss. As members of the younger generation, they shy away from the traditional *kgadi* and prefer instead to drink modern processed beer out of colorful aluminum cans. Most hold the blue and white cans of Ohlssons in their hands, the currently fashionable brand; only a few clutch loyally to cans of outmoded yellow and white Hansa or sadly archaic gold and red Lion. They are all having a good time, though, no matter what brand they are drinking.

"*Waii, monna*," Kubula turns to Sledge. "Where were you yesterday? We had a good old time at *Ema*."

"Really, I was at Ruth Semende's with Duanga and Oitsile. Penah Baise and Tsholofelo Sethwara were there, too," says Sledge jovially. His wide-sweeping sunglasses with teardrop lenses stretched thin to the sides reflect distorted faces and mammoth bowed trees as if portals to some fantastical dream world.

"*Iyoo!* Penah and Tsholofelo, you say? Two beautiful women like that at the same party and you didn't come get me? Trying to keep them all to yourself. No thought for your comrades." He taps Sledge lightly with the back of his hand and smiles. "So, *monna*, how was it?"

"*Naa, kgosi, o itse sent'e*," giggles Sledge. "It was just okay. We drank some good beer, listened to good music, danced and what-what."

"*Tsala*, I don't want to hear about beer and dancing. Tell me about the 'what-what.'" Twamanine has broken into the conversation and finishes by making all kinds of knowing grins and clucking sounds.

Sledge simply laughs. "Really, I think you do, *mogaetsho*, but, you see, a couple of BDF soldiers were there in their starched green uniforms, ready at a moment's notice to protect the ladies. Anyway, we had a good time. Ruth played the new Brenda Fassie tape on her cassette player."

"Another new tape?" asks Kubula incredulously. "Always new tapes, and a cassette player, too!" He grunts indignantly. "How can she afford all those things?"

Lebogang cackles with glee. "*Ao, monna*, you don't think she keeps the BDF around just for protection, do you?"

Kubula blushes and then snickers nervously to cover up his embarrassment.

Perhaps we shouldn't embarrass Kubula any more than necessary. Rather, let's turn our attention to the row of old men who are sitting in *kgotla* chairs over along the wall of the house. On the far left you can see Mohengi Nyangana, brother of the *kgosi* and his likely successor; next to him is Kuvumbira Nyangana, who on the one hand has enjoyed a long ride on the *Kgosi*'s coattails but on the other has felt himself unjustifiably eclipsed into obscurity; to his left sits his arch-rival, eternal verbal combatant and, well, his best friend, Nyambe Tuvumbudara; to Nyambe's left is the bodily swollen and mentally flatulent Kitchener Semumu, whose enigmatic gaze of self-contentment recalls that of the great sphinx of Egypt; farther on we see Mokgwasho Nkape, the owner of the butcher shop, and beside him Dunkirk Dumfries, owner of the general dealer and bottle shop, well-respected and ever-scheming gentlemen both; and lastly, there is the dispirited Moikokobetsi Ramphisi, who stares off resignedly into the distance and finds temporary solace in a *kgadi*-induced stupor. As the day progresses, they have changed their morose discussions about the recently departed *kgosi* into reveries of an increasingly lighter tone.

"No, no, no," says a somewhat tipsy Kuvumbira, "don't you remember the time we went hunting with the *kgosi* as young men and he killed the four francolins with one shot?"

"Really? You don't say?" Dunkirk Dumfries had grown up in Maun and thus did not take part in such early escapades around Shakawe.

Mohengi lets out a loud guffaw and spills *kgadi* all over his right foot. "Oh, yes, that was a good one. That is when Matengu—may his spirit not take offense—that's when he had some dead francolins in his bag, remember? And when the *kgosi* shot at one, he ran up to fetch the *kgosi*'s kill and he planted three more!"

"*Ija, bagaetsho,*" exclaims Mokgwasho, "and don't you remember how the *kgosi*'s tongue hung out in surprise when he saw those four birds lying there, and how ever after that, whenever telling the story, he would raise his nose and proudly describe how he had killed six with one shot. Before you knew it, the six had then become ten." Mokgwasho slapped his knee in merriment.

"You mean, you never told him?" cries Dunkirk.

"Never," says Mohengi with a happy sigh. "We didn't dare, and besides it was too much fun watching him gloat."

Their laughter subsides and Nyambe says, "*Naa,* but he was a good shot all the same."

The others agree and then fall silent, their thoughts reverting to times past. Each takes a drink from his cup, as if the infusion of *kgadi,* here and now, with its grainy feel against the back of the throat and its pungent tap in the nose, will somehow act as a kind of ambrosia to fight off death. If not that, at least it might free them of the iron grip of the past. But as it does neither, Kitchener decides to liven up their spirits and reminds them of the time when the first Motswana policeman came to Shakawe and how everyone mistook him for a salesman from Zimbabwe. They begin rollicking again and slapping their knees. Their gaping mouths show yellowed teeth and bobbing tongues, their chests heave and their noses crinkle like desiccated driftwood. Who knows, perhaps these grizzled old men, their stomachs brimming with *kgadi*, really don't exist but are instead merely ghosts from another time. Their minds overflow with vivid sensations—sights, sounds and smells—from the past; and, if there can be no reality without the mind, who is to say that the past is not the present for them and the present only someone else's memory?

Well, not for everyone evidently. There is poor Pono who still stirs away at the *motogo* over her hot cauldron. The debilitating heat is hardly imaginary for her. Between flinches at the bubbles of heat that hit her face, she glances longingly at her former teacher, Sethunya, and wishes so much that she could be like her: independent, intelligent and now happily married. She tells herself that someday she, too, will be a teacher or even something more important. Then she won't have to stand over a furnace all day stirring *motogo* until her arms drop off from exhaustion. In the meantime, she does have to stir, and so, with a sigh, she grasps her long wooden spoon and begins to sweep it in a circle around the pot.

And then there is Big Boy Kwanyana over at the far side of the compound. He is deep in conversation with a very attractive young woman. There is nothing imaginary about her shapely hips as far as Big Boy is concerned, although his imagination is no doubt galloping away unbridled at present. The woman is a new teacher at the primary school who has come from her home in Kanye, far away to the south of Botswana. Big Boy has kindly offered his services to the helpless damsel and has been so charitable as to take her under his wing. He is delighted that she is from the south and he repeatedly points out the natural bond that exists between them. Why, he says, the Bakwena, his people, and the Bangwaketse, her people, are almost like family, no? Brothers and sisters. Yes, she should consider him as a loving brother. He confides that she, also being from the south, will soon come to despise these northern barbarians as he does. He impresses on her that his door is always open to her and that should she encounter any problems, any problems whatsoever, she should not hesitate to . . . well, I perceive a delicate turn in this, at least what Big Boy believes to be, artful conquest. Let's remove ourselves discreetly and allow Eros and Prudence to battle it out alone.

Why don't we walk over by the—watch out, there! That damn Porridge Pot nearly ran us over. When Big Boy finishes with the new teacher, I shall certainly speak to him emphatically about that boy. Really, they ought to arrest him and take away his keys once and for all. He's much too reckless. You know, there was something different—do you think that was a new *bakkie* he was driving? As I was saying, let's go over by the jackalberry tree where there's a small patch of shade. Ah, I see it is already taken by Birgit Sveinnson and Joost Du Villiers. How kind of Joost to keep her company. As usual, Ms. Sveinnson is earnestly and energetically making a point to Joost in that uncompromising and overconfident manner in which the Scandinavian and Germanic peoples so excel.

"That's exactly my thinking, Joost," she says with her brows crumpled together, her guttural Germanic consonants gently gurgling out. "We must do something! The people here need a healthy diet. There is a river only meters away, all the water anyone could want."

"Mmm," nods Joost.

"And if we make a series of farms all along the river there would be enough vegetables to feed half of Ngamiland!"

"Ja, but . . ."

"Oh, but the cost. Yes, I know. That can be managed. We'll find the money from the donor agencies. Do you think the new *kgosi* will agree?"

"Well, I . . ."

"Oh, he cannot refuse once we have explained everything logically to him. Surely, he will not be so backward that he will deny the benefits of such a project?"

"I . . ."

"A lot of money will be brought into the village."

"Ja, he'll like that. But . . ."

"Of course, money is what it is all about and even though I do not like the idea of using profit as something to attract attention to the idea, if it brings about the same result, then I will use it."

Joost says very little; he is not a man of many words. Still, to be honest, I have seen him more gregarious when talking with the local people or with other bush-bred Afrikaners like himself. He is more reserved among the many greenhorn Whites who come charging into his backwater every year and proceed boldly to explain the region to him: its flora and fauna; its meteorological, geological and geographical characteristics; the various languages and cultures, the traditions and history; the systems of agriculture and hunting—all of which Joost has only been intimately aware of since a doctor first smacked his buttocks. Nevertheless, he bears their enlightened lectures with patience and courtesy. To tell the truth, he would much rather be speaking with some of the other villagers whom he knows well; but as Ms. Birgit is the only other *Lekgoa* present, he no doubt feels a certain duty not to abandon her, at least not until she finds someone else who will listen.

I see Kotlo Kutupura behind us in the center of the compound. She is serving up her *kgadi* out of that old dark green oil drum. Shall we have a cup? I don't know about you, but I'm finding the heat rather oppressive and there's nothing like swig of *kgadi* to set you right. It gives you the pluck to fight back. Afterwards, we can go over to the smaller reed hut and get some *motogo* and stewed goat meat from Pono—they simmer the meat with the goat's head, you know, to give it extra flavor. Wait a moment, it appears that Kotlo is preoccupied with Mrs. Nkape, the butcher's wife.

"*Mma, ga ke tlhaloganye tota!* What do you mean I am stealing your husband?" shouts Kotlo in amazement. "Have I been keeping him in my pocket or locked in my hut? *Mpolelela*, have I been using him to plough my fields? *Xx*, you are talking nonsense, *wena*."

Mrs. Nkape's face flushes starkly. "*Ao*, what are you calling nonsense, you thief?! Your *kgadi* is nonsense, that's what's nonsense. *Retsa*, stay away from my husband. *A o utlwa?*"

"Stay away? *Naa, mosadi*, is he sitting here in my lap? Do I have a rope tied to his nose like a hefty bull? Stay away?! He doesn't even come to get his own *kgadi* but sends his snot-nosed grandson, instead. What do you mean, stay away? *Wena!* And what do you mean my *kgadi* is nonsense? It makes more 'cents' than you do hacking away at that stinking bloody meat of yours." Kotlo laughs at her own joke.

"Stinking meat!" Mrs. Nkape spreads her feet and sets them solidly in the sand, her arms akimbo. "*Gao!* It's not too stinking or bloody for you to come and beg a free kilo every week."

Well, I suppose a can of Ohlssons or Hansa would be better, don't you think? No need to involve ourselves in that argument and risk getting burned—the hot sun will gladly do that for us. Why don't we walk down to the river, where they are keeping the beer cool. Watch out there! Best let Porridge Pot pass by first. I really think that's a new steering wheel he has, but I can't be sure—he went by so quickly. Now, mind your step coming down the bank. It's very easy to trip on the exposed tree roots. Hmm, he says the Ohlssons and Hansas are all on top. We'll take two Lions, then. They may not be the trendiest, but they will be the coolest. Here's to air conditioning! Now, doesn't that make you feel a little brighter?

I think I hear them calling everyone together for the reading of the praise poems, which are kinds of eulogies often composed for funerals or memorials. Let's go back up, shall we? In a way, these praise poems mark a turning point in the mourning process, for when they are finished, the celebrating can truly begin—not that most of us haven't tipped a few already. Uh oh, it seems they have invited the Deputy District Commissioner to open the ceremony; a very long and tiresome opening it will be, I can assure you. As if this infernal heat weren't already enough torture to endure, we must now push the limits of our sanity by sitting through one of his deadly speeches. Just look at the hair growing out of his ears and watch the way he scratches his crotch while speaking in public. Not attractive, but it will entertain you and help get you through the speech. That's an old wooden vegetable crate they have brought out for the speakers to stand on. It gives them more prominence. As I suspected, the DDC is beginning with the same formulaic opening in which he greets his fellow countrymen, his esteemed colleagues, the sadly bereaved family of the *Kgosi* and the loyal and worthy citizens of Shakawe, etcetera. Look, there's Porridge Pot driving behind the DDC. It seems he has his *bakkie* in low gear judging from the low wet spluttering of his tongue. I must admit, the DDC is doing a pretty good job of ignoring him; only a slight twitching around the edges of his mouth. Even those old men sitting in the front row are suffering from the banality of the DDC's address; and they like these formal events! Moikokobetsi, bless him, is already asleep, and Kitchener is only winks away. Kuvumbira and Nyambe are whispering to each other, and, in spite of their calm demeanor, they are very probably bickering needlessly about some trivial point. They always are. Oh, good, the DDC has finished. Polite applause . . . yes, yes, thank you.

Now Mohengi will recite one of his praise poems. Although he appears a little nervous, he is actually a very good orator and I'm confident he will speak magnificently. Let's listen to some of it; I'll translate for you.

> *O, you son of Lesego and Shonologa,*
> *You who kept the people's secrets,*
> *And who held the battle-axe*
> *And noble spear of the Hambukushu,*
> *Run and catch the broad-backed bull*
> *As once you did so long ago.*
> > *So few remain.*
>
> *You killed a mighty hippo*
> *As it charged young Cherekwe,*
> *Who sat among the river grass.*
> *And did not Mogantwa*
> *Shoot the savage lion*
> *That threatened your hallowed life?*
> > *Where is Mogantwa now?*

He is recounting events from the *Kgosi*'s life and, you might say, lauding them while also putting them into perspective. Cherekwe was the *Kgosi*'s younger brother who later died of malaria. As a boy, Cherekwe found himself between a mother hippo and her baby out on the flood plain one day. The mother attacked and the *Kgosi*, who fortunately had a rifle with him, shot and killed her. Mogantwa was a cousin of the *Kgosi* on his mother's side, who at the time was viewed as the bravest and strongest youth of the tribe. He came to be highly respected and lived for many years on the other side of the river, but he has been dead now for some ten years. Listen, Mohengi is finishing his poem:

> *And thus he ruled as one*
> *Who milks the speckled cow*
> *In the distant verdant bush.*
> *And thus the sacred ointment was applied.*
> *Now is the time to praise Motlhotlheletse.*
> *He nourished me and he nourished his people,*
> > *The broad-backed bull.*

Well-deserved and enthusiastic applause. He has produced a work as fine as any made by him in the past. Now, poor Abel Sirumbu is mounting the weathered crate to address the audience. He, too, composes memorable poems, but he is not so accomplished as Mohengi. He has the arduous task of following that breathtaking piece by Mohengi. By almost any stretch of the imagination he will come out the worse, laudable as his undoubtedly will be. There he's clearing his throat. Go to it, Abel!

ᢟ

Above, numerous white bulbous clouds hang in the pale blue sky like dazzling pussy willows. Thankfully, they bring a restraining hand to the sweltering heat of the afternoon. As nature's cooling vents, they avidly draw the swollen heat into their breasts where it is enfolded and transformed into milky wisps of rising moisture. The audience squints painfully in the sun while listening to Abel's poem. No one wafts a fan; they know full well how meaningless it would be: oven-hot air pushed rapidly forward has only oven-hot air to replace it just as quickly. Better not to move at all and pray that the ceremony does not take too long. At least the beers will be cooler by then.

As Abel recites his poem, a dung beetle appears out of the swirling convection of the rising air. A dung beetle. Why dung? Because of their habit of gathering large quantities of animal dung, which they then shape into a ball and roll backwards all the while collecting more and more until the orb is twice and then thrice their own size. These gooey globes are used as nests in which to lay their eggs. After the larvae hatch, they then munch away at the tasty snack, loving every rancid mouthful.

This, however, is not the dung beetle's only endearing trait. They also offer the most comic relief through their aerial antics, for these cumbersome creatures fly with less grace than they have table manners. Huge hulking masses of chitinous armor, they are extremely heavy and ungainly for their modest wings. At takeoff, they beat the air with thunderous strokes and then lurch ponderously forward into the air like black dirigibles. Nature's humorous counterpart to chivalrous knights, they hurl their lumbering bodies through the air, not with the delicacy of a butterfly or the acrobatics of a swallow but with all the subtlety of a drunken meteor. Their course is seldom true, though always honest, and any attempt at directed flight is a faint hope at best. They roar above the ground, rarely higher than a house, and gradually descend in accordance with the ineluctable dictates of almighty gravity, listing heavily all the while first to one side and then to the other like an oil tanker tossed on a roiling sea until at last they either crash to the ground or, as more commonly is the case, strike an intervening tree, pole or fence with an explosive *thwap*!

Now, as it so happens, this particular dung beetle flying in the air is hurtling towards the *Kgosi*'s compound in much the same manner, pitching first to starboard and now to port as it makes a pitiful stab at navigation. This is particularly regrettable, because had it not corrected from right to left, it would probably have slammed harmlessly into the side of the main house. After falling to the ground, dazed but without injury, it would have rested briefly and then taken off again in erratic flight. Instead, the beetle buzzes stupidly like a flak-ridden bomber towards the center of the compound and descends ever lower and lower until it finally stops with a loud and frightening smack against the roof of the sleeping Kitchener Semumu's gaping mouth.

Startled into panic, the violated Semumu sensibly spits the offending bug out; but in his shock and surprise, he manages to do so with such force that it rockets across the semi-circular open area of seated guests and knocks an unsuspecting Kuvumbira right behind the ear. Shaken, he turns to his right full of bilious rage and demands immediate apology from Nyambe, his neighbor to that side. Poor Nyambe has been deep in discussion with Mohengi on his right and is as profoundly surprised as Kuvumbira. Nyambe retorts that he has also been insulted by Kuvumbira's offensive behavior and would like an instant apology from Kuvumbira for having the insolence to demand an apology from him.

Argument ensues and rises to such a scalding degree of vehemence that none can hear the noble and impassioned words of Abel, who nevertheless continues to recite his poem with pretended aplomb. The two adversaries will not stop, however, and they begin to bandy about insults and exchange fusillades of angry accusation with increasingly vituperation. Indeed, neither of them is a violent person and blows are not expected; nevertheless, their gestures of disgust and disapprobation grow with each volley of abuse and finally Kuvumbira swings his arms in a roundabout arc to demonstrate his deep disgust at what he calls 'Nyambe's heinous deed.' In doing so, he accidentally strikes Sethunya's uncle Sarambo Dishero in the eye and this causes him to reel backward in agony. It just so happens that at this moment, Kotlo Kutupura is standing on her chair, the better to view the scuffle, and unhappily Sarambo falls into her, knocking her ass-backward into her fifty-five gallon drum of *kgadi*, where she becomes tightly wedged, her arms and legs flailing disgracefully and her mouth screaming words of very unladylike retribution. A crowd gathers round the rudely imprisoned Kotlo and studies her with avid curiosity and no small amount of amusement. As is usual in a village like Shakawe, no one moves to act or assist; they merely gawk, ponder and comment. Eventually, someone from the swelling throng approaches the poor old woman and makes an attempt to extricate her.

The crowd has now split into two: one around Kotlo and the other around Nyambe and Kuvumbira. Some avid spectators even run back and forth between the two fearing they might miss a crucial episode in either saga. Unfortunately, the idle rubberneckers around Kotlo have become so thick that they press in upon her. Suffocating from the crowd, she lashes out in a desperate search for air and whacks one of the bystanders on the nose with her thrashing left foot. This sends the group of people backward and outward like ripples from a stone thrown into a pond. At the outer edge of this human wave, Jackson Sedumedi accidentally steps on Big Boy's patent leather shoes, which have been especially polished for this occasion. Big Boy discharges a stream of curses that would make a porno queen blush. So terrible are they that Sedumedi is too appalled and embarrassed even to reply. This in turn only further infuriates Big Boy who threatens arrest, incarceration, bludgeoning and even beheading. Receiving no satisfactory answer to his threats, he shoves Sedumedi away from him in disgust and through this act loosens the cigarette which that dandy has been holding in his right hand. The burning stub somersaults through the air and lands squarely on the roof of the middle of the three small huts to the side of the compound. Dry as it has been after seven months of no rain, the thatch catches fire at once and proves to be a new event of such interest as to draw away and unite the two separate groups of onlookers, leaving the wailing Kotlo to writhe by herself in her drum and the two village elders to bicker by themselves. The entire body of spectators has also transferred its superb skills of commentary and inaction to the new crisis and stands passively ooh-ing and ah-ing while the flames build in intensity. Joost, however, quickly shouts out orders for two lines of attack on the blaze: one group of boys will fetch water from the river using pails while the other begins immediately to work at the sizzling tongues of fire with handfuls of abundant Shakawe sand. Big Boy feels ashamed and disgraced at this display of decisiveness and leadership, and not wanting to be upstaged, he runs back to grab one of Kotlo's serving bowls, with which he intends to take charge of the firefighting effort. But as the Fates would have it—and they do have it their way—Mothsithsi, the village rumormonger, has been busy scurrying about from contretemps to contretemps in search of juicy nuggets of gossip, which he hopes to wring through the rumor mill, and is running past the writhing Kotlo at this very moment. He suddenly collides with the retreating Big Boy and pushes him headlong into the drum holding the freshly fermented *kgadi* and its brewer Kotlo. The impact has the blessed effect of freeing Kotlo from her ignoble confinement but also the cursed effect of sending the two, Kotlo and Big Boy, lunging through the air. Upon landing, Big Boy finds himself positioned with his admittedly swollen head thrust up Kotlo's skirt and between her two spindly legs. She shrieks with maidenly discomfiture, causing the entire crowd to turn as one and witness the shameful and most embarrassing scene. Seizing the opportunity, Mothsithsi begins without delay to recount exactly how lecherous Big Boy attacked poor Kotlo while everyone's attention was averted, Mothsithsi being sure all the while not to let any scraps of truth creep into his narrative and, by so doing, spoil it.

With this last mishap, even Dr. Sveinnson and Moikokobetsi, neither of whom has so much as cracked a smile in months, both break out in unabashed laughter. Birgit is so overwhelmed that tears well up in her eyes and blur her vision; as for Moikokobetsi, he nearly chokes with loud cackles and finds the resultant rush much more satisfying than a whole drum full of *kgadi*. There is a moment of hesitation in the chaos, but then one of the young boys announces the extinguishing of the fire and this acts as a catalyst to release the tension from all the preceding confusion. Everyone begins laughing. Nyambe and Kuvumbira also stop arguing and join in without really knowing why they are doing so. The hilarity enlivens Porridge Pot who senses the change in mood and, in growing excitement, puts his *bakkie* into gear and drives in a boisterous circle around the whole group, making them laugh all the harder.

Suddenly, someone cries out and the others become silent. What can be the matter now, they ask themselves?

There is nothing wrong, though, no accident has occurred. The voice shouts again. It is Pono Kenyaditswe. She is yelling, "*Pula! Pula! Pula, e a nna!*" She must be mad, they say to each other. Rain? Little by little, though, they feel the drops: first one on the hand and then one on the nose. They look up and see a sky consumed by four mammoth clouds, dark and baleful. Indeed, the wind has picked up and rushes against their faces. More and more drops fall, hitting the sand at their feet, each one creating a tiny puff of fine dust.

Pula, e a nna. Pono is right. Rain has come.

The arguing and laughing and gawking halt. Even Porridge Pot stands transfixed with his vehicle in neutral. All watch with awe and gratitude as the first rain of the year descends. It soon begins to fall quite hard and people scamper left and right looking for shelter.

Only one person remains. Sethunya. Deeply inhaling the humid air, she walks eagerly down to the edge of the river from where she looks across at the flood plain, its blackened body already clothed in a new thin gown of bright green shoots. She knows that before long, the green papyrus will return as well as the reeds, tall and thick, and that families will drive their cattle inland, some across the river, to their cattle posts in the bush. The people will nervously watch their fields in hopes that their maize or sorghum will grow strong, that there will be food in abundance.

She relishes the warm playful drops that fall on her skin, drops that soothe her by nourishing her soul, and feels herself about to be reborn. She gazes at the river studded with silver explosions, at the empty brilliantly green-black plain beyond, at the trees with dancing leaves, and at the dark churning sky above, and she thinks of nature and she glories in the persistence of life and the wondrous bounty it so generously grants, even to an often indifferent human race. She marvels at the blunt smell of lightning, at the sound of groaning thunder and laughing raindrops, at the muted harmonious colors.

Sethunya closes her eyes and blesses everything. With slow deep breaths, she extends her arms to either side and gathers in the warm musty rain that falls in whispers from a purple-gray sky.

Glossary

Glossary

Setswana

ao / gao • interjection expressing surprise, scorn, contempt (women/men)

bona • look (also as an interjection such as 'look . . .' or 'see . . .')

bogobe • maize meal porridge

dumela • Setswana greeting word; hello

ee • yes [pronounced AY as in May]

ehe • 'oh really' or 'I see' [AY-HAY]

go ntse jang • How's it going?; What's up? [HOON TSAY JAHNG]

go siame • okay, all right, good-bye [HO SEE-AH-MAY]

ijo / ija • expresses surprise, distress, sympathy (women/men)

intswarele • excuse me, forgive me

ke itumetse • thank you, I am grateful (stronger than *dankie*)

kgadi • home-brewed beer, usually made in 55-gallon drums

kgokong • a wood-handled whisk made from a wildebeest's tail

kgosi • tribal headman; king; chief [KO-SEE]

kgotla • the tribal meeting place

kgotla chair • a wooden folding chair using leather straps for the seat

koko • said when knocking on someone's door or approaching a compound

kudu • a kind of large antelope with long spiralling horns

mma (pl. bomma) • Ma'am, Miss or Mrs.; someone else's mother

modimo (pl. badimo) • *Modimo* is the supreme god or spirit; *badimo* are guiding ancestral spirits of a village or tribe

mogaetsho (pl. bagaetsho) • comrade, fellow countryman [MO-HAY-TSOO]

mogolo • old; *monna mogolo* = old man [MO-HO-LO]

mokutshumo • a tree, the jackalberry (diospyros mespiliformis)

mokoro (pl. mekoro) • a dugout canoe

moloi (pl. baloi) • a witch; one possessing supernatural powers *monna (pl. banna)* • a man; also used colloquially as in the phrase 'Hey, man'

moraba • a bag used by traditional doctors to hold herbs or divination bones

morula • a tree, the marula (marula sclerocarya)

mosadi (pl. basadi) • a woman

motogo • a mixture of cooked white maize kernels and pinto or red beans

motsaudi • a tree, the African mangosteen (Garcinia Livingstonei)

naa • interjection meaning 'well,' 'say,' 'you know'

ngaka (pl. dingaka) • a traditional, non-Western doctor [NG-AH-KAH]

no mathata • no problem (English 'no' with Setswana for 'problem')

ntate • uncle; a term of endearment and respect used for elders

o bua nnete • That's right (lit. 'you speak truly')

o kae • What's up?; How're things? (lit. Where are you?)

o thlotse (jang) • How are you doing? (used in the afternoon) [OH TLOH-TSE]

o tsogile (jang) • How are you doing? (used in the morning up to midday) [OH TSOH-HEE-LAY JAHNG]

retsa • listen

rra (pl. borra) • mister; sir; someone else's father

ruri • really, certainly

sejeso • herbal mixture given to victims whom *moloi* wish to control; a potion

thebe • equivalent of a penny in Botswana currency

tla kwano • come here

tsala (pl. ditsala) • friend

tsenwa • crazy, out of one's mind

wareng • 'What's up?' or 'What's new?' Answered by *Ga ke bue (sepe)* or *Ga ke re sepe*

Simbukushu

ii • yes [EE]

maopinduka • 'How are you doing?'; answered by *maopinduka (thuana)*

mendengure • a kind of ritual dance used for healing, divining, discovering witches and expelling unwanted ancestral spirits

mokamadi (pl. hakamadi) • a woman

moroke • word of greeting; hello; good day

muanangeana • a sister's child or brother's child of a husband (used by a woman)

murume (pl. arume) • a man

nyakudiange • grandfather or grandmother on father's side

Afrikaans

bakkie • a pickup truck

biltong • beef jerky

dankie • thank you

kraal • an enclosure used to keep livestock in; a corral

lekker • nice; good; tasty

mealie • maize; corn

nartjie • tangerine

rondavel • a circular thatched-roof house

samp • cooked white maize

veldt • the bush; any wild expanse of bush savanna

vuitsak • 'Shoo!'; 'Go away!' Used for dogs; said to a person, it is the equivalent of 'fuck off'

wildebeest • the gnu; a large charcoal-gray antelope with a short stocky neck, short horns and a long horse-like face

British English

bottle shop • liquor store
paraffin • kerosene
petrol • gasoline
shebeen • a drinking stand; a bar
tin • can

Proper Names

Bakgalagadi • a mixed Khoi-Bantu people living in the central Kgalagadi desert
Bakwena • Batswana tribe living in and around Molepolole (southeast)
Bamangwato • Batswana tribe living in and around Serowe (central east)
Bangwaketse • Batswana tribe living in and around Kanye (far southeast)
Batawana • Batswana tribe living in and around Maun (near northwest)
Bayei • a people living in the far northwest of Botswana
Hambukushu • a people living in the far northwest of Botswana
Lekgoa (pl. Makgoa) • Setswana for a white foreigner
Matebele • Setswana for the Ndebele people of western Zimbabwe
Mosarwa (pl. Basarwa) • Setswana term for a Bushman or Khoi-san
Ngamiland • northwestern district of Botswana
Tsodilo Hills • two large rock outcroppings that rise up out of the flat, gently rolling bush of remote far northwestern Botswana; sacred to the Bushmen who live in the area

Setswana Orthography and Pronunciation

Vowels • The same as in European languages (a=ah, e=ay, i=ee, o=oh, u=oo)

Consonants • Mostly the same as English, with two notable exceptions:

1) G • This sound is pronounced as a hard *h*, somewhat like the *ch* in Scottish *loch* but softer. Thus, the name of the Kalahari Desert in Setswana, Kgalagadi, is pronounced *Khah-lah-ha-dee*. The capital, Gaborone, is *Hah-boh-roh-nay*.

2) H • Used alone this is a soft 'h' sound. Otherwise, this is used to aspirate a consonant, i.e., to produce a sound with a puff of breath. The *ts* in witty are aspirated while the *ts* in *nitwit* are not.

   Hence, *tsh* in Setswana is an aspirated (explosive) *ts* sound; it is not *t* + *sh*; a lone *t* is an unaspirated, soft *t* while *th* is an aspirated hard *t*, it is not the fricative *th* sound of English.

   As an example, *Go Hithla Motho* (to bury someone) is pronounced *cho-hee-tlah-moh-toh* where the *ts* are hard.

   Gh is a hard guttural fricative sound, like Scottish *loch* but made at the back of the throat.

Bushman Orthography

The languages of the Bushmen use a variety of 'clicks,' three of which are used in the story *Eggshells Are for Drinking*:

/ (e.g. /Gashay) • The dental click (front part of the roof of the mouth)

! (e.g. !Kung) • The alveopalatal, or glottal, click at the back of the mouth near the throat

≠ (e.g. ≠Toma) • The alveolar click at the top of the mouth between the '/' and '!' clicks

// , X, c (Xama) • The lateral click made with the side of the tongue against the teeth—often compared to the "tsk, tsk" sound used when prodding horses to trot. The symbol X is usually used when made directly before vowels and the // before consonants. The X and c orthography can still be seen in Ngamiland place names such as Xanekwe, Ncamasere.

Printed in the United States
23432LVS00005B/179